Reflection

Reflection

D.L. LAGONE

authorHOUSE®

AuthorHouse™ LLC
1663 Liberty Drive
Bloomington, IN 47403
www.authorhouse.com
Phone: 1-800-839-8640

Published by AuthorHouse   10/11/2013

ISBN: 978-1-4918-1793-3 (sc)
ISBN: 978-1-4918-1792-6 (hc)
ISBN: 978-1-4918-1791-9 (e)

Library of Congress Control Number: 2013916834

Contents

In Behalf of

Susan Sobol Hydo:

My Beloved Mother who
introduced me to the wonders
hidden on the shelves of a
library and the joys of Reading.

D. L. Lagone

*For Jim, A safe harbor whenever my ship becomes tossed
by heavy seas whose love and patience never falter.
James and Melissa your, "Mom you can do this", was
music to my ears,*
And
*The Wednesday afternoon Creative Writing Group of
Schenectady Public Library, talented, encouraging,
insightful and most of all supportive.*

To All This Book Is So Dedicated:

A Promise

Whatever you do, never sell my silver hand mirror. Promise me, it must remain in the family, Promise. These were my Grandmother dying words to me as I take her hand and she slips quietly away.

When I was eight my parents were killed in an auto accident, and I went to live with grandma she was my only living relative my father her only child. I never saw her cry or mourn at his death she said life went on, and that was that. Her name was Rose Black, but everyone called her Rosie even me. She was a lighthearted happy woman and her character was reflected in every aspect of life. The house a sprawling affair, she lived in her whole life belonged to her father, and before him his father is brightly colored and decorated with a whimsy Rosie loved.

As the last mourners leave, reassuring me Rose will be with me always. I shut the door turning to consider the mess of dirty dishes they can wait until morning I am just so tired. I start to wonder about the mirror and why Rosie was so worried about its safety. I want to look at it; I want to look at now. I turn off the lights, and climb the stairs, from the landing I can dimly see the entire ground floor, smiling how pretty it is almost as if spring lives here year round. I was fortunate to have had someone in my life like Rose Black.

Her room is at the end of the hall, I enter, turn on the light there on the dressing table I see the sliver mirror. A light creeps in through an opening in the heavy drapes its rays touch the silver giving it an eerie glow. This room is so not like Rosie I think to myself. The velvet drapes on the windows block out any life from the outside entering in; the furniture is dark and filled with ugly ornate carvings. The walls are papered with large red roses and scrolls, adding to the darkness that surrounds this space. The bed is a large four-poster at first glance you think could hide an army in the piles of pillows, and quilts yet somehow it still looks uncomfortable. At the far, end of the room stands an armoire grotesque in style with a large chair to match. I walk toward the window and the dressing table then sit down; on top of the table, are a variety of hand blown glass perfume bottles, a delicate lace runner, a small round tray, and the silver hand mirror aglow with a ghostly light. I pick it up for further inspection; it is made of the finest silver and feels refreshingly, soothing to my touch. The back is carved with morning glories and poppies, vines cascade down the bottom is a sunburst its rays reaching out towards the flowers. Beautifully scrolled initials are at the center LTG those are not Roses initials I whisper. Another unusual thing about the mirror is the handle a tangle of vines carved in silver that look like a crown of thorns making the mirror awkward to hold. What is it about this mirror that makes it unique? I turn it over and look at my reflection. Pretty enough with long black hair and dark eyes a bit haggard but that is to be expected considering the last few days. A dark haired beauty

2

that is what Rosie called me when I was little. We were exact opposites she fair with blonde hair and hazel eyes, cheerful people would say, Rose bubbles with enthusiasm, me quiet and shy with dark hair and eyes, a non-chance taker I liked to stay in Rosie's shadow where I felt safe.

I was about to replace the glass on the dressing table when I thought I saw something move in the shadows. Stop it now, in this gloomy room I am surprised ghosts are not popping out from under the woodwork. I turn out the light and leave the room. I am tired tomorrow will be soon enough to deal with mirrors, dirty dishes and what to do next with Roses estate.

The hot water of the shower feels warm on my body. Rose has kept my room pretty much the same since I left to get an apartment closer to the private school where I teach. I come back on the occasional weekend and holidays. Rosie said, "My room will always be here waiting for me whenever I need to come home". Yes, home is always a terrific feeling.

Dressing for bed, I wonder why my grandmother's room is so dark and depressing when the rest of the house is bright, cheerful, and inviting. I put on my robe and slippers deciding to look at the mirror again before going to sleep.

The room is quiet, and as I open the door nothing seems out of place, I walk over to the dressing table and sit down picking up the mirror to look at the reflecting side.

She is gazing deep into my eyes. I jump back startled for a second, who are you I whisper my heart pounding like a hammer against my chest. You do not know she answers her dark eyes staring into mine as if searching for some recognition from me. I am worn-out you must just a reflection of my overworked imagination running wild. No! She screams, did Rose not tell you about me. Look, take a close look I knew I was looking at myself, in the reflection younger a bit more flamboyant but me nonetheless. The same dark hair, hers longer and held back by a beautiful carved tortoise shell comb, her eyes dark like mine only they look like black pools of ice. Her clothes are of another time and country I think, Mexico, I say aloud, not knowing why. Very good, she says I am Louise Theresa Gutierrez Black your great-grandmother. No! That is ridicules, No! My great-grandmother's name is Tillie she was fair-haired with blue eyes, short and a bit plump I have seen pictures.

He never loved her it was me always me. They just wanted her money and the influence that came with it. I was not good enough for their beloved son. Her face becomes distorted with sadness her eyes darker. I showed her, she said I am still here Tillie could not get rid of me, however, hard she and her father tried, I showed her, Louise said with a sob.

Slamming, down the mirror I run from the room my heart pounding in my throat. I sit on my bed shaking, calm down, calm down, now remember your great-grandfather, Charles Black, yes, Rosie said her Father was with the Calvary when they invaded Mexico in search of Poncho Villa, Rosie has pictures somewhere of him in uniform. Great-grandmother and he married a year after his return. What happened in Mexico? Who would know after so many years? I can't sleep now, what shall I do?

The safe of course, with all Rose valuable papers it is behind the watercolor in the dining room. I fly down the stairs the combination was drummed into my head from childhood. You never know when you might need it Rose said. She is right I need it now 30 right 3 times, 50 left 2 times, 1 right 4 times, around to 0 twice; my hands shaking as the heavy safe door opens. Rosie has everything organized in small boxes marked with what contents. I remove the boxes and place them on the dining room table, looking to see what is marked on each of them. Will, House Deeds, Savings Information is on the first. The second has jewelry written on it, the third family information and important family papers, the last family photos. I concentrate on the last two I need all the information I can get.

I sit down and open the two boxes carefully they are crammed with old documents and photos. I remove the contents from one box gently on to the table. The old photos are yellow and delicate unfamiliar faces stare up at me as if saying look at me first I am the important one. I positioned them in rows to look individually at each. Quickly I find four pictures of great-grandfather one in his uniform. Then great-grandmother there is a college picture of her in cap and gown another of her in such a pretty spring dress, one in front of the Eiffel Tower and the latter a wedding photo. Her gown is elegant, satin with pearls Tillie is wearing a lace mantilla "so delicate" it looks as if it is woven of spider webs.

She looks so young and innocent great-grandfather stands next to her tall and impressive but with a look of sadness about him a perfect couple I wonder. I look thru' the photos of various relatives from the past I have never met, when something catches my eye, it is a photo wrapped in tissue, larger than the rest. Removing the paper an image jumps out at me great-grandfather in his uniform standing by a Spanish style church in what looks like a Mexican village. Next to him with his arm around her is Louise. I cannot understand what I am seeing; Louise is wearing the same lace mantilla great-grandmother wears in her wedding photo. The two look so in love around them are villagers and I think family members all beaming at the happy couple. My hands are like ice as I turned the picture over. Written on the back the words Charles and Louise wedding photo Guadalajara Mexico June. 1, 1917. I take the other wedding photo turning it over Charles and Tillie Hartford Connecticut, wedding June 20 1918. She is correct, I lay the two pictures down next to each other, and look carefully at both, Charles has a gentle smile on his face as he looks at Louise so in love. How at ease he seems with this woman by his side. The other photo is quite different; it is prim and proper, great-grandfather looking quite elegant standing stiff, however, not happy next to his bride who looks up at him adoringly. These are two different men, what occurred to change Charles so. I carefully put the other photographs back in the box only keeping out the two wedding pictures. The other box says family information I opened it cautiously not knowing what I will find. "As I check its contents" an idea starts to emerge Tillie's family has money, property, business holdings and influence in the community, Charles's family has spent their life trying to better themselves no matter what it took. There was paper work from a failed business ventures, liens, and mortgages against their home. As I search, I find a stack of letters held together by a tattered ribbon taking them into the living room; I curl up on the couch and open the first one:

Dear Charles

Father and I hope you are well. I think it just so unfair you are posted in such a God forsaken place as Mexico. I thought the Army would appreciate your value and keep you in Washington. Well never mind, do your best, I know you are under the command of General Pershing as one of his attachés be invaluable to him, and all the other officers I know you will progress through the ranks quickly. Everyone is thriving here. Make sure you write to Tillie she is just pining away waiting daily for your letters.

Love
Mother

I knew Charles was in the Army; however, his service in Mexico is a new revelation to me. The war between the United States and Poncho Villa is not widely taught in American schools. From what I remember from my university studies trouble had been growing between the United States and Poncho Villa in 1915. After years of fighting the tyranny of Victoriano Huerta and American oppression, Villa counted on American support in his bid for President of Mexico. President Wilson reneges on his promise and backs Venustiano Carranza for President. Villa swears revenge against the US and begins raiding along the border of Mexico and the United States in the hopes of discrediting the Mexican Government. Villa continues the raiding along the border, but Wilson will not intervene until Villa attacks Camp Furlong, and lays waste to the town of Columbus New Mexico, fourteen American soldiers massacred by Villa and his *Pistelerios* along with ten civilians. People living along the Mexican border have become hysterical. Wilson has no choice but to act he appoints Gen. Black Jack Pershing along with 4,000 Calvary troops to stop Poncho Villa but the expedition is doomed for failure. Poncho Villa easily blends into the populace, and no Mexican will help the soldiers catch him or his men. In 1917, President Wilson recalls the punitive expedition back to Ft Bliss Texas; clearly, Poncho Villa is the winner in the Mexican people's eyes

Dear Charles

Father and I hope you are well. We read in the papers every day of the hardships you and your men are going through trying to capture this villain Poncho Villa. However, Father and I are quite happy about your promotion to Second Lieutenant no one is more deserving. Although I thought, First Lieutenant more suitable. We are all reasonably well here a few sniffles nothing more. Only I must admonish you in your lack of writing to Tillie the poor thing waits daily for some word from you. Use the sense you were born with, Tillie will be the perfect partner for you and do not forget her father's prominence in this community will help make your own

fortune. Remember Charles the responsibility you have to your family.

Stay well

Love
Mother

I cannot help as I read these letters thinking how incredibly selfish this woman is. She seems to have no respect for her son only thinking of her own self-centered demands. The mantel clock strikes two a.m. the lateness of the hour has no significance, I need to finish what was started years ago I have to understand.

I pick up the next letter.

Dear Mother and Father

I know you have not heard from me for some time, many things have happened since I last wrote you. Our Command has been in a few skirmishes with Villa's men, but Poncho Villa is raiding to the north and has evaded captured. Most of the Calvary under the command of Gen. Pershing is being recalled to Texas, seems the war is over. However, some units will still be stationed here as an attaché' to the General there are still some matters I must finish so I will be staying, I do not know for how long but I am happy about it. I have come to love and respect the Mexican people they have suffered much by this undeclared war. Whatever we think of Poncho Villa

he is a benefactor to the poor of his country. The land is quite rugged and beautiful with much potential for expansion. An intelligent man could make his fortune here and have a decent life. Mother and Father I must now tell you my fabulous news. Soon after, I arrived in Mexico I met a remarkable woman and her family and fell totally in love. We were married June 1 in a beautiful Spanish church with her family, and all the town in attendance, her name is Louise Gutierrez. She comes from a prominent ranching family near Guadalajara. They provide most of the horses to General Perishing's Cavalry and to Fort Bliss; I have never seen such handsome beasts, Mother. I know this comes as a shock to you both, however, please, be happy for me, we are deeply in love, and I have never been so happy in my life. This is where I will live Mother in this place with Louise and her family. Within three, months when my unit leaves Louise, and I will come home. I am eager for her to meet the family. I know you will love her as I, how could you not. However, we have decided to return to Mexico, I will work beside Louise's Father on the ranch. I have so much to learn to start building my future now. Mother I have enclosed our wedding photograph you will see how beautiful Louise is and how happy we both are.

Your Loving Son Charles.

My hand trembles as I hold the letter so full of love, and hope for the future, yet underlying it all is a pleading for understanding and acceptance. I get up and put the letter down on the dining room table next to the wedding pictures. I want to keep all related information together to get a better idea of what went on in Charles, Louise and Tillie's life. Before going back into to the living room, I poured myself a tall glass of wine fortifying myself to deal with what I would read next.

Charles

How could you? This cannot be possible; you are an American Citizen with rank, and status do you honestly think this marriage to a Mexican peasant in a Catholic Church no less is legal. I think not, our government does not endorse the validity of this kind of marriage. What about your responsibility to Tillie you think you can just forget about your commitment to her it not being relevant anymore. I will not allow it you must return home immediately. Tillie's father knows influential people who can pull some strings. We will say you are sick and in of emergency medical attention. No one needs to know "especially" Tillie. I will write to Mr. Barnes tomorrow and you will be home before you know it. We can plan your wedding to Tillie then she will be so excited to see you when she returns home from Europe. Under no circumstance is that woman welcome in our home. Do you understand we will not tolerate her presence? In time, you will ignore this terrible mistake, and Tillie never needs to know anything about your folly. I will hear nothing more about this episode Charles the subject is close.

Mother

There are no more letters between my Great-Grandfather and his family. I put this letter next to others with a sad heart. How cruel how utterly heartless is Charles mother but I was not prepared to find out how utterly callous they were and to what means they would lower themselves to achieve this marriage between Charles and Tillie. I went back to the box saying Family Information, probing "for any other "I could find. I come across an envelope marked Birth, Death, and Marriage cautiously I open it. Oh God, What would I discover now? I remove all the documents, there are births, death, and marriage certificates for all the family. However, I know exactly the members of the family I am looking for. I find them tied with the same frayed ribbon that held the letters. I feel as if someone is guiding me through this voyage of discovery, quietly showing where to go. I sorted the papers quickly and find the information I need on the major players in this drama. The death certificates of Charles parents indicate their demise as one week apart October,12.1918 Charlotte his mother died, October, 19. 1918 his father Charles Sr. died strange coincidence no doubt. As I look for Charles and Tillie's marriage and death certificates, I come across a birth certificate. It reads Charles Marcus Black, Born: March 10,1918 Hartford Connecticut Mother: Louise Theresa Black, Father: Charles Black Jr. Attached to the birth record by a small clip is a death certificate : Louise Theresa Gutierrez Black died this day March 10,1918 in Hartford Connecticut Tears roll uncontrollably down my face. They have a son did Louise die giving birth to him.

I look up at the window; dawn is breaking over the Connecticut Hills how beautiful I think the beginning of a new day.

I have an appointment with Rosie's attorney at 10 this morning he must be able to shed some light on all this. I gather up the paperwork I have found and put it in my tote bag setting it next to the front door as if I would be likely to forget it. I need to shower and change. I fight the urge to enter Roses room. I need more evidence before I confront Louise again and I have no doubt I will.

The ride to the lawyers is uneventful; I gather the paperwork from the front seat of the car and walk through the door of the office. A young receptionist greets me with a smile, I am Rose Black's granddaughter I have an appointment, oh yes, she interrupts you are expected, follow me please. We enter a small office beautifully decorated with well-worn Mahogany and leather furniture; shelves of law books line the walls an Oriental rug on the floor adding to the air of professionalism that help put clients at ease. Behind the desk, an elderly man is standing, impeccably dressed with snow-white hair and piercing blue eyes. Hello, he says, extending his hand I am Isaac Burton, senior partner. He motions for me to sit in a leather chair near his desk. Your grandmother and I grew up together; our law firm has been the family's solicitors for over one hundred years." I hope you can help me understand", only before I could finish my sentence, he says, "I know I can, I came in today to meet you and tell you a story, are you willing to hear it?" "I brought some documents I found in Rosie's safe," I say, laying the pictures and papers on the desk. "Ah yes, Rose said you will have papers, with you when you came to the office", so it is Rosie who is guiding my way? Mr. Burton asks his receptionist to bring in some coffee as we wait he glances at the paperwork and pictures I brought. I search his face for some hint of emotion, there is none? "Nothing like a good cup of coffee in the morning to put things right," he says. I feel the hot liquid burn my throat as I take a sip.

I guess now is an opportune time to begin, will you tell me what you already know, please, it might save time. I take another sip of coffee and started. I tell him about Roses concern with the mirror on her deathbed, of Roses room dark, different from the rest of the house. Seeing the mirror holding it in my hand, but not about seeing Louise's image let alone speaking to her, somehow I could not. I speak of the wedding pictures, with both brides wearing the same lace mantilla, of the child's birth and Louise's death on the same day. The words were pouring from my lips only I am not sure I am making sense. Mr. Burton listens intently, when I have finished, he looks at me is there anything else you want to tell me no I say, "Are you sure, anything", he knew. It's all right my dear, some things we just cannot explain." Is it true then? Yes, he replies, and Louise is my great-grandmother. Yes, he answers quite calmly. Now take another sip of that coffee and I will begin. He has the two wedding pictures on his desk, beneath them the two marriage licenses and under Charles and Louise's picture are her death certificate and the baby's birth certificate. In his hand, he holds the last letter Charles received from his mother.

He begins, you see Charles did not return home in three months, he went to Texas where he mustered out of the Army, then immediately returns to Mexico and his wife. Charles learned the ranching and horse breeding business from his father-in-law it seems he was born to the saddle. For the first time, your great-grandfather was extremely happy. He loved his adopted country, but it was mostly Louise, she brought out in him the strength of his soul, and it shows, he was becoming a man of substance, someone trustworthy that could be relied on to do the right thing whether in business, the community or in his home. When Louise became pregnant Charles was thrilled, he was to be a father. The birth of a child in Mexico is a tremendous Blessing. Louise's family went to church, lit candles and Prayed that both mother and child will be well. However, Charles began to worry he wants his child to be an American Citizen born on American soil. When he voices his concerns to Louise, she readily agrees, Charles assures her they will go to Texas have the baby and come home to Mexico. Louise is happy with that idea. Then Charles begins thinking that when his parents find out they were going to be grandparents both him, and Louise will be welcomed home with open arms." No, they will go to Hartford the child will be born there in the roots of New England. When Charles tells Louise fear gripped her heart, she will be seven months pregnant quite far along for such a long journey to begin. She has never left Mexico or her family for that long a time, and she knows she will miss her mother. Louise thought that Mama would accompany them to Texas and help her when the baby is born. Now she will have her baby in a strange house with people she did not know. Besides, will Charles parents genuinely welcome her and the baby with opened arms as Charles says. Yet Louise voices none of her fears to her husband.

The Journey

In her seventh month of pregnancy January 1918, (28 weeks) they board a train in Guadalajara for Hartford Connecticut The journey will take 3 weeks give or take a few days, Louise's parents are worried though Louise is strong and healthy they believe such a long journey too much for her. Papa tries to convince Charles to have the child in Texas when the baby and Louise are strong enough travel to Connecticut. Only Charles will hear none of it, he is convinced his parents will be happy to see them and will be honoured to have their grandchild born in the house where Charles was born. With Mama crying, and Papa waiving the train pulls from the station belching out black smoke from its enormous belly high into the air.

The trip will be long, and challenging with frequent stops for water, along with wood to fuel the engines colossal appetite.

Louise seems to thrive growing stronger as the days pass. She begins keeping a small diary of her experiences, and what she sees as the train travels ever closer to Charles's family, and the future they all will share. However, Charles is not sure any longer as the miles pass drawing them nearer to the East coast doubts begin to overwhelm him. He watches Louise as she writes in her diary, sometimes drawing a picture of the countryside or pressing a flower she found when the train stops, between the pages. She says when the baby gets older she will show him the diary and tell him of the first trip he ever took.

The old lawyer takes out a cardboard box from under his desk. Opening the lid, he hands it to me commenting, "Rosie wanted you to have this", inside is a hand woven Mexican Blanket, the coarse fibers still rich with all the color and vibrancy of the country from which it came. A smaller box holds an elegant silver chain. I looked up Mr. Burton is smiling "put it on" he says, it feels cool on my neck. What is all of this I ask as I reach for a small leather bound book?

"Open it, is all," he said, the lock was old, however, the key "on a red ribbon" turned easily. The first page, it said, "This Book Belongs to, Louise Theresa Black" I gasped, my hands trembling I read aloud

Dear Diary

January 3, 1918

Our Journey has begun; I am afraid to meet Charles mother and father. He cannot know this. My first trip diary away from my beloved home and family God keep our baby and me safe.

"Would you like more coffee or another piece of cake," Mr. Burton asks, I look at my coffee cold in the cup "yes, please I whisper a refill would be nice" you know you look just like her, Louise was a beautiful woman someone you do not easily forget." The old solicitor has a faraway look in his eyes remembering years earlier. "Well yes, yes the story, I must not get off track, I find that easy to do now days, he says. As I had explained to you before our firm was the solicitors to the family, when Charles was in Mexico he wrote to my father, so we were quite aware of Charles plans, we drew up his new will, leaving his estate to Louise and the child. He wrote my father when he and Louise left Mexico to come east. His letters full of hope for the future, but he was worried about how his parents would react to their visit and the upcoming birth of a child. Furthermore, his fears were not unfounded Mr. Burton motioned for me to read on,

Dear Diary

January 4, 1918

The train engine is burping out steam and soot as we chug along, I always feel dirty. Everything is covered with soot the baby is kicking me, and I put Charles hand on my stomach we both laugh. My back is aching. Mama pray for me.

Dear Diary

January 6, 1918

Monterey today, the train stops for two hours. We eat at different food stands set up along the street. I smell the chilies cooking on the open fires. Mama and I love to shop at home for fresh fruits and vegetables. People visit with each other, laughing and talking about the latest news. This is our last stop in Mexico. I am not sure what we will eat on the train the rest of the trip.

I buy Charles father a hand woven blanket; the colors remind me of the desert sunset. Charles is not sure what his mother likes, so I picked out a silver chain for her to wear around her neck. I want to buy a small ristra, but Charles says no and I put it back. It is exceptionally hot and dry. I breathe in the colors, and sounds to keep in my memory so I will never forget. Diary I am giving you an Indian paintbrush flower to stay safe for me between your pages. I am frightened.

I reach up and touch the silver chain on my neck almost as an afterthought as if I have been wearing it for years. Looking at the beautiful blanket, I realize they were gifts purchased in love by Louise who hoped her new family would accept her. The old lawyer has a sad smile on his face, read on dear he said.

Dear Diary

The train is forced to stop today on an extremely lonely stretch of desert. President Carranza's Federalizes board with rifles drawn, they search for Poncho Villa or any of his *Pistelerios*. Rough coarse men, who do more, yelling than searching, they force us off the train, some women are crying as their children cling to them as the men try to reassure us all is right. Charles is composed; stepping forward he shows the Federalizes his Army papers and guarantees them no bandits are onboard. The men argue among themselves finally their leader seems satisfied and they ride off their horses kicking up a cloud of dust. I am so proud of my husband the passengers shake Charles's hand and hug him as we board.

Diary as I stood by the train I look down at my feet and there was a desert rose. I put it between your pages and ask you to care for it dear friend. Mama I miss you. I pray to Our Lady of Guadalupe.

Your great-grandmother was young, but she had the strength of her ancestors in her bones, when she stood next to Charles, he was a lion protecting the one he loved. Your great-grand father telegraphed my father from San Antonio and told him of the incident with the Federalizes, and now feels relieved they were on American soil. They will stay two days in Chicago, and he has reserved a room in one of the best hotels. He and Louise plan days of rest and seeing the sights that Chicago has to offer, Louise has never been further north than El Paso Texas this will be an exciting adventure for her, one she will remember forever.

Dear Diary

We have reached San Antonio I am no longer in Mexico. There are street markets full of food and clothing just as we have seen in every town along our way. The wide dirt roads are lined with stores, hotels, restaurants, and churches, there are so many automobiles I must be careful I am not rundown. There are so many people all in a hurry to get somewhere.

Charles takes me into an extremely fancy restaurant to have dinner. The manager will not give us a seat he says we do not serve Mexicans in this establishment: furious Charles grabs the man by his shirt. I am afraid he is going to kill him. I beg Charles to let him go, and we can just leave. Charles throws him to the ground and storms out. Oh, diary is this just the beginning of trouble. How will I be treated in Charles hometown, will they respect me or throw me into the street? Dear friend I am placing a piece of sweet grass between your pages. Keep it safe, it makes me think of home and Mama.

I look at attorney anger filling my heart, yes my dear prejudice, for the first time in Louise's life she is the recipient of prejudice. Read on dear, his voice is soothing.

Dear Dairy

The land is different now as we travel eastward everything is so green the trees are extremely tall and full of leaves surrounding large farmhouses. Growing on the land is row after row of corn. So much food is grown on this land, everyone must be very rich, when I tell Charles this, he shakes his head and smiles at me. Well they must be rich all the same. We will be in Chicago soon I wonder what it will be like. Diary

I found a maple leaf I will put it in your pages to stay safe and show Papa.

After four, days, the train arrives in Chicago. The first thing Charles does after they settle in their room is to wire my father saying they arrived safely. The weather is cold, and he must take Louise shopping for warm clothes, as hers are not suitable for the New England winters. He will wire my father when they arrived in New York.

Dear Diary

I only have a moment as Charles is telegraphing his lawyer. I must tell you about Chicago. The buildings reach the sky, higher than any church in Mexico and so many people, and automobiles', noise oh, the noise, horns beep, and people shout loudly to one another, whistles and sirens, I have not heard anything like this before. It is also extremely cold how people can live in such freezing temperatures I do not know. When Charles comes back he is taking me shopping, he says I need warm clothes to wear. I wish papa could be here to see all this.

Charles enjoys watching Louise try on different outfits each one makes her look more beautiful than the first, the eyebrows of some of the shop girls raise as it is not the rule for a pregnant woman to be seen being so bold in public. Charles cares little about society's opinions his thoughts are only for Louise and her happiness.

Dear Diary

Oh! The beautiful clothes I have, I look just like a rich American lady Charles says. I have velvet dresses with lace and jewel trims, fur coats, and muffs all with hats to match. Leather boots with high heels and so many buttons. Charles bought me pretty clips for my hair. He says I must wear it up now to look fashionable. I know his family will love me now that I look as they do. Diary, I am putting between your pages the theatre tickets from last night's show. Charles and I saw Sarah Bernhardt the actor on stage. She has only one leg and reclines on a beautiful couch, where she performs, so elegantly. I had such a lovely time people are extremely polite, now that I have on my new clothes, I wish Mama and Papa can see me.

They cram as much as possible in the two days they have, museums and shopping during the day, theatre, and restaurants in the evening. Wherever they go Louise enchants, all around her, her genuine passion for what she is experiencing becomes catching. However, the two days pass quickly before they know it, they are boarding the train for their last leg of the journey, in, less than a week they will be in Hartford, meeting Charles's family.

Dear Diary

We must leave Chicago now I do not want to, I feel like a fairy princess here. Diary your pages are getting full of all my treasures. I have seen and done many things on this journey, but I want to be home. I know you will care for my memories,

how I love Charles. The baby is always kicking now I think he is happy.

After they board the train, time goes by quickly before the two realize it they are approaching Grand Central Station in New York City. Charles decides they should spend the night in a hotel to relax from the long journey and start out fresh in the morning. Hartford is only a two-hour trip from New York. Your great-grandfather wired my father asking if he would let Charles parents know of their arrival. He was not quite sure that surprising them is a good idea. My father agreed it was a better plan, allowing the Blacks time to prepare for their visit. Louise stayed in the hotel as Charles went about the task of telegraphing Hartford, she was tired.

Dear Dairy

Feb. 19.1918

My body is so enormous it is a challenge to walk any distance. Both my ankles are swollen, and my backaches I tease Charles that the baby will be a strong Vicario able to rope and ride as soon as he is born. Charles just wants the baby to be born healthy and cares not whether it was a boy or a girl, but I am convinced the child will be a strong healthy boy, and that is that. We are staying this evening in our room. Charles promises we will come back to New York to see the sights on our way back to Mexico. Now we just need a decent night's sleep. We must board the train for Hartford at 8:00 am

tomorrow morning. Mama, I am afraid and desire to return home

Dear Diary

Feb. 20, 1918

Well diary we are almost there

Charles is fussing, and fretting am I comfortable, am I warm enough, even though I have put on my beautiful dark blue velvet suit with fur trim and muff. Do I need something more to eat? I assured Charles I am quite comfortable, warm, and full. Diary I feel Charles anxiety and try to reassure him all will be well. Nevertheless, his hands are cold. I tell him how much I loved him, and no matter how this day goes, we will always be together. Mama I am frightened pray for me.

Your great-grandfather told my father several times of an uneasiness he felt that he could not stop. Hartford Connecticut the conductor yells as the train pulls into the station Charles sits frozen in his seat. Louise is up, and on the moved, hurry Charles she says handing him his hat and cane, she is down the train aisle almost before he could move; the conductor helps Louise down the train's steps and deposits their luggage on the platform. The day Charles dreaded has arrived. My Father meets them at the station and falls utterly in love with Louise. She has him in the palm of her hand with one smile.

My father tells Charles he has gone to prepare his parents for their coming arrival and, they seem pleased, his mother especially, ordering the housekeeper and cook to arrange everything just the way Charles likes. When they arrive at the house, Charles asks my father to accompany them inside, still not sure of their reception, Louise comments she knows everything will be just fine with a shaky voice. Before they can ring the bell, the door opens, and there stands Charles mother.

Charlotte is an imposing figure dressed entirely in black; however, she reaches out towards her son clasping his hands in hers welcoming him with a kiss on the cheek. Come in, come in she exclaims, your father is in the living room, she seems to ignore the fact Louise is standing next to Charles. Mother this is my wife Louise, Charles says as he put his arm around her, ah yes your wife, well yes come in dear, Charlottes voice is as cold as ice. As they walk into the living room Charles father stands up from his armchair, the men shake hands and exchange pleasantries, father I would like you to meet my wife, Louise this is my father. The old man stands like a stone, the room is quiet, Charlotte clears her throat. Sit down everyone you must be tired from your long journey. Charlotte rings a small bell the housekeeper enters carrying a tray of coffee, tea, and small cakes, Charles jumps up grabbing the tray he plants a large kiss on the housekeepers cheek. Bertie you look beautiful, are my parents treating you well, Oh! Mr. Charles it's so lovely to have you home, Bertie this is my wife Louise, the housekeeper smiles from ear to ear, so happy to meet you Miss Louise. Enough now Bertie serve the refreshments, please. Charles Sr. has been quietly observing every move Louise makes scrutinizing her every gesture, in almost a whisper he asks when is the child expected to be born. Charles turns abruptly towards his father, the words seemed to hang heavy in the air. However, Louise answers quickly in five weeks, he nods and seems to dismiss her, I feel fine, and the baby is extremely strong I know it will be a boy. I am sure you are my dear, and the baby will be healthy whether a boy or girl Charlotte says. The atmosphere in the room is intense, and the air is heavy, Charles parents exchange small talk with my father only as a courtesy and seem relieved when he gets up to leave. Charles walks him to the door if there is anything I can do for you or Louise you just have to call, remember I said anything Charles. Your Great-grandfather puts his arm around my father and thanks, him for what he has done so far, saying he will be in touch and closes the door.

My dear Marie this is all I can tell you now, the next chapter of the story you must hear from Louise, he says. I do not know if I can go back into that room and, face Louise after what I have learned today. The old man gets up and comes around the desk taking my hand in his, Oh my dear you must, you not only owe it to yourself but also Louise. She is your Great-grandmother, and she has a right to tell her story in her own words. She and she alone know what happened in that month she lived in Charles parent's house. I can pick up the story after her death and I will. However, it is her account you must hear. I put the dairy back into its box and get up to leave, Mr. Burton hands me a card on the back is written his home phone number. If you need me just call my son and I will come to you in minutes. I reply, I will call after I speak to Louise and perhaps our next meeting can be at Rosie's house. I would like that he says, yes, I would like that very much.

Getting into the car my feelings are mixed, I genuinely want to know the next chapter in this family drama then I do not. I tell myself forget everything, call the real-estate place Rosie's house on the market including the contents and let someone else worry about it. But I know I cannot, this is as much my story as Louise's, and I will see it thou' to its end.

Arriving at Rosie's a quiet cheerfulness pervades the air, Hi Rosie I say as if she will come out of the kitchen any minute to give me a hug. You sure left me a mess to clean up old girl. I put the tote with all the papers along with the box containing Louise's treasures on the couch, all of a sudden I feel hungry, going into the kitchen I find food left over from the wake. A sandwich and glass of wine will do the trick. I settle back on the couch and start to thumb through the diary. The wine is relaxing me. Read the diary and decide what to do after I think. The lawyer might be right Louise should be able to tell her story, and I need to listen to what she has to say.

Birth and Death

Funny, I think of Rosie's room as Louise's now. I cannot figure out why Rose did not use another room as hers. She could have chosen from four other rooms, all decorated so much prettier. Was this atonement Rose must do for the forgiveness of some sin. My mind is spinning this question must be for another time. Today will be hard enough for both Louise and I so one thing at a time. I open the door to Louise's bedroom and gloom the lifts a bit; I walk straight to the windows and open the heavy drapes to let in the sun, its streaming light makes the heavy Victorian furniture less foreboding. I call out Louise's name as I cross the room taking a seat at the dressing table. I breathe deeply to calm down. Louise is waiting for me as I hold up the mirror. *Buenos Dias Abuela* I say hoping my Spanish is not too amateurish *Buenos Dias*, Louise answers with a smile you look beautiful today the sun is glistening around you, like an *angel*. I feel the glass wishing with all my heart I could reach out and embrace the great-grandmother I never knew about.

Abuela, I went to see the family Solicitor, ah Signore Burton yes. He gave me some of your things, Louise smiles I see you are wearing the silver chain I bought in Monterey. My hand went to my neck touching the delicate silver of the chain. I am glad you have it I think I bought it for you all the time. *Abuela* he also gave me your diary, I have found and read the letters Charles wrote to his mother, Louise nods, and whispers Charlotte. Mr. Burton told me a good deal of what he knows about you and Charles marriage and your journey here. Last night I read much of your diary. I know you are my great-grandmother and Tillie is not, however, I am extremely bewildered by this turn of events, and am trying to hold on to whatever reason I have left. I think there are things only you can tell me, things that only you know. I will tell you, the day Marcus was born she says without my asking. "Yes and the day you died." As I look in the mirror, I see tears in Louise's eyes. I am sorry maybe another time this must be terribly difficult for you. "No", Louise says, this is the time, there is no other. Have I made a cruel mistake asking Louise to relive her own death? Then again, I am drawn to the mirror like someone with no will of her own. I sit quietly as Louise starts.

The hurt wakes me, tearing through my body like a butcher knife. I lie perfectly still and wait, looking out the window at the night I see no stars, no moon just shadows. Another pain rips violently into my groin and down my legs. Mama says the pain would be extremely hurtful but not to worry when it is over a beautiful child sent by God will be in my arms, and I will forget the pain. I look out the window into the night trying to see into the darkness. Count, count the minutes between the pain, one, two, three I grab at the sheets, tearing into their white starchiness pulling hard, I can smell the sickening scent of lavender in the air around me. I stare into the blackness outside, lay still it is not time to wake up Charles yet. I feel his breathing next to me, but it does not comfort. Another pain rips and slashes at me Oh Mama help me. No, no count the roses on the wallpaper. Large red roses, again one, two, three, four they are all blurred, just keep counting five, six the pain. My body is drenched with sweat my hair sticks to my neck like glue. You will be fine Mama says, you will be fine do not scream, look at the roses. Ugly roses I hate them.

At home, the cactus flowers are blooming, horses are running free in the desert, I see them their tails and manes blowing wild in the hot wind, they stop to look, their mouths opened in horrible smiles screaming, screaming at me.

Water is running down my legs it is me, I am screaming Mama, Mama Help me. Charles jumps up, I feel his movement, yet everything seems to be a blur.

"My God Louise," he pulls the white sheets back, the bed is soaked with blood and water, my nightgown is stuck to my body, the pain, I must get away from the pain I'm struggling to sit up cannot move. Charles runs to the bedroom door calling for his mother to come at once. I try to see, to focus on Charles as he quickly dresses. "Louise", he says, coming to the bed, his hand stroking my wet hair, you will be OK I am going to call the doctor, do you hear me"? I try to nod but can only scream in pain. My stomach is moving downward, and my legs are tearing from my body.

"Damn it mother hurry"! Charles yells as he runs into the hall. Do not leave me, I murmur, but maybe not, maybe it's not me, I feel so far away like I am looking thru a dark glass.

"I will not be spoken to in that manner in my own home," someone snaps" mother shut up, Louise needs you this minute, I'm going to call the doctor." I see a shadowy figure standing by the bed staring down at me with a look of utter disgust on her face.

Someone is stabbing me in the back, why is she hurting me. I push the knife away, but it is still going deep into my flesh my arms are moving fighting, to stop the horrible stabbing pain. The bed is hot and sticky; I am drowning falling ever deeper into the red hot water surrounding me. The shadowy figure moves ever closer, quietly it says stop you are acting it will do no good. Acting yes, a play like one Charles and I saw in Chicago, someone is acting on the stage I am only watching from far away. I hear Charles talking to the dark person, something about a doctor; I hold out my wet hand to him and feel his warmth as he touches me. Louise darling listen to me, can you hear? Am I nodding? I think I am, the doctor is out tending a farmer, the people have no phone father, and I will go to get him and bring him here. Do you hear me? I feel him grab and shake my shoulders, say you hear me my darling, I shout out yes as my body is racked again, I'm coming back soon I love you he says. I hear Charles speaks again to the dark shape about towels, string, and scissors help if the baby comes. What baby, is someone having a baby, how nice, a baby. I hear the door slam, Charles please, do not leave me, please. I see the shadowy figure walk over to the window then look out, the blackness is gone, the sky is cloudy, I can see the rain hitting the window as a hand pulls back the curtains, the air smells fresh and clean. The dark figure moves from the shadows, its Charlotte a smile on her face as she stares out into the bleak daylight. I watch her walk to the bed, well my dear I will leave you now. I am sure a woman like you can cope with the birth a baby, think how lucky you are here in a nice bed or would you prefer being out in a field somewhere. I can hear a faint please, in the air, Charlotte walks to the door and turns to look at me for just a moment, I hear the door close. Yet, I feel her evil presence lurking in the shadows, is she still here watching quietly. The pain is tearing my flesh I arch my back as another and another slash at me. I am "having" a baby! It is me screaming. Mama help me, I look over at the chair across the room the giant ugly one I hate. I can see the towels stacked on the seat with string and scissors on top, I have to get to them. I slowly move from the bed, blood is everywhere covering the once white sheets, sticky and foul smelling. I fall to my knees on the floor I can feel the hot puddle around my legs, the roses on the wallpaper drip their petals on the floor, I drag myself to the chair their redness is everywhere I must protect my baby. I pull the towels onto the floor the scissors and string fall near my hand I cannot crawl back to the bed I am to weak. Then the tearing, screaming, and pushing happen at once, I bend my knees and open my legs the pressure becomes unbearable. I grab one towel and bite down hard on it. Another I place on the floor between my legs, push, push I see Mama sitting on the floor next to me my body explodes with a flood of pain. Sit up Louise she says the baby is here, it is a healthy boy, hold him up and pat his back until he cries, I struggle to sit up that's it, get a clean towel, and wipe the blood from his face and eyes, good girl. Now

33

the scissors and string tie the cord extremely tight and cut it. My hands are blood soaked; the scissors slip from my fingers. I try again yes, that is it, you see I knew you could do it Mama says. Now listen to me wrap him in a clean towel, hear how he cries a strong *Vaquero*. Do you see the cradle over by the dressing table you must put him in it cover him to keep him warm until Charles returns? I feel Mama's arms help me up I hold my son tight to my breast, the rose petals are everywhere, and it is hard to walk through them. I lay my precious bundle down on the clean white quilts in the cradle and cover him. His voice is powerful as he cries out for life. I think I should sit here now in the roses and rest. Wait Mama do not leave yet, Charles will be back soon we can all go home together, Papa will be so happy to see us. I need to rest here in the petals for a while stay with me Mama.

Except, I see, Charlotte is standing over me, well, well what a mess you have made, I see the little bastard has finally arrived. I grab Charlottes dress as she tries to walk to the cradle, do not you touch me, you filthy devil, but I will not let go. I hear running men's voices in the hall, Charlotte is telling them to hurry that I have gone crazy, and I am attacking her.

Dear God, its Charles' voice I hear, he picks me up from the floor, the baby do not let her near the baby I whisper, Charles carries me to the cradle and sees his son for the first time. He is beautiful my darling, he is beautiful. There is another person in the room he is giving orders to Charlotte, sheets, hot water, and, clean towels now. I am so tired, but I know I am safe, my husband is holding me in his arms no one can hurt me. Charles lays me on the pure white bed I can smell the lavender in the air. *Amor mio* I will never leave you ever, I reach up to touch his face, but he is gone. Louise is silent.

I sit shattered, fragmented as autumn leaves blowing in the wind. Charlotte my Great-Great-Grandmother stood by and watched her daughter-in law bleed to death on the floor in this very room without lifting a finger to help. Revulsion and disgust spread through my body. Wrenching from a hate I never knew I could feel bile it raises in my mouth like a vile poison. Knowing her blood runs through my veins horrifies me. I want to rip my flesh to purify myself of her evil within me.

Louise breaks the silence, Maria do not weep so hard, *amour, amour.* I am here with you. I wasn't aware I was crying, I pull the mirror close to my cheek whispering I am so, so sorry." No", Louise says, you see Mama is right the pain it is gone. My son is born he grew to be a man then had a son and now there is you. I have waited for you all this time my beautiful *angel* it was for you, I stayed.

Louise what happened after, I just cannot say the words, "after I died", "yes". Before I can say more, call Signore Burton, and have him come here, he and I will tell you together what happened. I am tired and must rest Louise closes her eyes. I lay the mirror down on the dressing table. Shivering with more questions than answers running thru' my brain. I sit in the silence of the past. This room of heartache, where the red rose wallpaper dropped its petals to the floor stares sadly back at me. The large ugly chair Louise hates, the one that held the towels, scissors, and thread is still in the corner, and on the floor beneath it my grandfather was born struggling for life. Here at my feet was his cradle where with her last once of strength Louise placed her beloved child guarding him against Charlotte until Charles returned to keep him safe.

The large bed calls out to me, I get up and walk over to it. Among the clean white sheets in the arms of her beloved husband, Louise died. I lay down, curling up among the pillows and with a scent of lavender still in the air fall asleep.

I have made up my mind I am going to go to Mexico. I want to see my family. Start a new life shake off the ropes and chains that keep me captive to myself. I want to take Louise home out of this nightmare into the sun. This is a reckless move for you my dear Mr. Burton comments "Yes", I know, and it is about time, safety, walls, comfort, my life, now I want to start living. Only you do not know the whole story yet my dear "NO', that's why I called you, But after what I have heard from Louise nothing can change my mind.

The sun fills the room as I pour coffee into the lawyer's cup. My dear selling everything and starting over in another country is not easy especially for someone, he pauses, someone like me who honestly never left the nest or traveled far from her safety zone, Well I would not have said it so harshly but yes. You see that is just why I have to do this; anyway, I will not be a waif out on the streets. With the sale of the house, my inheritance from Rosie, and my saving, I will be quite comfortable. If not I will begin teaching in Mexico. You see I do have a plan. Have you told Louise yet, the Lawyer asks, no I thought when we are all together I will say something. Hum, have you seen her today, "yes" this morning I told her, you were coming, she is happy to be seeing you. Well, he said, no time like the present getting up from the couch there is a spring in his step as the old gentleman climbs the stairs to Louise's room, me following behind.

Louise dear, Mr. Burton quietly calls as we enter the bedroom; well the place is at least tolerable with the drapes opened and the sun coming in. I use to tell Rose, pull the drapes back, open the windows, let the light in, she was too terrified to change anything, fearing what might happen if she did. Rosie terrified I thought, the concept is hard for me to embrace, she is Rosie the rock, Rosie the glass always full, Rosie the mighty, not Rosie the terrified.

Louise are you awake, He calls picking up the mirror "ah" there you are as beautiful as ever. Thank you for coming I have told my great-grand daughter all I could tell without your help. I am here now and together we will finish your story, thank you my amigo I know I can count on you.

I sit quietly as these old friends speak words of comfort to each other hardly aware I am in the room. Louise dear are you sure you are up to this Mr. Burton asks, Maria must know she says, the lawyer turns to me, Marie are you ready all I could do is nod yes like a bobble head doll. Well then, he says making himself comfortable in a chair near the dressing table, his hand cradling the glass, so Louise has a clear view of me sitting next to him, he begins.

When the doctor quietly tells Charles Louise is dead, he shrivels within himself; becoming an old man right in front of everyone. There is nothing the doctor could do you see Louise and Charles both died on that cold March day. Charles senior quietly slips out of the room telephoning my father to come to the house immediately. On his arrival, the scene he witnesses is chaotic. Charles will not let go of Louise he clings to her as a drowning man clings to a life preserver. Charlotte is telling the doctor he must remove the body quickly, her voice is getting shriller, and more agitated with every word. The poor man is trying to convince Charles he must take Louise away only Charles hears nothing. Yet above this clamor, the baby sleeps a contented sleep, only a child can. You must do something Charles Sr. says, father walks over to the bed where Charles holds Louise and whispers in his ear, "It is time to let go now Charles, the doctor will take good care of Louise, not to worry." Charles looks at him and slumps back into the chair a broken hollow man. The doctor works quickly wrapping

Louise's body in clean white linen sheets, all the time Charlotte keeps saying, "Just get her out of here." Mr. Burton pauses for a moment looking at Louise asking, "Are you all right my dear to continue." Please, yes she says I want Maria to know everything. He starts his narrative again; within minutes, the mortician arrives and finishes wrapping the body gently placing her on the stretcher and with his burden starts out the bedroom door, Charles lets out a strangled sob. Charlotte runs over to her son, soothing his forehead, I will take care of you now Charles, I am here dear, Mothers here. The doctor gives Charles a sedative making him lie down to rest. Charlotte says she will take care of all the funeral arrangements, dismissing the doctor with, "we no longer need your services." Charles father asks the man to follow him downstairs to the study where he will pay him and see him out. My father turns to leave; However, Charlotte asks him wait. As Charles slowly drifts off into a drugged nightmare, she walks over to the cradle where the child gently sleeps. A look of pure hatred flashes across her face as she hisses to my father, get rid of the child, I do not care what you do with him; just take him from this house. That is an excellent idea, my father answers, I will keep him for a few days at home, and my wife will love fussing over him. When things are back to normal, and Charles is on his feet again, he can come and get his son, yes-good idea. You do not understand I said get rid of the baby, I do not care what you do with him, keep him or give him to an orphanage, do whatever you will. Charles never needs to be reminded of his tragic folly, and this is just what the baby will do, remind him every day. I know what my son needs now, that is rest, and to start his life over in a respectable marriage when the time comes. Her words shake my father to his very core, yet he prevails, I think when is well again Charles will need his son with him to give him strength to accept his new life without Louise. The only strength my son needs is his family that being his father and me. We will make the right choices for Charles about his future, and the one I am making now is the child must go do you understand. Either you do it, or I will, hearing a veiled threat in her voice my father agrees to take the child home with him until Charles calls him with further instructions. So with the baby in tow, and the things Louise lovingly made, and purchased for Charles Marcus, to start his new life in my father leaves this sad house.

Weeks go by, and my father does not receive the awaited call. Mother is in her glory with two babies to care for. I am eighteen months old, and Marcus is so small and helpless, she appeals to my father if Charles actually does not want Marcus could they be the family to adopt him. Father is reluctant and tells her Charles will want his son with him, to raise him and to love him, adopting the baby is out of the question. Father wonders to himself just what is happening in that house, yet every time he calls the Black home, he is informed the family is in mourning and not receiving calls.

Charles fades away with every passing hour, spending his days quietly in a drug-induced hangover never leaving his room, his nights in the hellish nightmare of twisted truth only sleeping pills can reveal. Charlotte, hovers, stroking his forehead and caring for her son not leaving his side but for scant moments to speak to her husband about calling the funeral home to have Louise's body cremated immediately or the housekeeper as to what she wants prepared for dinner. She and she alone will exert her will over Charles, she will bring him back from his recklessness, and he will acquiesce to her plans for him and the family. Only she does not have the friendship of time, In Tillie's last postcard from Paris she writes, she and the family will be returning to Hartford by mid-April, Charlotte must now concentrate all her strength of will showing Charles in his weaken state he should trust her to make the right decisions for him.

Charlie the Magnificent

Escape is so close, in his terrifying dreams, Charles sees how his first disobedience in his young life helps seal his fate shaping him into the reflection he sees looking back at him in his shaving mirror as he readies to meet with the lawyer Mr. Burton Sr.

He knows he will be in trouble, his mother Charlotte told him if not once than a million times not to swim in the filthy Connecticut River that flows behind the house. His mother never lets him do anything his friends can, after all he is ten already but it is always the same do not climb trees, do not race your bicycle to fast, you will get hurt no, no, no is all he hears from her. His friend John is beginning to call him a Mama's boy and Charles hates that. Today he will sneak down to the river, and swim with his buddies, no one will be the wiser especially Mother.

The morning has dawned hot and sultry the air a heavy wet curtain hanging over everything it touches a perfect day for a swim, and the day will only become more oppressive as it wears on. Good he thinks all the adults will stay indoors trying to avoid the heat and foul air that is as still as a graveyard and he will be free to swim to hearts content.

Quietly creeping up the extravagantly carved staircase hoping he will make it unnoticed to his room, where he could change into his bathing costume and waite for the opportune time to make his escape.

Rats! Charles what are you doing skulking around like a criminal, Mother is at the bottom of the stairs looking up at him, I want you to spend the day in your room she says, Oh! It is so stifling a mere movement will cause one to fall in a faint. Do you hear me Charles, read a book or something, just keep quiet I do not want you getting ill? I will send Bertie up later with some lemonade. I feel giddy quite giddy from this heat. I have to sit down; running the house in this weather is more than I can endure. Lunch will be light I think; we can have something more substantial tonight when it is cooler. Now up, you go, Mother may I skip lunch today, he asks politely, it is just too hot to eat, please Mother, Oh very well, you may be right.

Bertie, fresh lemonade now hurry Oh this heat. Charles watches as Charlotte retreats to the cool darkness of the parlor with a smile on his face closing the door to his room, safe at last. All he has to do now is change and wait until lunch is over and the house is still. It feels like an eternity in time has passed, but it is little more than an hour, Charles opens his door without the slightest sound poking his head out ever so slightly to listen, good, not a peep. Bertie is in the kitchen cleaning up after the midday meal mother is in the parlor. Now is his chance, grabbing the towel from his bed Charles starts down quietly, pressing himself against the staircase wall with only the carved gargoyles as sentinels watching? He looks like a small-lost caterpillar in his woolen stripped swimming outfit trying to find freedom in the outdoors. He makes it, bolting across the side of the house as fast as his legs can move, down the hill, and into the woods where he finally slows his pace, he can hardly breathe the heavy air into his lungs, panting he drops to one knee for just a bit, feeling he is now out of view of the house. Mother might be giddy from the heat, but Charles is reeling from the pure excitement of his escape.

He can hear his friends laughing and splashing in the water as he runs out of the woods to the river's edge. Hi, Charlie his friend John calls out come on in the waters great, dropping his towel in he jumps. Yes, he is Charlie, Charlie the fantastic, Charlie the magnificent, swimmer extraordinaire, he thinks as he paddles his way out to his friends in the river.

The boys splash and wrestle each other diving under the water and bobbing up like corks, spitting streams of the dirty water in each other's face and laughing until their sides ache, unaware the current is getting stronger pulling them further into the deep murky Connecticut River.

The afternoon is now waning, and Charles knows he had better head for home before his mother misses him. The other boys have already swum to the shore and are lounging on the grass skipping stones into the water to see who can throw the furthest. It is just he and John in the water now, both boys are tired from the day's antics, and the bank looks miles away. As they start swimming, Charles pulls far ahead of his friend, hey Charlie wait up I'm getting tired John yells as Charles stops swimming and turns, he can see John floundering in the water, flapping his arms in the air trying to stay afloat. Help help, Charles hollers to the boys on the shore as he starts swimming back towards John. Two of his friends jump in and start swimming out as fast as they can the third he can see is running for help. Charles is exhausted the water pressing against his chest with such force he feels crushed his arms are like heavy logs as he raises each one out of the water to take a stroke forward. John is screaming now as he keeps sinking under the water then fighting his way to the surface. Charles's muscles burn like hot coals, but his only concern is to save John, he can hear his two friends coming behind him as he surges forward. The three boys reached the spot were John is struggling only to find nothing, each dive under the dark murky river repeatedly grabbing and pulling up anything they can feel until they have no strength left, but John is gone. They can hear the rowboats coming toward them, the boys are holding each other to stay afloat, unstoppable tears run down their cheeks and mix with the unrelenting tide. The men in one boat get the boys on board wrapping each in a wool blanket to stop their shaking keeping them warm as they row back to shore while the other searches for John. Charles can see a crowd has gathered on the riverbank it seems as though half of Hartford has heard the news and have come to see what happened. Charles feels nothing only the wet cold that has seeped into his bones. As the boat reaches the shore men pull it up onto the land. People all speaking at once wanting to know what occurred surround the boat. The crowd only parts when the police officers push them aside to allow the boys desperate mothers through. Charles sits with his head down pulling his blanket tight over his body he knows the wrath of Charlotte to come. Two of the boys are carried from the boat, upon setting their feet on solid ground, are smothered with hugs and kisses by grateful parents and taken home. Charles looks up to see his mother and knows there will be no kisses for him. As the man in the boat goes to pick him up he pushes him away drops the blanket and stepped out of the boat on his own, Charlotte makes no move toward her son, dragging his feet in exhaustion slowly the boy walks to his mother. He can see the fury in her eyes and with the full force of that anger; she slaps him across the face. How you dare disobey me, she hisses. Seizing him by the arm her grip like iron she drags him home. Charlie the fantastic, Charlie the magnificent, swimmer extraordinaire has drowned with his friend John.

The freedom he feels for such a short time again was with Louise, only she is dead also. Everything good Charlotte's spirit touches withers and dies like the red roses in winter. Now flight is impossible he is a prisoner for life. Only he could spare his son, there is an escape for him, Mexico where Louise's family can raise him with love, and he can grow to be a man of honour.

One day with no advanced notice, Charles shows up at the Lawyers Office alone. Father at first says he does not recognize him, he is thin, and haggard, his pallor grey and dusty the once tall young man with the look of love and ease is no more, he is replaced by a dim shadow. Sit down my boy, can I get you a drink, how about a whiskey, Charles nods and drinks the amber liquid down in one gulp. I expect you have come take Marcus home I wish you called first, but never mind I will ring up my wife, give her an hour and the baby will be ready. My father knows mother's heart will be broken, but right is right and Charles is his father. Marcus is such a happy baby, I hope you do not mind we call him Marcus instead of Charles I am sure you can call him what you want naturally. Father is rattling, something he rarely did. My son Isaac loves the child, I am sure they will be true friends growing up. Charles sits in silence, looking off into the distance. Well, let me make that call as father reaches for the phone, Charles grabs his hand, no, not yet. I have come to convey my wishes about whom I want to raise the baby, your son my father corrects, yes, my son. Well what is your decision; my father sits back in his chair and listens. I cannot raise my son on my own. My life will be different now, and Marcus must be raised in a home where he is loved and wanted. I am not able to give him that, he stops, the life I wanted, Louise and I wanted, is gone. I want Marcus sent to Mexico his Grandparents can raise him there. My Father is stunned, Charles do you know what you are saying, you are giving up the right to raise your son, your own flesh and blood, Mexico, Charles are you sure? Yes, he belongs with them he belongs in Mexico. Louise's family will care for him, Charles you are Marcus's family, you are his Father, he is your son, and he needs you. Is this your decision and yours alone, tell me Charles. Yes, it is my decision; make all the arrangements have him sent there along with his mother's ashes. Marie gasped loudly, and Mr. Burton stops in mid-sentence, did you say ashes she asks the lawyer, yes Maria, Louise answers her. Charlotte had me cremated; there is no anointing of my body, no mass for the dead, no words said for my soul. Charles never came to say good-bye. I thought Catholics did not believe in cremation Marie asks visibly shaken by what she has just heard. You are right my dear one, that is the way of the unbeliever, Louise answers. Is that why, why you are trapped in the mirror? That is only part of the reason I am here my angel, only part of the reason. Can you tell me why? In time, my angel, you will see in time. Louise looks at the old gentleman and smiles. He continues as I said, my Father shocked by Charles decision, tries to change his mind, believing his mother is influencing him. Only nothing my father says can dissuade him from his course of action. Charles hands my Father an envelope containing a large sum of money and instructions as to where to deliver baby Marcus and Louise's ashes to her parents care in Mexico. Charles you are making a terrible mistake one you will regret your whole life. I know Charles says and leaves.

Enough for today, I am exhausted in the telling, and I know Louise needs to rest also. I want to holler no, no I must hear the rest but looking at Louise and Mr. Burton I know he is right. I will have to wait for another day. He gently lays the mirror to rest on the dressing table, and we quietly leave the room. Marie I have paper work I need to find, I need a few days let us say midweek I will call first. He can see the disappointment on my face, not to worry a few days, I promise, he pats' my hand and closes the front door. I know the days will seem more like an eternity; I stop the urge to go back upstairs to ask Louise more questions, she is worn out and, I must wait. Suddenly I feel hungry, and I have to smile at myself, "Life goes on", Rosie would say, I go into the kitchen and raid the fridge.

The next morning, Mr. Burton calls saying he would return on Monday week at 10 in the morning. It is hard keeping the disappointment out of my voice a week a full week, the lawyer laughs and soothes me suggesting I ask Louise questions about her childhood on the ranch to know her as a little girl growing up. Brilliant I think to get to know my Great-Grandmother as a young girl. I thank Mr. Burton saying I would see him soon and hang up the phone. I am excited at the idea of asking Louise about her childhood, and go up the stairs to her room.

Abuela I call out as I enter making sure every day the room is light and airy; the drapes pulled back and the windows open to let in the freshness from outside. I pick up the mirror, good morning *Abuela,* good morning my angel what a beautiful morning, I hear the birds singing and can feel the sun on my face. What have you planned for today? I thought we could sit and talk, you see I know how you died, and I read in your diary about your travels here to Connecticut. Now tell me how you lived, about your family what you were like as a little girl. The horses, the ranch everything and especially how you met my great-grandfather. Louise smiles, such a long story you want to hear my *angel.* "No", *Abuela* need to hear, Please, where to start she says? What did you like to do as a little girl, did you go to school and church how many brothers and sisters do you have, did you have many friends, who were your best friends? Louise starts to laugh oh my, let me think.

I have two older brothers Miguel and Peter I am the baby. Mama and I are extremely close, she taught me everything, to cook and sew and take care of the garden and the house. Only Papa taught me about horses. I love to ride since I could remember, to sit high on a horse, and fly across the desert so fast no one can catch me. Mama will worry and scold. However, Papa will say Maria leave her, she loves horses, and they love her.

My horse is a small filly named sage (*Sabio*) because she is so wise, I love to brush and feel her soft golden coat under my fingers. I hug her strong neck, and she nuzzles me for a carrot or piece of sugar. She is my best and truest friend. She knows all my secrets. When I left Mexico, I missed Sabio as much as Mama and Papa.

Funny what we keep in memory, School, Church on Sunday and Holy Feast Days. The processions thru' town, Louise is smiling with a faraway look in her eyes. We venerate the Saint whose name day we are celebrating. Only the most holy men can carry the Saint and must be careful not to drop it or any flowers or money the people pin to it that would be a sin. The priest walks behind carrying an enormous gold cross and the altar boys carry incents that filled the air. My brothers always fight about who's turn it is to carry the incents. Mama will bless herself and wonder what she did to deserve these two devils as she tries to separate them. Then the mariachi band comes playing their best music hoping to get a specific favor from the Holy Saint. The procession marches into the Church and all the people follow, for the solemn mass, we will ask forgiveness and guidance from the Saint for a whole year. My favorite saint is Our Lady of Guadalupe she is so beautiful Her Holy Day is December 12. The faithful from all over Mexico came to Mexico City to pay homage to her image. La Morita, Our Lady of all Mexico, Mother of all Mexicans. Mexico City is bursting with pilgrims, coloured lights and flowers are everywhere the city is dressed in its finest on this special day. I remember Mama braids my hair, and I yell and make faces I cannot stand my hair in braids I like it just to be free, but no, I have to have braids. Mama weaves ribbons through them that match my dress. On this feast day we must look our best, Papa is extremely firm about this, he says we are not peasants; we are *Dueno* (owners) powerful people the town respects. That we should celebrate Our Lady's Special Day in Mexico City only proves our influence in Papa's eyes. When everyone is dressed Papa brings the carriage to the front of the house and with proper dignity, we start on our journey to the city. We see pilgrims all along the roads many on bicycles or walking, some even crawling on their hands and knees as a sign of their devotion and gratitude for a favor they received from Our Lady. There are alters decorated with flowers and flags that are waving in the breeze by the sides of the road. The closer we get to the city the more excited I become my brothers stop their bickering as Papa scolds they sit quiet now until we arrive at the cathedral. The High Mass is a most solemn occasion; the cathedral is dark and chilly, a stark change from the burning heat on the outside. As we enter through the huge doors, the only sounds we can hear is the rustling of the priests and altar boys vestments, hundreds of lit candles fill the altar and there before us, she stands Our Dear Lady aglow with a heavenly light. She is covered with flowers of every kind they were so beautiful except for the red roses, funny I didn't like red roses then, and I still don't now, but never mind, She is gorgeous and I am in heaven just seeing her. Mostly I ask her to watch over

Sabio and me as we go riding, so Mama does not worry so much. I pray to her still.

After church, the city becomes one giant fiesta, the streets are filled with family, and, friends all up dressed in their best clothes to celebrate the day. There is music and food, what food, Mama, and Palomar (dove) our housekeeper will go from a food stall to food stall in search of the tastiest for us to dine on. Hot, spicy chili's that burn your tongue and tamales, Frijoles, blue Corn tortillas, Pollo, tomatoes, mole' sauce just everything, if I close my eyes; I hear the music and laughter and feel the excitement. Papa will select the best and most decorated courtyard full of tables, alight with colors shining brightly in the night it is there we will celebrate this festive day. Palomar has a surprise she brings her fabulous cakes, filled with fruit and honey dripping down the side. I can taste their sweetness now. My friends and I play games and dance what a happy time. Before leaving for home, I see Mama and Papa sitting on the terrace holding hands smiling. My brothers and I sleep a contented sleep on the way home. I wake up snug in my own bed in the morning wondering how I got there.

It sounds so lovely *Abuela*, maybe one day I will attend the Feast of your dear Lady of all Mexico and join in this magnificent celebration. Please tell me more of your life, Marie asks.

`Miguel, Peter, and I go to a mission school near our church in town. The nuns are extremely strict. Papa says just because I am a girl is no excuse not to learn and do my best then maybe someday I will go to Mexico City to the University. Sister Mary Patrice says I must get those silly notions out of my head my responsibility is to make a respectable marriage and be a true Catholic. Papa is always at war with Sister and her old religious ideas. He is a decent man just not a good Catholic. Mama says Novena's and lights candles for his mortal soul, but Papa keeps up the war of words with the old nun over my education.

I remember times Papa took me along with him and my brothers to buy horse stock for the ranch. He teaches us how to select strong healthy beasts to look in their eyes, to feel their coat and legs make sure the hoofs are healthy with no cracks only the finest horses will be breeding stock on the ranch. On one, trip, Papa tells me I am old enough to choose my own horse. I am so excited; my brothers have their own horses and tease me, saying there is no horse small enough for me to get on. I pay no attention this is my day, and I know my precious horse will be waiting for me.

The corrals fill with horses as we arrive at the auction house. Ranchers look over the stock before the bidding starts to choose the horse right for their needs. I run ahead of Papa and my brothers pushing my way to the front of one of the corrals. The horses are running around kicking dust high into the air, most have never been in a pen before and with the noise from the crowds of ranchers talking and yelling, the smell of tobacco and sweat, they are frightened. Yet in all this confusion, I see her, my horse. Her eyes are intelligent and calm she looks right at me as if saying what took you so long I have been waiting for you. I remember climbing to the top rail of the corral with Papa hollering for me to get down. Sabio walks over to me, I reached out and hugged her neck her gold coat is warm and soft to my touch at that very moment we become best friends. Papa ties her to our wagon, I sit in back so I can talk to her all the way home, and it was one of the happiest days I can remember. *Abuela* what about my great-grandfather how did you met him, her smile is warm and happy and the shadows around her eyes vanish. In time my *angel* in time.

How easy it is to get lost in the past, but the present is encroaching on my time, there still is paperwork to do involving Rosie's estate and calls must be made regarding my decision to take a leave of absence from my teaching position. I am giving up my apartment and staying at the house, no need to have two places to live, and it will be easy to sublease my apartment. I only have to pack my clothes and bring them here that I can do in an afternoon.

Abuela There are things I want to do today, I want to move back here for a while, so I have to see about bringing my clothes and some things home then talk to my landlord about sub-leasing my apartment. Sub-lease? I have never heard that before, smiling I explain to my great-grandmother modern day real estate procedures. A good idea Louise is quick to understand what I am explaining to her. What about teaching, when must you go back to your school? Well here, it is, should I tell her about my intention to bring her back to Mexico, I think not I will wait just a bit. I am taking a leave of absence from my teaching, a leave of absence she asks, *Abuela* it means I am taking some time off from teaching, can you do that, she says, I explain, I have the time, and I think this would be an excellent opportunity for me to take it. I have been teaching for twenty years, and a year sabbatical is a good idea. What will you do she asks how will you live? I can hear the concern in her voice. There is no worry about living expenses. I will receive a financial grant, I have money saved, and at the end of the year, I will find a new teaching position probably in another country. We can spend time together, and you can help me study. I want to learn all about your life, Mexico, what the war was like, how you met Great-Grandfather everything. Louise looks at me smiling. This is a good idea, will you also tell me about your life, I only know what Rosita would tell me when we talked before going to bed at night. I know she never told anyone about me only Senior Burton, but he already knew everything, and so does his son: I think she was afraid of what people would think. Yes! You may be right; I find it hard to believe Rosie was afraid of anything only this I guess so. *Abuela* I am leaving now I have much to do today. I will be back before dinner and tell you what I have accomplished. See you later I love you my angel. Putting the glass down I leave the room to develop a plan of action.

I don't realize how difficult it is to sub-lease my apartment, not the legalities and paper work my real estate agent takes care of most of that. It is what to take and what to leave behind, maybe Mr. Burton is right starting over is not an easy matter. I decide to take what I brought with me from Rosie's house. I will pack these things along with my clothes and sort later. This way I will not overlook something that might mean a great deal to me now that

Rosie is gone. I go to the moving and storage store purchasing as many boxes, bubble wrap, tape as I think I need, and began working. I want to be home before dark, so Louise does not worry. I think to call her to let her know when I am on my way, I laugh to myself as I realize our modern phone service does not connect to someone confined in a mirror. Locking the apartment door behind me, I drive to a fast food restaurant to pick up dinner and hurry home to eat with Louise. The house is dark when I arrive I forgot to leave a light on, I quickly remedy it as I enter and call out to my Great-Grandmother I am home hoping she could hear me. With fast food bag in hand, I climb stairs to have dinner with Louise. *Abuela* I'm home I say picking up the mirror, she is there looking a bit forlorn, are you all right I ask, just a little lonely, for years I visited with very few people and there were days when there was no one to talk to at all. Now when you go I feel lonesome waiting for your return, silly is it not? I reach out to touch the reflection in the mirror, never worry about being alone again, I am here and have no plans to leave, and you are stuck with me whether you like it or not. Louise smiles, I think I love the idea she says and with her next breath asks what smells so bad in that bag you have on the table. My dinner I reply as I unwrap the burger and cold fries. No! You cannot eat that it is not fit for the pigs on the farm. Where does food like that come from she asks? I am not sure myself, I reply, throw it out Louise says making a face to put her point across. I wish I could make you a warm hardy meal, the kind my mother made me growing up in Mexico. Maybe someday we will be able to have dinner on the terrace of my family's *hacienda* in Guadalajara. I like that, I like that very much, I say. We talk awhile longer before saying an early goodnight. Mr. Burton is coming tomorrow with more papers for me to sign regarding Rose's will, promising to spend the day with us finishing his story as how his father brought baby Marcus and Louise's ashes back to Mexico.

Before going to my room, I go downstairs to the kitchen to do some early lunch preparation so I would not miss anything the lawyer has to tell.

The next morning dawns sunny and warm, promptly at 10 o'clock the front doorbell rings there stands Mr. Burton in a dark grey suit, his silver white hair and piercing blue eyes gives me a sense of an anchor stabilizing a still rocking ship. I can count on his advice being sound and his friendship true. Good morning Marie ready for our momentous day he says smiling, please come in I am more than ready.

After signing the last of the papers settling Rose's estate, we go into the kitchen for a cup of coffee. I also want to finish lunch preparations, so I only have to grab the tray and carry it to Louise's room when we are ready to eat. I would like to ask you a question dear if you do not mind, he looks serious, what is it? I know you have not told Louise of your plans to take her back to Mexico, have you thought this thru' as to why you have said nothing to her. I am terrified to bring the subject up I say, I know she will ask questions I have no answers to. Louise has not left her room in one hundred years. If anything happens to her, I can never forgive myself. Whatever decision you make I am sure it will be the right one for you both. Well no time like the present he says getting up from the table let us go upstairs and see Louise.

I was about to learn more about my family's past, but I must never let go of today for it is the decisions I make now that will ensure who I truly am, and the person I will become in the future. Before opening the door to Louise's room Mr. Burton puts his hand on my shoulder and says" when Rose was a young woman she had a promising career as an artist, yet somehow she seemed tied to this house and the past within its walls. When she tried to step away, it always pulled her back, and each time the courage it took to leave dimmed until it finally went out. You spoke to me the last time we met about leaving and taking Louise back to Mexico, starting over, I was hesitant then, now I know it is the right thing for you to do, you have your life, and you must live it away from the shadows that will eventually smother you. Louise he calls out as he opens the bedroom door, enough of an old man's philosophizing he says smiling at me.

As we settle ourselves, he quickly picks up the mirror, you look lovely today my dear I could swear I see Louise blush, are you ready I still have much to tell. Oh yes Louise says, I have been waiting to hear about my son. Then let us get on with it my dear, him trying to setting his old bones comfortably in a hard chair. I went thru' my father's journal to make double sure my information is correct, and found a few surprises myself, he says.

When my mother is told of the plan, to take baby Marcus to Mexico she will not be dissuaded there is no way my father can go without her, and there is no way she can go without me. Therefore, it was settled we are all going together including a nurse for Marcus and me and our housekeeper Mildred. I was sure my father would be frantic with my mother's decision, but when I read his journal, I find he is quite pleased. The housekeeping and baby care could be my mother's responsibilities, and he could get on to what he is skilled at, managing the travel plans, money, also making sure there will be no problems along the journey. Mother is not about to dump baby Marcus upon his Grandparents without her first scrutinizing home, hearth, financial status and their ability to care for a baby. I think she never gave up hope Marcus would stay with us and be part of our family.

Interview with Louise's Father

As I walk up the path to the courtyard of the *hacienda*, its beauty overwhelms me. The terra Cotta color softly glows as the sun bounces from the ceramic tile roof into rays of light so vibrant you want to reach out and touch them. The light caresses my hand as I reach for the brass knocker and quietly tap on the heavy oak door its rich wood stained with age.

The door opens, and a tall handsome gentleman stands in front of me Signore' Gutierrez, I ask, yes how may I help you? My name is Carla of the Mexicana Daily News Paper. I show him my papers what can I do for you, he says quietly. Our Paper would like to do a memorial story on your daughter Louise, with your permission of course. I have come to speak to you about her life from a father's point of view if you are willing. The old gentleman smiles graciously, come let us sit here in the shade. Now what is this all about he says?

We heard of Louise's death in the United States as you know her passing sadden the town and our paper would like to do a story honoring her life. I watch a deep cloud shadow his face and think this is not a convenient time for an interview.

He kindly takes my hand, saying, "What would you like to know", her life, about her life. Mio Madre' such a life, my baby, my girl such a life. She is a blessing to my bones and loves the ranch from the time she is a little girl, she would follow me into the corals, and pastures to be with the horses, you see my daughter loved and respected them. Whatever her mother and I taught her, she quickly learned. She was an outstanding student in school. That silly old Nun says it was a waste of time sending a girl to school, what does she know. Louise went to University in Mexico City and was head of her class. She came home to be with the family after her brother Peter died. She wanted to help. If only she would have stayed in Mexico City perhaps things would be different, she might be alive today.

She married an American Soldier you know, they met when he was buying horses for General Perishing Army. She was so happy, so happy she was in love. Only such a long journey to America she had to make. I like her mother wanted her to stay here and have their child, but it was not our decision to make Louise must obey her own husband. Charles wants their child to be born in the same house he was, and be an American citizen. I can understand that, children leave home to follow their own way that has been since the beginning of time. Yet it has been extremely hard, my wife is suffering, and I miss my daughter's teasing voice.

A dark shadow returns over his eyes and his body becomes tense as he stares at his hands. That evil woman let my daughter die like a mongrel in the street; she stood by and did nothing to help Louise as she bled to death. I am sorry sir, who are you talking about, his mother, Charles's mother, a cruel wicked woman. How do you know that sir, it is terribly hard to believe a woman would not help another in the birthing of a child and you were not there, you could not know? His eyes looked into my heart and said, Clara "a father knows these things, a father knows." I am uncomfortable and want to bring the interview around to happier thoughts.

Louise has a baby boy we have heard he is coming to Mexico for you and your wife to raise here on the ranch. A smile faintly touches the corners of his mouth and all shadows disappear. Yes, my Grandson Marcus is coming; the travel arraignments are being made by my, he stops, by Charles's lawyer. They will be arriving in a few months. My wife is making things ready; it has been many years since these walls heard the cry of a baby.

You both must be extremely happy, yes, Senora' Gutierrez has lit candles to our beloved Mother of Mexico for the babies safe arrival. She believes the Lady will heal our hearts when our grandson arrives. I will wait and see. They are also sending Louise home you know. I look at him confused; I thought they buried her in the Black family plot in "Connecticut". No, sadness again outlines his face his mother would not have it. No, my daughter was cremated not a mass for the dead or a priest praying for her soul was said. She is coming home with her son back to the land she loved. A ray of sunshine touches my hand the old man smiles, I know the interview is over.

On a warm May day Isaac Burton Esq. along with his wife Abigail, his eighteen month old son Isaac Junior twelve week old baby Marcus, one wet nurse, Mildred the housekeeper and more luggage than anyone will ever need boarded the train in Hartford for the two hour journey to New York City. Fathers journal said, and I quote", we looked like a troupe of players, moving from one performance to another." I smiled as I tried to picture the chaotic scene of the dignified lawyer trying to manage this band of travelers, making sure no one or nothing is misplaced or left behind, quite a daunting task to do, first arriving in New York City then in Chicago. Senior Burton, yes Louise he answered where was I when all this traveling was going on? Well my dear it seems my mother had the urn with your ashes strapped securely in among her corsets, there she thought you would be safe as no decent gentleman would search through a ladies undergarments. Quite a sensible solution if you ask me. This time I had to laugh aloud, the shocked look on Louise's face was beyond words. Her ashes had traveled from Hartford Connecticut to Guadalajara Mexico in Abigail Burton's underwear. Not to worry my dear you arrived quite safely along with my mother's corsets the lawyer said with a smile.

The trip in general seems without incident, father reserved two sleeping compartments for each leg of the trip. They had private baths and comfortable upholstered seats that folded down at night by the trainmen making four cozy sleeping beds. Father and mother made sure we all ate together like a family in the dining car. Under these close circumstances, my parents felt it would be the right thing to do. At night, the wet nurse and Mildred our housekeeper slept in one compartment with Marcus and Mother and Father along with me slept in the other. Yet a train trip of this distance could not have been easy for anyone.

Friday May 20 a train pulled into the Laredo border crossing station, my father wrote in his diary, this was the time he dreaded most. The world is now at war, and he knows this American traveling extravaganza will be questioned and, searched most thoroughly on both sides of the border. The American patrol officers could not understand the truth that he is the Blacks' family lawyer in-trusted with the task of delivering this baby on the death of his mother to his Maternal Grandparent in Mexico to be raised. It seems there has to be a more sinister motive than that. Father writes Mother was an unmovable pillar of American womanhood supervising the luggage search, becoming quite modest when called for and indignant at the intrusion as what she saw as her families rights to privacy. The border authorities finally acquiesced to her resolute stand actually helping us cross the border into Mexico with a great sigh of relief to be rid of us. The Mexican Federally greeted us most cordially, Father thinks they saw what mother put the Americans thru and wanted none of that. A quick check of our paperwork and passports and we boarded the train that would take us to our final destination and the waiting arms of Marcus's Grandparents.

This train was hugely different from the last, comfortable sleeping compartments were replaced by hard wooden benches extraordinarily much like church pews. People sat wherever they could find a spot, there they would eat any food they brought with them, chat with their neighbors, and sleep whenever it took their fancy. The bathrooms look like outhouses for the common use of the passengers. The women were appalled at these conditions. Yankee ingenuity was called for and pushed to its maximum. Louise interrupted; tell me Senor Burton what is Yankee ingenuity please. He smiled, it is what New Englanders do when facing a difficult time. They think of ideas and ways that will ease their hardship. Oh, said Louise, but I took the same trip just months before and did not find it a hardship. However, my dear you were in love, yes she said, I was in love her voice breaking with emotion.

Abuela, should we stop for a while have lunch downstairs and Mr. Burton can finish a bit later, how would that be. No, no, please I have waited so long to hear do not stop. All right I will go to the kitchen bring up lunch for Mr. Burton and me, he can tell us more as we eat and relax how that would be. The lawyer answers before Louise brilliant idea Marie bring up lunch I am getting hungry myself.

It took me just minutes to load the tray as the coffee brewed, sandwiches, brownies, and hot coffee. Within ten, minutes, I was back in Louise's room, and we were savoring our food as Mr. Burton resumed the story between bites.

The weather is hot and dry writes Father, you do not notice at first until slowly it overtakes you in an all-consuming wave pressing against your chest. You feel you are drowning, unable to escape; breathing becomes a sheer act of will. Soot is another enemy, try as the women might they could not fight the black greasy dust that covered everything and everyone it lands on. Our noises became black portholes, and our mouths filled with the sweet oily taste of coal. The three women fretted and fussed trying to keep Marcus, and I as soot free as possible, worrying what this filth would do to our health. The lawyer inspected his food making sure it was soot free before taking another bite.

The benches were hard and unyielding, backs ached, and we babies whimpered and wailed. Mother and the wet nurse stripped us down to our nappies trying to keep us as fresh as possible, but nothing helped. The heat and hours on the train took their toll on everyone. Father could see a mix of sorrow and concern on Mothers face as she struggled to accept the fact Marcus would soon be out of her care and living with his Grandparents who were strangers to her.

I asked Mr. Burton if he remembers anything about the trip he answers, Marie I was too young, what I am relating to you is from my Fathers journal, and what he and Mother told me later. We lawyers are extremely accurate in our rendering of a situation, so I think you are getting a better idea of what happened from the journal then if I could recall anything of the trip.

Louise looks anxious, are you all right *Abuela*, I asked, oh yes my angel, just excited as we move nearer to my home and parents. I could understand how she felt I too was traveling closer only on a journey to find the truth of my like.

Dear Senor, will you continue please, Louise asked. Reaching for a brownie, he repeats the heat, long hours aboard the train, the ever-present dirt and smoke is getting the best of everyone. Yet there is a pleasure in seeing the change in the countryside as the train travels southeastward on its trek. The limitless desert is hugely different from the large congested cities of the East and the golden wheat fields that covered the flat prairies of middle United States. This land has colours my parents never saw before, Vermillion rock formations spring up from the desert floor with shapes and outlines that seem to reach the sky. The treeless landscape stretches on for miles giving the awareness of not only beauty but also a danger to.

When the train stops, which is often passengers, get off to stretch, wash off some of the grime and purchase food to eat. Father writes, Mother would ask questions of the locals at these small train stations. Her Spanish flawless and the people are happy to chat with her about anything from custom to cactus flowers, clothes, religion and the spicy food being cooked in every stall in the open air markets. Red dried chilies hung in ristras from stalls with enticing smells and bright colors. She tried all the food offered her without a single wince when it was obviously extremely hot and spicy. Father was not as brave a true meat and potato man he was more cautious in what he chose to eat. One of Mother's solutions to the hard benches on the train is to purchase the beautifully woven blankets in rich colors and detailed patterns for sales at every station. Folded on the benches of the train they became almost comfortable to sit on. Her curiosity endears her to our fellow travelers, and she receives many invitations to visit. Father says", I am proud of my wife, she is kind and caring to all those around her as she recalls a train ride in the opposite direction taken by Charles and Louise in a happier time." Now she will help her husband oversee the safe return of Louise's ashes and her newborn son to the land of their ancestors despite the ache in her heart.

In the Village of "What If"

"What If 'I would have said to my daughter, please do not go. Those words are with me always,' WHAT If" crying at me during the day and haunting my nights. I should have been strong in my convictions told Marcus no; she cannot leave home. He has always given in to her wants since she was a baby, she just had to say oh Papa, and he would melt. See what it has brought us just misery. What Father would let his daughter travel *so* far and in her condition with a stranger. He was her husband, and I know Charles was an upstanding man still he was a stranger to us with strange ways not one of us.

She loved him so much, ha; what is love. A dream nothing more just a dream. Marcus says it changes nothing. Louise is dead, and all the "What If "cannot bring her back to us. Still the question troubles my heart "What If" what if, she and Charles never left to go have their child in his family home." Was ours not good enough? What If", they had just gone across the border into Texas, I could have gone with them, and been there to help. The baby would be born an American citizen that was what Charles wanted an American child. Why travel so far, what was in this faraway place, and why did Charles have to drag my daughter there for whom. My thoughts cannot rest, "What If", what if she never left college to come back to the ranch after her brother Peter died. She would not have met Charles. "If" she met and married a wealthy businessman in Mexico City, she would have been just as happy.

I am her mother I should have taken her aside spoken to her from my heart, not left it to her father. I could have shared with her my fears telling her how terribly I wanted to be with her when the baby was born. How I could have cradled her to ease her pain, comforted her told her how much I love her, and how extremely proud I am of her. Now she will never know I was silent. My silence will torment me all my life.

Could I have prayed harder to our Dear Lady of Mexico "What If" I lit more candles beseeched heaven with my fears, would Our Lady have intervened for me, she is a mother to she knows the heartache. Our children both died only her son rose from the dead, my Louise cannot.

The sin in my life that I did not confess is that why Our Lady could not help me. I search deep into my soul I know I am a wicked person. The church says I must suffer for my sins is that why my daughter is dead for my pride and anger. Did I remember to tell the priest how willful I can be all the times I was angry with my husband calling him unkind names and telling him how I wished my father had chosen someone else for me to marry? That day at the market, I know I should have helped that poor beggar in the street calling out only I was busy buying food for our ancestors to celebrate the Day of the Dead and he was dirty and smelled, why didn't I just throw him some coins? No, I thought he was just a lazy Indian like all the rest, and he would spend my money on drink. Yet the priest says it is our duty to help the poor, but I thought let someone else help, I do not want to get my dress soiled, and you never know he might be sick. I can still see his face looking up at me. *Madre Mio* help me.

I feel pain in the palms of both my hands upon looking down I realize I have dug my nails into them. The blood is dripping on to my clothes is that a good sign? If I suffer and bleed for my sins as Christ died on the Cross, will I be forgiven? I think not forgiveness cannot come to me with just a few scratches on my hands. Marcus must not see the wounds he will be angry and say I am being silly. What if he is right, my husband is a practical man seeing things clearly for what they are. Only he can never see what is buried deep in my heart.

For now I will listen to what he says, our grandson will be here soon and much needs to be made ready for him. It has been many years since a baby has lived within our walls that I have listened for its soft cries and soothed its restless sleep. Enough of this thinking about the past, Marcus is right, I must make ready for our grandson. Now where did we put the old cradle, I will ask one of the ranch hands if he has time to look in the barn. I am sure it is there somewhere, and with a little cleaning, it will be good as new.

Tomorrow I will go to confession early then light candles to Our Lady of Guadalupe for our baby's safe arrival. "What If" I am not a good Grandmother?

The train arrives early in the morning, Guadalajara station is buzzing with activity, travelers hurry along all with seemingly important places to go. The building is beautiful and can be easily mistaken for a gothic cathedral, with carved spirals and stained glass windows. Father writes how he and mother are surprised at this beautiful bustling city. Waiting until everyone leaves the train and few people are on the platform, the Isaac Burton family, mother-holding Marcus gets off the train. There is no problem locating the babies Grandparents. Marcus Sr. and his wife Maria stand waiting with a restrained dignity for their grandson arrival. That dignity all but collapses when Maria spots the child, she runs forward with arms outstretched, but suddenly stops as her husband calls her name. Decorum is restored the two families approach and introduces each other. Father writes Mr. Gutierrez tall, well dressed in a dark suit and tie, his silver hair in stark contest to his suntanned skin. His eyes sharp and intelligent with a direct look that says nothing passes his scrutiny. I like him immediately. Maria Gutierrez is almost as tall as her husband heavy but with a comfortable look about her. She is dressed in black as she is still in mourning.

A quiet cry of Mama comes from Louise, shall I stop the lawyer asks concerned. No, please go on are you sure, my dear Mr. Burton asks. Yes, please Louise's says.

My father writes; at the arrival of baby Marcus, I could see the sadness in Maria's eyes replaced with a sparkle, a smile of pure joy lights her face. I know at seeing this couple Charles is right in his decision. This is where Marcus belongs, and I am proud to be the one to bring him home.

With Marcus and me in tow, we walk out of the train station into the hot Mexican sunlight. Signore Gutierrez has two large touring cars waiting at the entrance of the station one packed with all the luggage and paraphernalia we brought along on our journey, including Mildred and the wet nurse. The first car in line reserved for the family, Mother gives the baby to Maria after she is settled in the back of the car and then climbs in and holds me on her lap, two women from different worlds with one thing in common the love they share for these two little boys they hold close to their hearts.

Louise speaks out, in an excited voice, does your father write about the house and the horses, how about my brother Miguel and his family, I want to know everything. The lawyer smiles yes my dear my father is impressed with the ranch and thinks the *hacienda* is beautiful. We stay for a week that is all the time father writes he could spare from the office. However, during that time, our families become close.

The first day of our arrival, your mother, and father settle us into our room, where we unpack and freshen up. Mildred and the wet nurse have a room close by they will help take care of Marcus and me while your mother and mine get to know each other. Did she show your mother the baby's room, did your father write about how it looked, Louise asks. In a minute dear, allow me look through the notes Mr. Burton shuffles thru' the journal to find the correct place. Yes, here it is, Maria is quite proud of her home and is eager to show Abigail around. Yes, that is Mama she loves our family home, Louise interrupts, and Mr. Burton smiles and continues to read. After Abigail and I rest, Maria knocks I would like to show you around the house especially how we fixed the nursery for Marcus if you are not too tired from your trip. Absolutely I would love to see everything, this is such a beautiful setting I am overwhelmed at all, I see, and you know Maria, Abigail says taking her hand, I feel unusually energetic funny after such a long trip must be the warm weather. The two women leave the room chatting like old friends. In the main parlor, standing in the corner of the room a tall clock chimes the hour like a sentinel keeping watch. How handsome the tall clock is and what a musical chime it has Abigail remarks, my grandfather brought it back from Spain Louise interrupts, again oh, sorry, Signore Burton quite all right my dear he says as he continues. We have a tall clock at home I do not think it chimes as pleasantly as this does Abigail says. It comes from Europe the chimes sound like the cathedral bells along the Spanish Coast calling people to prayer Maria tells her. You must love this clock, I know mine gives me immense comfort in hearing it, and it is not as grand as this one.

Out of the corner of her eye, Abigail spots a large religious statue across the room. What is this she asks, walking toward the figure; it is a shrine to Our Lady of Guadalupe, mother of all Mexico. Abigail is not familiar with Santo's and their shrine as she is of the Protestant Faith as she approaches she knows instinctively its Holiness. I Prayed to Our Lady that your journey was not dangerous, and you would take proper care of Marcus and bring him home safe where he belongs. Thank you Abigail says as she absently fingers a lace mantilla covering the Alter. He does belong here with those who love and cherish him, Charles was right he made a smart decision.

That is Louise's mantilla, Maria says in a hushed voice Abigail looks down at the beautiful lace covering she has been touching, she wore it the day she married Charles. I have never seen anything so lovely Abigail whispers as a tear slowly rolls down her cheek. Do not be sad the baby is here, part of Louise has come home to make us smile again. Yes, you are right Abigail takes Maria's hand, now let us go see that beautiful nursery you are telling me about, Maria makes the sign of the cross and they both leave the room. Does your father write what the nursery looks like, Louise asks I have interrupted you again haven't I? I am so sorry she says, it is fine my dear, but at this rate I will not finish until next week the lawyer comments. Marie has been sitting in the large ugly chair across from the lawyer *Abuela* we must let Mr. Burton finish then you can ask all the questions you want how is that, yes you are right Louise said, please Signore go on, I will try to be still. Well my dear let me say this before you make such a vow the lawyer remarks. Your old room was made into the nursery, both the lawyer and Marie wait for a passionate response from Louise, but none comes only a quiet yes Mama did the right thing.

Maria opens the door to the nursery revealing a room filled with light, windows are on two of the walls making the room bright and cozy. The terra Cotta color has a warm glow that accentuates a large carved oak crib on the far wall filled with blue blankets and an assortment of stuffed toys. In the corner near the crib is a handmade rocking horse its mane a bit tattered from loving use. Mr. Burton pauses looking at Louise, my brothers and mine she quietly says, he nods. Beneath one window is a chest that matches the crib and next to it a large comfortable looking rocking chair., on the walls are pictures of storybook characters except above the crib where there is an assortment of photographs of the baby's mother Louise. What a delightful room this is Abigail says, noticing the room is divided in half, on the other side a bed, chest, nightstand with lamp and wardrobe. Not far from the bed is a cradle and above it a rosary. Abigail looks questioning at Maria, we have hired a nursing sister to come after you have gone to help take care of Marcus for a few months. It has been a long time since a baby lived within these walls. Maria finishes showing Abigail the rest of the house and gardens when the bell sounds for dinner. I did not realize I was hungry Abigail says, I will just go wash up, get Isaac and be back in minutes. Today has been a lovely day she thinks to herself as she opens the door to her room to ready for the evening meal and see if Isaac is awake.

The conversation around the dinner table is cheerful meeting Miguel, his wife Gabriella and their three boys let us know instinctively we would be a part of this family no matter how far away we lived. Yet a question has not been asked," Did you bring Louise's ashes home"?

It is an early night even the children fell into a deep sleep after filling their stomachs with a warm hardy meal. Good nights said, tomorrow promises to be a busy day. Father writes Marcus Sr. and his son Michael want to take him on a tour of the ranch on horseback, and he readily agrees. Although he has not ridden a horse since a child on his grandfather's farm, and that was the old dapple mare Sadie. Mother asks before falling asleep is you sure about this Isaac, he answers sleepily not really and begins to snore.

The lawyer looks at his watch, and Marie takes the hint, *Abuela* it is getting late I am sure Mr. Burton must be getting back to his office. We have taken up enough of his time today. Yes, my dear I must get back I have a client at four today and have to prepare. Louise looks sad I understand she says, thank you for coming today you have been an immense help to me. Not to worry I promise to return Saturday to finish the story the lawyer says getting up from the chair rubbing his stiff back. Collecting the journals belonging to his father that he has been reading from and some papers both he and Marie leave the room, Louise is alone with her thoughts.

What time Saturday should we expect you Marie asks the lawyer, around ten in the morning. The office is closed on Saturday, and we will have more time together? I am hoping to finish telling you and Louise what I know about the trip to Mexico to bring Marcus and Louise's ashes home. Then we can discuss what your next move should be. Yes, I was wondering about what to do next to find out the rest of the story.

The Horse Ride;

A soft knock on the bedroom door and Isaac is out of bed in an instant, it is not as if he slept much. Waking with a start in the middle of the night after realizing what he has agreed to, riding and on a horse no less, a horse. Isaac opened the door, and Palomar stands in the hall holding, a riding costume. Signore thought you might need the proper riding clothes she says handing Isaac the outfit. Thank you; closing the door behind him, he looks down at the outfit with a groan. There is nothing to do but get dressed.

Pulling on black trousers with silver medallions down the sides, a white cotton shirt, and black vest with the same medallion design, Isaac sits on the bed pulling on soft brown leather riding boots and leather chaps. Isaac turns to look in the mirror, not too shabby he says to himself for an old New England lawyer. Well if, it is not my handsome caballero, Abigail is up smiling at him, he blushes, come over here and give me a kiss she says. He picks up his sombrero and gives her a peck on the cheek. Have a good day she says as he leaves the room. Maybe he is worried over nothing, he is an educated man how hard is it to ride a horse. I just need to show it whose boss that is all.

Marcus and Michael are seated at the breakfast table having coffee, looking up they both smile their approval as Isaac enters and sits down to eat a hardy meal, hoping it isn't his last the three men finish their breakfast and walk to the coral.

A groom is holding Isaac's mount a Chestnut Stallion about sixteen hands high. As the two men mount their horses Marcus says to Isaac, Coca is a gentle creature not to worry. No thinks Isaac this beast is a mountain who can do me much harm. After several unsuccessful attempts to mount the horse, which has only caused Isaac's sombrero to become askew on his head making him look quite ridicules. Then adding to his embarrassment the groom brings a small ladder from the tack room to help him get on Coca, which he does with much trepidation. Ready Marcus asks as he and his son gallop out of the coral heading for the open range. Getty-up Coca, Isaac commands the horse and the two set off following the other riders. Bumping along and hanging on for dear life Isaac Burton Esq. of Hartford Connecticut rides the open range of Mexico.

That evening dinner conversation is a lively blend of laughter and the account of the mornings ride. Although a bit sore and stiff Isaac feels strong, this Connecticut lawyer has just come in from riding a horse on the open range of Mexico, life is good.

After dinner, the men go outside to sit and talk more about the day's events and smoke cigars. Quietly Abigail asks Maria to come into her room, she knows now is the time to give Louise's ashes to her Mother. Please sit down Maria I have something to give you. Opening her trunk Abigail reaches in and gently unwraps Louise's ashes from her corsets, the porcelain of the container feels cold against her hands, she turns holding out the vessel towards Maria tears spilling down her face. Maria reaches out hands trembling; neither woman speaks the sound of soft sobs fills the room. Maria with all the strength she could muster stands holding her daughters ashes close to her heart. Abigail puts her arms around Maria steadying her. Come with me please, Abigail, the two women slowly walk into the parlor towards the shrine of Our Lady of Guadalupe as they approach Abigail stays back to allow Maria time alone, but Maria takes her hand, please she says pray with me. Both women kneel as Maria places the container with her daughter's ashes at the feet of the statue. Holding hands, the two mothers, pray for Louise's soul to rest in peace.

The old Lawyer sits back in his chair, I have come to the end of my part of the story, both Marie, and Louise simultaneously asked why? My parents left for home the next morning and did not keep a journal for the trip back to Connecticut. The families exchanged letters after about a year they stopped. I have them here, Mr. Burton opened his case and hands Marie a brown envelope you can read them at your leisure.

The Evil Eye and the Woman in White *La Llorona*

Maria rings the rooster's neck with ease, there the job is done with hardly a feather out of place, she, then slits his throat with one stroke of her sharp knife, and hangs the bird up by its feet on a hook near the chicken coop to bleed into a small clay bowl she places on the ground. A fitting end to a proud, haughty cockcrow that prances around the hen house thinking himself better than his human kind and cannot keep his mouth shut. I do not need much blood she thinks to herself, some for Our Lady and the rest to sprinkle around the outside of the *hacienda*. Enough she says aloud, and sets about burying the creature.

One of the Rancheros hired to help break the stallions this season has come up to her this early morning as she is leaving for mass. Hat in hand he asks if he might tell her a tale told to him last night. She is in a hurry and not interested in old tales and legends until he mentions the rooster. Interested now Maria sits down on the bench by the front of the courtyard, please tell me what you heard, she says. Last night the story begins as I was sitting alone by the campfire the old rooster came close to warm himself. I told him to make himself comfortable, and he perches on a log near the fire and starts to talk, quite full of himself, he puffs up his chest feathers saying, the burrow told him, he heard *La Llorona's* wails and saw her walking in the desert, the moon light falling upon her white robes. The ghost stops and tells him, she is starting her journey, and on the night of the full moon, she will be here to take your infant grandson to her bosom. With him, she can enter heaven and be at peace. She swears the animal to silence, but he like the rooster cannot keep a secret.

Are you sure, the rooster is telling the truth, Maria asks. Oh yes, he could barely get the story out as he pranced and paraded in front of the fire telling his tale. Thank you Maria says as she hands the man a peso, she knows what must be done, and she must be the one to do it, tonight the moon is at its fullest.

Her grandson Marcus has only arrived just a few weeks ago and she is delighting in caring for him. He makes her feel young and alive again with a purpose to get up in the morning just to see his face. Now like a mother lion taking care of her cubs, she will fight heaven and earth to keep him safe. Mass will wait.

She grew up hearing the legend of *La Llorona* how she drowns her two children in a lake to be with the man she loves, but when he rejects her. She then drowns herself in the same lake, and is doomed for eternity to walk the earth looking for her lost children. She can be heard weeping and calling out "aaaay, mis hijos". "O-h-h my children." Maria's mother told her many times if she miss-behaved *La Llorona* would come and take her away not to be seen again.

She picks up a shovel digging a deep hole near the entrance of the *hacienda* Maria wraps the dead bird in a clean white linen cloth and puts him in, she then places a Crucifix on top of the corpse saying ten Hail Mary's and one Our Father as she covers the body with dirt. Without stopping, she next picks up the clay bowl of blood from the bench where she has placed it. Dipping another crucifix in the bowl, she begins praying and walking around outside the house sprinkling blood on the ground. Maria is determined in her objective *La Llorona* will not take her grandson, not this night or any other night. When she is finished, she blesses herself and takes the remaining blood into the house. Maria entered thru' the French doors walking into the large receiving room. It takes a few minutes for her eyes to get use to the cool dimness surrounding her. Holding the small bowl in her hand, she feels a strange quiet envelope her. She knows The Mother of All Mexico will not abandon her, not now, she will accept the sacrifice offered and keep her grandson safe. Maria loves the room it is her favourite of all in her house, the tall clock stands in the corner like an old town crier announcing the noon hour. Maria can remember her father purchasing it on a visit to Spain when she was just a child. The excitement the clock caused in the village when it arrived by steamship. Nothing so magnificent can be seen in all Mexico she felt. Its chimes sound like the great Cathedrals along the Spanish coast calling the faithful to prayer. The terra Cotta tile floors covered with Moorish hand woven rugs depicting significant events in Spain's history. Their bright reds, blue, and yellow soften the effect of the overstuffed dark leather couches, and chairs that furnished the rest of the space. This is the heart of the house and the pendulum clocks ticking its heart beat. Maria quietly walks to the corner in the room, toward the shrine to Our Lady of Guadalupe. A delicate white lace mantilla covers the altar; Louise wore this mantilla as her wedding veil when she married Charles. In the center flanked by two tall silver candlesticks, stands a statue of Our Lady of Mexico. Maria sees it as her sacred duty to attend to Our Lady's every need. Her soft blue robes she dusts daily and garlands of fresh flowers she places surrounding the statues feet and head. The candles are of the finest pure beeswax Maria trims the wicks every night herself so in the morning when she lights the tapers they burn clean and bright as she kneels to pray. With head bowed in respect, she places the clay bowl of blood at the feet of the icon, praying this sacrifice will be found worthy in the eyes of the Virgin, and she will stand guard-protecting baby Marcus from the fiendish clutches of *La Llorona*. However just to be safe Maria does not intend to sleep this night; she will stand guard near the cradle of her grandson and do battle with this evil aberration until her last drop of strength, sending the weeping woman back to the desert to continue her wanderings.

Maria can hear the nursing sister talking and playing with baby Marcus as goes about her day helping to care for this precious child.

At dusk, her husband returns from the day's work in the corals, helping to select the strongest and most beautiful stallions to be broken to the saddle, Marcus loves this part of horse ranching best, being out with the Rancheros selecting and training these magnificent beasts. He takes a certain pride in knowing each animal's traits, his or her strengths, and weaknesses. It is as though he has a primordial tie, a golden thread that reaches back to the beginning of time, to connect both horse and man.

Dinner is the time where the two of them share, the day's events with each other, Maria knows her beloved husband will have much to tell her of the happenings in the corals, and she is just as glad, for she has no intention of revealing her day's events and her plans for the night. Marcus will scold calling her a silly woman believing in old wives tales; nonetheless, she will take no chances with their grandson's well-being. She sits listening to her husband's chatter while she plans her night's vigil.

After dinner, they both go into the baby's room for a good night kiss before the nursing sister puts baby Marcus to sleep. Watching her husband gently hold this small infant in his arms brings back memories of other times and other infants he cradled close to his heart. The baby looks at his grandfather with deep intent eye, he smiles, and goo's wrapping this tough rancher around his fingers. Maria is thinking of their two children that died, only Miguel their oldest son is alive, now this tremendous blessing is in their midst, and Maria will see to it that he will be safe.

The evening passes slowly with Maria having one eye on the rising moon thru the window and trying to keep up conversation with her husband as though nothing is happening. Why doesn't he go to bed she thinks. Stretching finally Marcus set off to the bedroom, are you coming my dear one he asks, soon she answers, I want to check on the baby then sit out for a while; the night is so beautiful with the full moon lighting up the sky. He yawns, blows her a kiss, until later, he says, and leaves the room.

She must hurry now there is little time the full moon is reaching its zenith and *La Llorona* has begun her journey. First, she kneels praying at Our Lady's shrine asking for her protection and reminding her of the offering, Maria placed at the statues feet earlier in the day. She next ties her rosary over her belt like the Nuns, dipping the crucifix in the sacrificial blood making extra sure, of her protection she also dips the crucifix she wears around her neck. Now she is ready to do battle, the baby's room is next as she enters she can hear his gentle breathing from the crib, she removes the crucifix from her neck and places it on the sleeping child. The nursing sister is softly snoring as she sleeps on her bed across the room. Maria closes the door and goes out to the veranda to await the weeping woman.

Settling herself in a chair her weapons at the ready Maria listens to the sounds of the night. The gentle hooting of the desert owl waiting for his dinner to pass by, scurrying lizards, and scorpions as they to hunt for dinner maneuvering thru' the desert so they will not become some larger creatures meal. Then she hears it the distinct sound of crying, La Loraine is near. Maria sits on the edge of her chair like a lioness ready to pounce. Her heart thumps to a beat she has never felt before, fingers clutching the crucifix, she jumps up holding the cross out in front of her, now ready to face the woman in white.

I have come for my child the apparitions says, Maria is silent still holding the cross high in front of her scrutinizing every detail of this ghostly woman. What Maria sees is not the flowing robes, bare feet, and unkempt hair, but sorrow, sorrow in human form. All the fury drains from her body as she speaks. The child you seek is my grandson, my daughter died giving him life. I know the grief you carry, my Louise is gone, but she left her father and me part of her to soothe our heartache. Can you take this child from us? I must La Loraina says, No! Maria shouts you cannot see that nothing will soothe your soul, you murdered your children, and your penance is to walk the earth for eternity in the form of sorrow. Quiet sobs shake the ghostly woman as she turns to disappear into the desert. Maria starts to pray her rosary aloud she knows she has won.

What to do Now

What do I do now? Where do I turn for information? I can tell you this Tillie's family was quite prominent in Hartford until the death of her father Mr. Josiah Barnes in 1934 says the lawyer. Was your firm the family's lawyers also, Marie asked? No, we just represented the Black family, but at times after her father's death, I handled legal issues for Tillie concerning Charles and the Black family's estate. I am sure there is information in the state archives only I imagine it deals more with the Barnes family's business legalities, the census, birth, death, and marriage statistics. Yet give it a try you never know.

How can I thank you for what you have already done, Marie says taking hold of the old man's hand, and bringing it up to her cheek, his countenance turning a bright red, however; a brilliant smile crosses his lips. I am not going away just pick up the phone and call if you need me. I will keep looking for any more information and let you know what I come across. Please keep me up dated on your search also. The lawyer turned to toward the dressing table where the mirror was propped up so Louise could see both the lawyer and Marie, your unusually quiet my dear are you all right, I suffer with a deep worry in my heart that I will never be free. *Abuela,* please, do not think that, one day waite and see, yes Louise Mr. Burton says one day I promise you will go home to the land of your ancestors and be free again. Home, is it still there, do I have a home Louise murmurs. Of course, you have a home he says. What am I thinking, I am not thinking, a phone call yes, a letter followed up by a phone call, I do not follow Marie questions the lawyer? I will have my office research the old address in our files let us see if it is valid and if so who is living there. Do you think the family still lives on the ranch Louise asks excited now? Peter died before he could marry, but Miguel was married and when I left had two sons and his wife was expecting, yes there must still be family. I wish Tomas your father would have gone back; he also belonged on the land. Rose told me Marcus wanted Tomas to come to America with her. Rose should have told him the truth so he would not forget his father and his family. Waite a minute Marie interrupts, Louise, my Father was Rosie's son, Rosie's husband my grandfather died in World War 11. No, my angel, your father was Marcus's son and my grandson. Marie grabs the edge of the chair and sits with a thud; she looks at the old lawyer for some truth. Marie dear he says, Tomas was Rose's nephew. When Rose found out, she had a half-brother she went to Mexico to find him. Marcus was in a tragic riding accident; both his legs were crushed and have to be removed leaving him confined to a chair for the rest of his life. My family is cursed Louise says in a sad voice, now, now my dear none of that talk, the lawyers replies. When Rose arrived at the ranch, things were hard, the war was just over, and money in Mexico is scarce. With Peter dead and Charles Marcus now crippled, the running of the ranch fell squarely on the shoulders of Miguel. Our law firm made her travel arrangements now let me see after the war I know, roughly the summer of 1946 I think. I will look thru' our files and see what I come up with. The elderly man stood to leave, my advice is to see what you find in the state archives and get up into that attic God knows what is up there. Louise my dear I will come again as soon as I find more information. Louise looks at the lawyer, thank you Signore for everything; you have been a faithful friend to me, no need for thanks my dear no need. Marie Mr. Burton says as he turns toward the door Marie looks directly at him and in a whisper says why did Rose lie to me, why, what do I believe now, who am I seriously can you explain that to me, who am I, her voice tinged with sadness. Dear you are Marie Louise Black and Marie Louise Black can be whoever she wants to be and do whatever she wants to do. Why did Rose lie to you, the same reason Tillie lied to her to protect you from being hurt right or wrong it was done out of love. Rose is not my grandmother she is my great aunt. Mr. Burton looks at Marie patting her hand she loved you Marie and, in that, there are no lies.

At the front door, the old lawyer gave Marie a quick peck on her cheek, remember dear we all have the opportunity to create our own destiny, and do not let this chance slip away as Rose did. I promise, Marie watched as this friend drove away, waving, saying see you soon.

Marie went back to Louise's room, I have an idea she said *Abuela*, I think we should work together, and I will do all the legwork, Louise giggled kind of silly thing to say, Marie smiled. What I mean is I will go to the places Mr. Burton suggests and bring everything back here together we will find the answers. Good idea perfect Louise says, can I ask you a question *Abuela*, of course my angel. Have you ever left this room I mean have you ever been to any other part of the house? No, my angel I have not ever left this room. When Charles was alive he spent all his time here with me, only at night did he leave and would come back to me in the morning. Did Tillie know about you, yes Charles told her and tried to have her speak to me, only she just looked at me with tears in her eyes and did not say a word she then turned and left the room. After Charles is taken away, Tillie shut the room up, locking the door; I do not know for how long, I was so alone. Oh *Abuela* how awful I am so sorry, no, no my angel I have you now, Charles told Rose everything, and she would come some night to visit, when did she move in this room? After Tillie moves Rose brings Thomas to America to raise him as her own and Tillie wants no part of it, after all, she tried most of Roses life to shield her from everything, she moved to a small cottage an Aunt left her, and she lived there until she died. Do you know where Tillie moved? No, said Louise, I know Rose went to visit her mother but never took Tomas Tillie would not have it. Do you know why Rosie never told my father she was not his mother, but his aunt and his father was in Mexico and did not die in the war? We spoke of it some yet Rose would never say a thing to Tomas, she too was keeping the families secrets. Did you ever see Thomas did she ever bring him to meet you? I guess I knew the answer by the look on Louise's face, she whispers a faint no.

Rosie, Rosie I cannot believe you could do such a cruel thing, after all he was your grandson *Abuela* the more I am learning about my family the sadder I am becoming, such cruelty and lies all to protect what can you tell me, please someone tell me? Marie walks to the window to look out over the Connecticut hills. Maria, Louise calls out apprehension in her voice do not leave yet please, realizing Louise cannot see her Marie walks back to the dressing table. I am not leaving *Abuela* I was just by the window looking out. Sit Maria Louise asks, Marie pulls out the chair and sits facing her great-grandmother. My angel people will do anything to protect their name, and those they love from the hurt of finding out they are not what they want others to think they are. Rose did that, she loved her father, and when she found out about what made him ill, what his life was like, she would do anything to keep the family and her father safe from scandal. Then there was Tomas to hide the story from and finally you.

I think Rosie at the end of her life wanted me to know, her final words to me were to make me promise never to sell this silver hand mirror. She knew I would become curious, she wanted us to meet I know she did, maybe she was sick of all the secrets and wanted me to know the truth. That is the reason, Rosie was not a mean person, she might have had reasons to hide the truth, but I think the overwhelming goodness in her prevailed, and she wanted me to know. I have to believe in that, *Abuela* I have to believe there is good somewhere in this family. My Angel there is good in our family never let the evil overshadow that or Charlotte will win. I am sorry *Abuela* you are right please forgive me. No, no nothing to forgive; now what is our first step in finding more information,

Louise said with a smile. The archives first I should think, I will go tomorrow to see what I can find, then bring everything here, and we can sort through it together. How does that sound? Yes, that is an excellent idea Signore Burton says many legal documents for both families are stored there. That is what I will do tomorrow, however; now, I know you have never left this room, *Abuela* do you think you can? I do not know what will happen if I do, Louise replied should we try just out to the hall before Louise can answer Marie picks up the mirror and carries it to the door, both women hold their collective breath, Marie opens the door and with Louise in hand steps into the hall, *Abuela*? I am fine Angel look I am fine, tears start to run down Marie's face if anything happened to you, no Angel look I am fine, look, Louise can hardly contain her excitement. Then how about a little walk around the house, yes, oh yes, answers Louise cautiously Marie holding the mirror so Louise could see starts down the hall. After about an hour walking through the house, both Louise and Marie feel encouraged as they sit and talk together back in Louise's room. This day there is much to discuss, Louise describes to Marie how the house looked when she first arrived, the heavy dark furniture she hated so with its overstuffed oppressive feel. How pretty everything looks Louise sighs I wish I could tell Rose how free you have made me feel. Maybe the garden, should we try going into the garden tomorrow Marie said, Oh yes lets' do, outside warmth and fresh air I how I long to feel the breeze around me. Plans are made to spend time out in the garden the next morning for now Marie feels overwhelming exhaustion and wants nothing more than to grab a bit to eat and lay down to think about what she has learned today. *Abuela* I want to get something for dinner then rest awhile, could

I say good night I know it is early, but I am tired. It has been a busy day my Angle go rest now and tomorrow we will explore the garden and talk some more. Good night *Abuela*, Marie says as she turns out the light and leaves the room. Going down to the kitchen Marie makes a quick sandwich and pours herself a glass of wine, then goes into the living room and gets comfortable on the couch. The changes in her life have come so quickly with everyday a new revelation to take in and try to understand, at times she feels as though she is drowning in a vast tidal wave destroying everything in it path. Yet now the only thing she can think of is sleep as her eyes shut and the relaxing of her mind and body transport her to a place of quiet slumber.

Morning dawns bright and sunny as Marie wakes stretching her sore muscles she realizes she has slept on the couch rubbing her legs. Two things Marie wants to accomplish today, taking Louise into the garden and, going to the city archives. She will worry about going up to the attic another time.

City Hall

Dressing quickly Marie tells Louise she must go out for a while, and when she returns, they will spend the evening in the garden talking. She knows her Great-Grandmother is disappointed, yet Marie wants to gather as much information as possible, then she and Louise will be able to sort through it, clearing up some lies in her family's sordid past.

Getting into the car Marie heads out driving in the direction of Hartford. The traffic on the road is light getting into the city, and within a half hour, she is pulling into the parking garage near City Hall. The archive is located on the third floor of the building, taking the elevator up, Marie, as the door opens feels overwhelmed by the vastness of the room. She realizes this is the entire top floor of City Hall and there are rows upon rows of boxes on shelves reaching up to a vaulted ceiling with massive dark Gothic beams. The room with its overflow of seemingly endless cartons appears without rhyme or reason. How will I find anything in all the clutter she exclaims? A tidy white head pops up from behind a desk. Hello, I am Miss Kenny the archivist, standing behind a large wooden desk just visible above a mountain of books a small elderly woman smiles in greeting. I am sorry I did not see you and thought no one was here. I guess I do blend in at times the archivist replies how may I help you. Marie looks around this vast space and replies I am not sure if you can. Oh, do not let this mess deter you my dear I know every inch of this room, and where everything is, coming out from behind the desk smoothing her drab brown dress and touching her snow-white hair making sure every strand is in place. Miss Kenny holds out her hand taking the papers Marie has brought with her. Hum let's see now reaching for her glasses that hang around her neck on a lanyard, Black, Charles senior and Charles junior, Barnes, Josiah, not a problem, I will be back in a few minutes why not take a seat over there at the table. Thank you, Marie walks to one of the large tables that are located throughout this part of the room. Sitting she runs her hand over the top of the wood it feels rough and uneven; its color has a dark, rich patina from years of use. Settling into the hard chair Marie get ready for what she feels will be a long wait. Within minutes, Miss Kenny returns, here we are dear, all we have on the family names you have given me, and she has only two folders in her hand, which she places, on the table in front of Marie. Is that all Marie asks I thought there would be more? Yes, Miss Kenny replies I did also, tomorrow my part-time helper will be here and together we will search again, if we find any more information, I will call you. For now this is all there seem to be, the Archivist returns to work on her desk, seemingly to disappear amongst the books and folders.

Marie opens the first folder marked Black all it contains are the birth and death certificates that Marie found in the safe at home nothing else for that matter there seemed to be more information at Rosie's than here. Putting the Black folder down Marie picks up the other marked Barnes, this one has even less that the other, something is wrong. Marie asks Miss Kenny if anyone can remove paperwork from the archive. Oh dear no, you can make a copy of the papers you want that is five cents, but no one can remove anything. I was just thinking there is so little information on these two families that maybe someone might have taken it, both families have been in the Connecticut Valley for over two hundred years, and these files have so little in them. Yes, I thought it odd also, but please let my assistant, and I do another search and see what we find, now do you want me to make you any copies of this information? Yes, Marie says as she hands Miss Kenny the folder marked Barton although there is little information in it Marie thinks it best to make a copy of the papers to take home. Is that all Miss Kenny asks, yes Marie answers if you find anything else you will call, let me give you my number. Most certainly, Miss Kenny replies as she hands the copies of the Barnes folder to Marie and takes the phone number Marie has written on a scrap of paper. Thank you, you have been extremely helpful as she turns to leave, you will call Marie reiterates. Please do not worry dear if we find anything I promise I will call, Miss Kenny says as she returns to her desk, looking as though she has already put the matter out of her mind.

Marie opens the door to Louise's room calling *Abuela* I am home as she picked up the silver mirror, Louise is waiting I was becoming worried you seem gone so long. I stopped to have dinner before I came home, I do not feel like cooking tonight, you look sad my angel is anything wrong. I guess there is I thought I would find more information at the city achieves on the family's history, yet both files were nearly empty. It is as if the paperwork has been stolen, Charlotte, Louise whispers could be *Abuela*, but why take the Barton's papers also there is no logic in that. The Archivist says, no one is permitted to take out folders from the room, yet I know something is terribly wrong. Miss Kenny, by the way, is quite likeable and efficient made these copies for me of what is in the Barton family's folder. Marie spread the few papers on the dressing table in front of Louise so she could see, is that all the papers, yes *Abuela*. I think you are right someone must have taken the information. I think so, the archivist assured me when her assistant comes to help tomorrow they will search again, I have an idea they will not find anything. Louise shook her head in agreement.

I will call Mr. Burton in the morning he may be able to shed some light on the situation. Until then, I will go change I think a walk in the garden is in order. I thought you forgot Louise says with a smile that brightens up her whole face, never Marie calls over her shoulder, be back in a minute.

The evening is warm with just a slight breeze rustling through the trees; Marie holds the mirror up at a slight angle, so Louise is able to see the garden and Marie, as well. Everything is so green, and there are so many flowers, there is the river down over the hill, Louise is speaking excitedly, Charles told me about the river and how his best friend drowned there. I did not think it was so close to the house. Such a beautiful place yet so sad, but the flowers different from the ones in Mexico I love the colors, bright and cheerful. I would pick so many bouquets; I have always loved flowers as a young girl I would pick handfuls to bring home to my mother. She would put them in a glass of water on the table and give me a loving kiss. Her voice became quiet almost a whisper I love flowers just not red roses. Changing the subject, I ask when you came here as a bride did you walk in the garden with my great-grandfather? I could imagine the two lovers holding hands slowly walking through the flowers yet in a world of their own. No, my angel I was never in the garden we came during the winter, there was so much snow I did not like the cold and stayed in the house. It was still cold and rainy in March when Marcus was born after that there was nothing. Oh! I am sorry *Abuela* I should have realized, please, do not be sad. My sweet angel look I am not sad this is all too beautiful for me to be sad. I walk with Louise through all the different parts of the garden to the small fishpond with water lilies floating like small sailboats upon the water. I picked Daisy's and weave a chain of them around the mirror, so Louise looks as if she has them pinned in her hair. I cut a bouquet of lilacs to bring into the house later. I show her the colorful bed of Zinnia's and the bright yellow Marigolds, we walk past the large ferns that hug close to the shade of the tall trees. However, I keep far away from the Bed of Roses they are all red.

The sun is beginning to set, Louise and I face the western sky, someday *Abuela* we will follow the setting sun all the way home to Mexico I promise. When my angel, I have waited so long to go home, I think we must wait until Mr. Burton locates the information about if the ranch is still there and if so who owns it. In the mean time I will find out as much as I can about the family in Connecticut, it should not take long. I am planning to sell this house, no loose ends here to drag me back and . . . . Wait Maria, Louise interrupts when did you decide to live in Mexico and why are you not coming back to America this is your home, all you know is here and your teaching work. Maria do you know what you are doing; Louise's voice was full of concern. *Abuela* I think for the first time in my life I am making the right decision, I have lived a lie, now with the truth, I am free to be Marie Louise Gutierrez Black, and she, can do whatever is right for her, angel you sure. I have never been sure of anything in my life. Marie raises her hand to touch Louise's face. Never surer *Abuela*, I think we had better go inside now it is getting dark, Marie picks up the bunch of Lilacs she cut earlier and this curious duo head toward the house Marie holding the silver mirror up high so Louise will see the inky night sky just starting to sprinkle with stars.

After saying good night, and making sure, Louise is well after their walk in the garden as this territory is new the two are exploring.

Marie decides to look up in the attic, it is still early, and she is disturbed about the outcome at the Achieves. The door is at the far end of the hall away from any of the bedrooms; Marie brings a flashlight with her just in case. Opening the door she notices a long cord dangling from the end of a light bulb, she is not hopeful as she pulls it that anything will happen and is surprised when the light flickers on. She remembers the steep staircase she climbed it many times as a child when Rosie wanted to store things away.

The dust and the cobwebs also remembered Marie gives a shutter climbing the stairs, turning on the flashlight just in case. Reaching the top there is another cord hanging pulling it a dim light goes on Marie could see the family's life for generations stored in this dusty dry place as if waiting for someone to tell its story. Where do I start Marie says aloud shining the flashlight she still holds in her hand around the room. There is old furniture everywhere covered in a thick layer of dust, steamer trunks and blanket chests all piled together with no apparent rhyme or reason. Gas lamps and electric chandeliers tossed in a corner some broken, the glass making a kaleidoscope of reflected colors on the floor. Marie decides to look through the chests first thinking that might be where she would choose to store family information. I think I will just chose that one over there Marie says aloud, walking over to a large red walnut hope-chest, she opens the lid, finding it filled with old clothes and nothing more she sighs closing down the top. Next, she chooses one of the large steamer trunks, clothes to Marie says, struggling to pull open the large container. To her surprise, the inside has cardboard drawers filling both sides in the trunk. The interior and the drawers papered with the same hideous red rose wallpaper that covers the walls of Louise's room. Marie sits down on the floor, amid the dust and the dim light pulling open the first of the drawers. Inside a small metal box and nothing else, what is this she says, putting the box on her lap opening it. Inside a small leather journal and an envelope marked Charles's commitment papers. Oh! No, she cries as she opens the envelope in it is a single sheet of paper that states Charles Black was committed to Meadow Brook Sanitarium on the, 16th of August 1934. Diagnosis; Nervous Breakdown,

Witnesses: Dr. Henry; Psychiatrist,

Isaac Burton Sr.; Attorney

Marie puts down the paper, why did not Mr. Burton tell me, why. Picking up the small metal box Marie turns out the lights and climbs down the staircase closing the attic door behind her. Walking slowly down to the main floor of the house, Marie feels the burden of this discovery. Sanitarium is not that a nicer name for mental institution she says, opening the box Marie looks at the paper as if reading it again will change what it discloses. How and why did this transpire and why didn't Mr. Burton tell me his father was one of the witnesses signing my great-grandfather's commitment papers. Looking at the mantle clock on the fireplace, she sees it is too late to call the lawyer. Tomorrow first thing, I want to know why and who wanted him committed. Unable to sleep Marie lies on the sofa and opens the small leather journal that is in the metal box.

What Tillie Conceals

Sun shines thru' the window of Tillie's room, she rolls over in bed and stretches. Morning she sighs, there are times Tillie dreads waking up and wonders if today is one of them. She was tired last night and did not wait up for Charles to come home from his night wanderings. She sits on the edge of the bed dangling her legs over the side, when the door opens thinking it might be Charles up and dressed for work she smiles, its Molly the housekeeper." Good morning" Mrs. I have your coffee, thank you Molly, is Mr. Black up yet. Not a stirring from his room shall I knock. No, No I will wake him Tillie says, very good, breakfast in an hour, Molly says as she leaves the room. That is all I need, Molly seeing Charles first thing in the morning after a night of who knows what, she thinks. The housekeeper is a good woman and can be relied for her discretion, yet back door gossip is extremely tempting. Putting on her robe and slippers Tillie walks down the hall to Charles's room and opens the door, there she finds Charles curled up under the covers sound asleep. Good she says aloud, quietly shutting the door behind her as she leaves. I must hurry and get dressed, on her way back to her room she stops to wake Rose. Tillie pokes her head in her daughter's bedroom. Come on sleepy head up and ready for school. Molly says breakfast in an hour. Rose groans

Mom, yes dear, and hurry. Tillie closes the bedroom door behind her leaning against it, she feels exhausted. How much longer can she keep up this charade, at what time will the mask of civility be stripped off? Stop she says aloud, I have no time for this, not now not yet. Rose is fifteen, and in two, years she will leave for college, just two more years. Her father promises he will take care of everything and no one needs ever know. Tillie dresses thinking how grateful she is to her father for managing her life and affairs ever since Rose was born. He has kept Charles on as a full partner in the business, even though he shows little or no interest in anything to do with commerce or for that matter Rose. Just two more years Daddy, just two more years, Tillie says aloud as she closes her bedroom door and hurries downstairs. Molly, Mr. Black is still sleeping after Rose leaves for school fix him a tray and I will take it up to him. Yes, Mum Molly says as she leaves the dining room. An aroma of crisp fried bacon and freshly brewed coffee fills the air.

Morning Mom, what smells so yummy Rose exclaims as she pulls out a chair and picks up a piece of toast, is Dad coming down. Rose is everything Tillie is not, although small in stature Rose occupies every inch of space in any room she enters. Outgoing and likable she can charm the most disagreeable person. Mom I will be staying after classes today for choirs then a bunch of us will go to Von Leasons for ice cream. Be home for dinner. Rose jumps up from the table blonde curls bobbing in every direction, as hard as she tries her hair will not be held back by the large blue bow that is part of her school uniform. Like her hair, Tillie knows her daughter can never conform to what society expects of women as she did, the word coward flies through her brain to describe herself. Rose still munching a piece of toast kisses her mother good-bye and is gone. Tillie smiles my tiny whirlwind she mutters to herself. If there was anything good about the union between her and Charles it was Rose, and she must never find out about her father affliction, surely Tillie could do that.

As she checks her day calendar, Molly comes into the room carrying a tray with Charles breakfast. Should I take Mr. Charles' food up she asks. No, I will do that, but would you check the pantry and make a list of what we need, I would like to go over it this afternoon before I see my father. Tillie takes the tray and starts up the stairs, yes miss the housekeeper says, Tillie pays little attention.

She hates facing her husband when he has been out all night. Coward she silently says again as she stands in front of the door mouthing a prayer before entering. Good morning Charles, it's a beautiful day, I'm sure you won't want to miss any part of it by sleeping in, Tillie says as she places the tray with his breakfast on the bed stand and moves it closer to Charles. Molly made the most delicious food for you this morning. Tillie is babbling an unusual phenomenon that only happens when she is uncomfortable. Charles groans and says something she cannot understand as he struggles to sit up. Tillie walks over to the windows and pulls open the heavy red drapes to let in the sun light when she hears a thud, turning, she sees Charles has fallen onto the floor and is struggling to get up. Waite she says as she hurries over to help. Putting her arms under his shoulders, she lifts him up and sits her fragile husband on the bed. Are you hurt she asks as she pours him a cup of coffee, I am fine a little dizzy from all the sunlight he says reaching for coffee with shaking hands. I am sorry, shall I close the drapes: no Charles says I will be fine in a minute. His eyes are sunken watery with dark circles under them; his skin the color of sand bleached by the sun, "this once handsome man" is old, aged before his time. Tillie feel a sudden contempt for her husband and wants to lash out at him for trapping her in this dried up withered marriage from which she cannot escape. However, she swallows her feelings saying, I thought you might feel up to going to the office today. Father and I will have lunch at his club, you could join us, it might be enjoyable for a change, and if you would like we could take a walk in the park the warmth of the air will make you feel stronger. No, not today, please Charles if not for me than for Rose she loves when you are up, and about, she hardly get to see you anymore, she is growing up so fast soon she will be leaving us to go to college and, I said NO! Not today. Tillie knew it was fruitless to argue any longer and turned to leave the room, wait Charles asked I would like to speak to you about something. All right, Tillie answered as she sat down on the edge of the large carved chair in the corner of the room. She hated this room with its dark drapes and ugly ornate furniture. If she had her way, she would close and lock the door forever. This is Charles family home, and this room was his parents. They gave the room to Charles and his first wife Louise when they came from Mexico. In this room, his son was born, and Louise died, yet still lives Charles would never leave it, and she has certainly never slept in it ever. What is it Charles, Tillie asks her husband, Rose is getting older he answers I think she should know she has a brother, half-brother

Tillie corrects, all right half-brother, but I think she should know. Tillie felt the anger rising up in her with all the pressure of a bomb ready to explode, she jumped up and faces Charles, you think, you think, she screams how dare you. You have not had a rational thought in years, or are you forgetting Rose is only fifteen still a young girl (born May 1918). All you want is to ease your conscience at the expense of your daughter, oh but my mistake, she is not the beloved son born of the cherished Louise she is the second child and a girl no less, of a contemptible pretense of a marriage, why should you worry about what effect it will have on her. Tillie's whole body is shaking, why not tell her the whole truth that her father is a liar he never told her mother he was married before and had a son until after they were wed. He married her only for her family's wealth and prestige he never loved her or felt any affection for her. Do not forget the best part her father is a morphine addict and prowls the street of Hartford at night until he reaches the "Seven Moon's". I know Charles I know everything. When people ask me why you look so pale, why you are not by my side at church or town charities. I tell them you have been ill since you came back from fighting in Mexico and the death of your parents soon after your return was more than you could bear. Therefore, you see Charles I am a liar too, only I lie to protect Rose. He has never seen his wife in such an emotional state as this, her usual response to his pleas is to acquiesce calmly and move on to another subject. She needs to know he says pressing the point, she will know, now is not the time. I will not allow you to rob Rose of her carefree youth for the easing of your conscience, I will not allow it, she shouts and runs from the room slamming the door behind her. Anger is turning into fear Tillie wants to wait two more years until Rose leaves for college if Charles tells her now what should she do. As Tillie reaches the bottom of the stairs she turns, walks into the library, and she picks up the telephone it seems an eternity until someone answers. Mr. Burton this is Matilda Black Charles's wife, I was wondering if you were not busy, would you have lunch with my father and I at The Mercantile Club. There is a problem; I would like to speak to you about concerning Charles. Today at noon, thank you, thank you so much I will see you then. Tillie hangs up hoping she has done the right thing.

Leaving the library, she goes to the kitchen going over the list of things needed for the pantry with Molly. Why don't you go to Klein's Grocery Store and shop tell Mr. Klein I will stop on the way home and pay our bill. Yes, Mrs. better yet make sure they deliver everything I do not want you to carrying anything heavy home. Tillie turns to leave the room, Mrs. should I leave lunch for Mr. Charles. No, do not bother if he is hungry, which I doubt, he can eat dinner with us in the dining room this evening. Food is not what Charles is craving Tillie thinks.

Going to her room, she changes getting ready to go downtown and have lunch with her father and Mr. Burton. Before leaving Tillie knocks on Charles door and enters. I am going to have lunch with father Charles at his club, can I get you anything before I go. Charles is slumped in the large chair near the window, no he says almost inaudibly. You have not touched your breakfast Charles you have to eat something, please, Charles. I'm fine, well you don't look fine, you look dreadful, I said I was fine, his voice hoarse and restrained, Charles, Tillie tried one more time, just go, he looked up at her with cold unfeeling eyes and Tillie leaves the room. She had no misgivings now as to what she was about to.

Tillie leaves the house and walks two blocks to catch the trolley that would take her to downtown Hartford. Her father always wants to send a car for her, but she likes the trolley ride, it gives her a sense of being her own person. She meets neighbors, and they chat amiably about the weather or local news, anything to get her away from the everyday problems that seem to plague her and frankly, it is fun. Today she needs time to calm her emotions, Tillie does not like confrontations, especially with Charles, except Rose must be protected, and it is her responsibility to do that.

The trolley stops in front of the mercantile building and Tillie gets off, standing for a minute in front of the revolving doors she takes a deep breath and goes through'. In the lobby, she sees her father deep in conversation with Mr. Burton the lawyer. She can just make out what they were saying as she approaches. Father, Mr. Burton, Ah! My dear I was just telling Mr. Burton how pleasant it is that he could join us for lunch today. Yes, father it is kind of him to come on such short notice. Her father could see the tense lines around his daughters eyes, come my table is over in the corner it is quiet, and we can talk.

The wine is poured, and, lunch ordered before Tillie's father asks; tell us dear what is troubling you so. She looks first to her father then the lawyer, Charles wants to tell Rose that he was married before, and she has a half-brother living in Mexico. Please, please not yet, she is too young to understand. I know Rose must find out, why now, why cannot Charles wait until she is older. Allow her to have her youth, and freedom for just a little longer. Tillie's father looks as he is about to explode as she speaks. Damn him, he says clenching his fists, the only thing that man can do is ruin everything good in his life. Let us think rationally the lawyer says, Rose must know someday, not now, Tillie's father says under his breath. I agree, now is not the time, let me meet with Charles. I will try to make him see reason before we go any further with this. Tillie is picking at her food tears welling up in her eyes, now, now my dear everything will be fine wait and see. I do not think Charles wants to see reason, I do not think he has a reasonable thought in his mind anymore. Is he as bad as that the lawyer asks, yes, Tillie says, he just sits in his room all day, and in the darkness of the night, he leaves to skulk through the streets until he gets to the Seven Moons? There are times he does not come home for days if Rose asks where he is; I say he is away on business. I am terrified she will find out what her father is, and now he wants to tell her about his other life before we were married and she was born. Father, Tillie looked up with tears in her eyes I will do anything to keep this from Rose Father, anything. He pats her hand and looks at the lawyer I know you are the family lawyer and have Charles's best in mind so I will waite until you speak with him. However if, nothing comes of it, I will take over, and we will do things my way. I will not have my daughter and granddaughter hurt by Charles no matter what his reason. Have I made myself clear, yes, the lawyer says, I will do what I can to make Charles see, telling Rose about his life is ill advised at this time, and he must waite until she gets older and hopefully can understand. I will call him, myself when I get back to my office and ask him to come to see me, Tillie looks at him sadly I don't think he will, then I will go and see him. I will let you know the plan if I must go to your home, I do not want you there when I am speaking to Charles I think it will only complicate matters further, Yes you are right Tillie says. Look, her father says whether you go to the house, or Charles goes to your office after the meeting wherever it takes place the three of us will meet at my office and go over the outcome. This way we can formulate a plan of action as to what to do next if Charles is not agreeable to what you have to say. The lawyer gets up to leave, and Tillie takes his hand, thank you, thank you so much she said. Such sadness he thought, how the sins and manipulations of Charlotte, Charles mother has affected everyone's life and now it is threatening Roses, something has to be done and quickly. He can only hope he chooses the right words and Charles listens.

By the time, Tillie arrives home, Mr. Burton already telephoned Charles, and he left, to Tillie's surprise to meet with the lawyer. Tillie walks into the kitchen, asking Molly has she bought everything needed for the pantry, in an around about way trying to find out what time Charles left the house, and did he say when he was coming home. However, the housekeeper was of no help, she only knew Mr. Burton had called as she answered the telephone and soon after Charles left the house. Thank you Tillie said leaving the kitchen to go upstairs and change her clothes. She stops in the parlor and places a prettily wrapped box of chocolates she purchased for Rose on the table. She knew it was extravagant but did not care, Rose loved chocolate and will be surprised. Tillie tries to keep her mind occupied so she will not be thinking about what is going on in the lawyer's office. She changes, goes out into the garden to cut flowers for the dinner table, smiling to herself flowers and candy all in one day, what is she thinking.

Well Charles I am happy you agreed to come see me today there is something serious we need to discuss. I think I know Charles says as he sits down opposite the lawyer's desk. Mr. Burton is shocked by his client's appearance, a once healthy intelligent young gentleman has been reduced to a walking dead man, damn Charlotte to hell, he thinks. However, says, let me get you a drink Charles before we begin, scotch, and water, fine Charles says, his hand trembling as he reaches for the glass. How have you been my boy, you look a bit under the weather, to say the least, Charles says as he gulps down his drink. Let's cut thru' the small talk and get down to why you called me in here today, well I've heard you would like to tell Rose she has a brother Marcus, half-brother Charles reminded him, yes, well half-brother then. I can guess who told you, did Tillie cry on your shoulder, did she complain about how difficult her life is what a vile husband I have become. Charles unsteady slowly gets up and walks over to the window. Now, Now my dear boy, nothing to get so upset about, Mr. Burton gets up and puts his arm around Charles, Tillie is worried that Rose is too young to understand and maybe you should waite to tell her when she is a little older. What do you think Charles asks, I tend to agree with Tillie, Rose is only fifteen her concerns should be about school, her friends, football games and dances, give her this time to be young and without care. Charles turns and looks at the lawyer, I knew you would side with Tillie, no, I am not siding with you, or Tillie I am trying to think about what is appropriate for Rose. Charles's body is rigid his eyes staring vacantly into the distance. I am going to tell her he says, why? Why now Charles, why is it so urgent you tell her now the lawyer asks. She should know I have a son, yes; but are you forgetting you have a daughter also, and what kind of father are you, have you been a loving father Charles, have you? I think before you make any decision on the matter you need to think about just that, and then maybe you will agree to waite a little longer to tell her about Marcus. You see you cannot tell Rose about her brother without telling her about Louise the circumstances of her death, and where she is now, why you made the decision to give Marcus away to be raised in Mexico by his Grandparents, it's more complicated than you think Charles, will you have all the answers when Rose asks you why. Charles turns and looks out the window, it is dark now, and the lights of the city shine like stars below him. I have to go he says walking slowly with some effort to the door. Will you think about what we talked about today, please Charles? Think of Rose give her a little time to be young, just a little time is all we ask, think about it, Mr. Burton is almost beseeching Charles as he speaks, only Charles has other matters on his mind it is dark, and the House of the Seven Moons is calling.

Every City has its Tenderloin

Every city has its frayed side, and Hartford is no different. Cold-water tenement buildings stand next to ram shackled wooden houses lining the narrow unpaved streets that become a quagmire during the slightest rain and freeze solid during the winter with deep ruts making any means of travel life threatening. Store fronts some with colorful awnings compete for customers with horse carts that fill every space along the crowded road loaded with the daily needs for human survival. Vendors hawking in loud voices the benefit of shoppers buying from them, "chickens get your juicy birds, killed fresh this morning." Shop owners try to entice people into their stores with bargains holding up less than fresh vegetables, they barter with weary shoppers for the best price. A stench of recently dropped manure, rotting food, feted red meat, and fish with an occasional decomposing horse carcass overpower the human senses. On these, mean streets children play amongst the chaos, stealing when possible an apple or other delicacy eating it quickly before it is stolen from them.

Women hurry home with purchases of food to cook the families evening meal as darkness settles over the city, calling out to children and husbands alike to come in to eat.

As night falls, the area takes on a sinister, tawdry atmosphere, people of the evening creep out into the shadowy alleys, and side roads to sell what darkness must hide. Reputable, wealthy, men who have reached the pinnacles of New England society seen every Sunday in Church with wives and children, come nightly to purchase what they crave, that home does not provide. Charles now inhabits this world as he quietly walks towards The House of the Seven Moons.

He knows the way it is imprinted on his soul. The squalid streets hold no fear for Charles only an unsatisfied want he knows will be filled when he reaches his destination.

A lady of the night in a short fancy dress with brightly coloured feathers and beads wore for professional purposes stands in a doorway breasts all but exposed trying to entice a potential customer inside. Her face painted to hide the pillage of time presses against a willing customer with erotic gestures, her hips gyrating to rhythms that delight, come inside sweetie let me make you feel happy she whispers stroking his leg seducing her prospective customer. Charles is never approached everyone knows the comfort he seeks comes in the form of a syringe. He walks through' the darkness eyes fixed on a house at the end of the ally, a sign hangs above the door an arch of seven golden moons painted on a dark blue background nothing else needs written. The dimly lit front room engulfs Charles in a smoky haze as he opens the front door.

Madame Yang the proprietress of the Seven Moon's stands silently clothed in a red silk kimono delicately embroidered with flowers, she wears matching red shoes on her diminutive feet. The woman's black hair arrayed with pearls and diamonds, her long crimson fingernails point the way down the hall, she nods in greeting to her frequent patron, and there is no fanfare here. Anonymity comes with the service offered inside these walls. With shaking purpose, Charles, walks to the back of the house to a room familiar to him moving the curtains aside he steps in walking over to a bed covered with a filthy sheet. Removing his coat, he hangs it over the rusty metal footboard of the bed and sits down. Everything he needs for a night of forgetting he finds laid out for him on a table within easy reach. Wasn't it only months ago that a few drams of laudanum brought him some peace, he tries to remember as he rolls up his shirt sleeve and tightens a band around his upper arm hoping to find a vein that hasn't collapsed. He slaps hard at a distended blue snake popping up under his parchment white skin. Clutching the syringe filled with morphine, not bothering to tap out the air bubbles, he injects the blunt needle into his arm. Drawing out the serpent's lifeblood into the glass syringe, he presses the plunger down releasing the fire that will calm his tormented soul. Blood streams down his arm as the hypodermic slips from his hand onto the floor. The burning flames course through his body as he collapses in a heap on the edge of the bed. Euphoria grips his mind as the journey to oblivion begins.

Hi! Charlie what took you so long hurry up come on in the water it is great. I will beat you this time I have been practicing, boy you look old like my grandpa. I am stronger than you are now Charlie, but I wish you were here with me, I wanted you to come I tried to bring you remember. We would have a grand time, I can swim all day if I want hurry Charlie, hurry. Charles is at the edge of the water, wait John have you seen Louise, who is Louise, Charlie. My wife John, your wife? I do not know a Louise stop joking Charlie you do not have a wife. Come on lets go swimming last one in is a rotten egg.

Beads of cold sweat cover Charles forehead, his breathing is shallow, hot dry air fills his lungs. Cactus flowers with colors beyond belief swirl and dance through his vision their sickening sweet smell heighten his senses. He can see into the ages, eternal as the desert, free.

It is after six when the telephone rings, Tillie hurries to answer, hello Mr. Burton, yes I have been waiting for your call. The lawyer tells her he spoke to Charles but is not sure he has made any headway with him. I didn't think you could have Tillie says, Mr. Burton informs her that he has called her father and they set up a meeting for tomorrow at four pm at his office to discuss matters further. I will be there Tillie tells the lawyer, not to worry he says we will sort this out my dear, but I wouldn't expect Charles home until late tonight as I am sure he will go to The Seven Moons to deal with this dilemma he has placed himself in. See you tomorrow at four then, good-bye dear he says as he hangs up, Tillie places the receiver down on the phones cradle and quietly leaves the room. She is torn between the feelings of pure disgust and fear what Charles could do next.

Hi, Mom how was your day; Rose is home, Tillie taking a deep breath, goes to meet her daughter. Fine dear how was yours, wonderful just wonderful, Rose drops her school books on the hall table, guess what Tom asked me to the homecoming dance, and I said yes, I can go can't I. Yes, of course, you can go and maybe a new dress is in order, Oh, Mom do you think I can, it will not be too expensive will it, Rose was so excited. No dear a new dress it will be, now go wash up Molly has dinner waiting. Rose runs from the room, than stops is Dad eating with us, I want to tell him about the dance, No Tillie answered he has business tonight, you can tell him tomorrow if he is not tired. Tillie walks into the dining room placing the box of chocolates near Rose's plate and sits down feeling suddenly terribly old.

Rose chats all through dinner excitedly yet Tillie hears half of what her daughter is saying, Mom, Mom when can we go shopping, how about this Saturday, Tillie is tugged back from her thoughts. Yes, dear this Saturday will be acceptable we can go shopping and have lunch at Grandpas club how's that. Oh that sounds like fun Mom, Rose answers as she grabs her box of chocolates and goes to her room to do her homework. Not to late Tillie says I will be up later to say good night, but Rose is already gone, she smiles, how she loves her daughter and vows she will protect her no matter what she has to do.

Tillie sits quietly alone with her thoughts, how did her life become this hollow shell. Rose will soon be leaving for college, the next two years will go by quickly, and then she Tillie will be alone. Oh, Rose will come home on school holidays and vacations, but she will be busy catching up with friends, not wanting to spend her time at home with her mother. Tillie must start thinking about what to do with the rest of her life she knows she will be spending it on her own no matter what happens tomorrow. However hasn't she been alone most of these last fifteen years, when she and Charles were first married she explained his quiet aloofness as strain and nervous exhaustion from the war than the death of his parents so soon after they were married. Then again as a new bride, she was busy setting up house and learning to be the proper homemaker. She doted on Charles even though his sullen mood swings alarmed her at times; she loves him so dearly there is nothing she will not do for him, yet she cannot seem to make him happy.

At night when he comes to her room, his love is cold and mechanical there is no warmth in his touch or words of affection, he quickly falls asleep or departs the room leaving her feeling used and dirty. When she was pregnant with Rose, the visits stopped Charles showed little interest in her or the birth of their child. Tillie is struck by the wonder happening inside her. Every move or twitch the baby makes excites and gives her purpose in her life she spends hours going through baby name books studying hard to choose the right one for their child. She decides if it is a boy, her son will not be named Charles and one will convince her otherwise. She makes lists of things the baby will need she and her mother spend days shopping and decorating the nursery. Tillie knows if it is not for her father's generosity, the baby will have little, and they would be drowning in bills.

Charles attempts at showing up at the office are woeful at best, no employer would keep him on, and she is thankful her father has made him partner in his business, if only for title sake.

The nine months go by quickly, Charles spends days in his room and leaves every night at dusk returning in the morning, sick, and hardly able to walk, yet if Tillie tries to help him, he pushes her away, seemingly repulsed at her touch.

Late one night Tillie feels a dull pain in her lower back, then another, getting up from the bed she goes to Charles room to see if just maybe he has come home. She opens the door only to find the room empty as another pain grips her lower back, holding on to the door tightly. The plan is to call her parents if Charles is not at home so Tillie slowly walks back to her room and picks up the telephone, Hello daddy can you please, come get me, the baby is coming, please, daddy I'm alone.

On May 1, 1919, Rose Elizabeth Black is born to the delight of her mother and Grandparents, her father is at the House of the Seven Moons. Finally, after three days Charles goes to the hospital to visit his wife and new daughter accompanied by Mr. Burton. His feeble attempt to show some joy at the birth of Rose angered Tillie, and she asks the lawyer to take Charles home. Tillie will not let her husband spoil this moment with his presence.

Looking back now Tillie knows she and Charles's lives were doomed from the very beginning, however; there is still time for Rose and, Tillie will make sure she has her chance at happiness.

The day drags on slowly Tillie keeps up the charade that nothing is out of the ordinary. Telling Molly, she has a meeting in the city at four, to please prepare a light dinner ready at 6:30 and Mr. Charles will not be eating with them. Tillie does not go into Charles room during the day she wants nothing to deter her from her plans.

Her father calls asking if she wants him to send a car for her, today Tillie says yes. The thought of seeing people on the trolley and having to make small talk is just too much to bear she wants to be alone with her thoughts.

Arriving at Mr. Burton's office promptly at four p.m. she finds her father has already arrived. Both men stand as Tillie enters, my dear sit down her father says, how was the ride downtown, making small talk. Fine father it was fine can we get on with it Tillie replies as she sits in the chair nearest her father. Certainly, as the lawyer starts the discussion, your father, and I thought of a set of guidelines Charles must follow to stabilize his life, I know an exceptionally good psychiatrist, I will make an appointment for

Charles, I have already spoken to him, and he is willing to meet with Charles. He must also go to work every morning without fail, go to church with you and Rose, and under no circumstance go to the Seven Moons the psychiatrist can help with that problem. He must never reveal to Rose his past and that she has a half-brother until we deem it the appropriate time. In general, he must start acting as a loving, caring husband and father. I will have my secretary draw up a contract with this guideline, and, anything else you can think of, we will all meet next week here with Charles present, and he must sign the contract. Tillie sits in silence as Mr. Burton speaks, well dear what do you think her father asks. Tillie is quiet a moment longer, how do you expect to enforce this so-called contract she questions the men. That is where the psychiatrist comes in he will at every appointment work with Charles on these issues and monitor his progress. Tillie looks at her father, and you believe this is the solution, no dear, but I think it is a start. I do not father, I would like the psychiatrist to admit Charles in hospital for evaluations, and from there into a mental hospital, I was thinking of Boston there is an exceptionally skilled sanitarium in the city. He will have time" to get well, and take stock of his life, for the next two years" he will remain there, and all his visits will be supervised all his mail checked before sent out, and he will not have access to a telephone. I want Charles to know I am serious if he wants; a decent life he has two years to show us, if not I will commit him stating mental incapacity, and he will never be released. Both men are shocked what will you tell Rose the lawyer asks, the truth her father is an opium addict, he was married before his wife died giving birth to his son while he was engaged to me and I knew nothing of this until years later. By then she was a baby, and we tried to hide the truth from her until she was older. My dear Tillie, what if Rose asks why you stayed with her father, then I will tell her the truth I love him and thought I could make things better, but I couldn't.

I will also tell her, she has a half-brother living in Mexico and refer her to you. If she asks, give her all the information you have, the rest is up to her what she does with it. Rose will be in her twenties by then old enough I hope to deal with whatever she feels is right. Tillie her father interjects are not you being a bit harsh, no I want Rose protected for as long as possible. You promised father if I stayed with Charles, and not bring scandal down upon our family by divorce, you would make sure Rose never found out about him until she was old enough to understand; at fifteen, she is not old enough to understand. But Matilda dear, Tillie turned to the lawyer Mr. Burton, please, make the arrangements necessary for the physiatrist to admit Charles for evaluation as soon as possible and then to Meadow Brook Sanatorium in Boston. I want Charles out of the house away from Rose and myself, I will not be held captive by my husband and his family secrets any longer. Inform the doctor where he can find Charles I am sure he will be at 'The Seven Moons" for the next few days. I am going home now to have dinner with my daughter. Tillie arose from her chair, thank you father, Mr. Burton I will hear from you both soon, leaving the both men speechless as she closes the door.

The Seven Moons

Weeks pass or is it just days Charles has no recollection of time, he is only aware of the quiet shadowy figure entering his room to replenish his opium supply; keeping his feelings dead in a world of the living. Charles struggles to sit up on the filthy bed he has been lying on, however, his mind is foggy, and his reflexes slow he tumbles on to the floor. Snickering to himself, well mother look what the prize son has become, no bright future here, where's wealth and prestige I was responsible for bringing to the family. There goes' Mr. And Mrs. Black pillars in Hartford society and their son, he is a billionaire you know. He took over his wife's inheritance and tripled the income, a financial genius. Is not that right Mother what you pushed and strived to achieve, rich, social, pillars no matter what the cost. Well Mother take a close look at your son, laying on the floor in the filth of his addiction that you helped create, what do you think of me now, am I the pillar you wanted, am I mother? Charles starts sobbing. Crawling to the chair he pulls himself upright on shaky legs looking down he sees his trousers are wet, he has urinated all over himself and the floor, pillar of society muttering as he strips off the wet clothes and kicks them to the corner of the room. Charles hears voices out in the hall but pays little attention until the curtain opens and Mr.

Burton is standing in the dim light of the hall with another person. My God man have you no shame the lawyer says coming into the room, he grabs a filthy sheet from the bed to cover Charles's naked body. What has happened, he says quietly, Charles you are ill I have come today along with my friend Dr. Henry to take you to the hospital? Charles backs away from the men, I am not crazy you know, no one said you were crazy Charles, you are physically sick and need care in hospital until you are well again, Charles, please, and we have an ambulance outside waiting to take you to Hartford Hospital. No, Charles murmurs and with his last bit of strength tries to push past both doctors only to end up in the arms of two hospital orderlies that have been out of sight in the hall. One quickly restrains him while the other pulls the straight jacket tightly around Charles fastening it behind him. Charles knows there is no escape now and drops his head in defeat. All the lawyer's principles seem shattered, and he feels dishonest, trickery and lies have never been part of his business ethics to Mr. Burton "the ends never justify the means."

The ambulance proceeds through the streets of Hartford without sirens or speed this is not an emergency. In the back, Charles in straitjacket lays on the gurney quiet, staring as if he is in some far way place. Dr. Henry keeps up a steady conversation trying to comfort his patient. Charles this is for your own good, you need to have a medical examination, and if we find you in reasonable health you will go home the Psychiatrist reassures Charles. Yet he makes no progress in reaching his patient with soothing words, Charles knows he will never go home again, Louise he whispers, Louise and starts to sob uncontrollably.

Mr. Burton is following the ambulance in his own car there are legal papers he must sign and file with the city regarding Charles commitment as the family's lawyer. He is visibly upset, I never thought it would come to this he utters, Charlotte I hope you are happy seeing that your lies and ruthlessness has destroyed your son, all in the name of money. He shakes his head sadly; his car pulls up to the entrance to the hospital behind the ambulance. Mr. Burton watches as the doors open the driver and orderly remove the gurney and wheel it through the doors of the hospital, Dr. Henry is still talking; only no one is listening.

The ease at which Charles is admitted to the hospital is surprising, Dr. Henry called ahead to have a room waiting on his arrival. Charles is quickly whisked away with Dr. Henry following, before the lawyer could say good-bye, all that is left for him to do is sign the commitment papers and call Tillie's father. Before leaving, Mr. Burton inquires as to when Charles might have visitors, the Charge Nurse tells him to call Dr. Henry as he is in charge now and will make that discussion, thank you the lawyer replies and leaves the hospital commitment papers in hand.

Marie sits silently on the sofa she now knows why her Great-grandfather was committed to the Sanitarium Tillie wanted to protect Rose if only for a little while. Why didn't he fight back? Why did he let his mother control him? Marie said, and then he was willing to destroy his own daughter. Marie felt disgust for Charles, he like his mother seemed to devastate all who love them.

Marie picks up Charles's death certificate from a stack of papers next to her on the sofa reading it, Charles died Oct 13, 1943 age 50 years old, cause of death Heart Failure. Looking again at the commitment papers Marie sees he was committed to Meadow Brook Sanitarium on Aug. 1934. Nine years, he was in the Sanitarium nine years, suddenly she starts looking through the pile of papers next to her, it is not here there are no divorce papers Tillie never divorced him. She said she might but did not, was Charles willing to wait and not tell Rose about his past until Tillie felt it was the appropriate or was it true she still loved him, I guess I will never know.

Marie wakes to find herself on the living room sofa again; I seem to sleep here more than in my bed she says stretching the kinks out of her back. First things first coffee as Marie walks into the kitchen she passes her reflection in the dining room mirror agh, she groans shower next. Within an hour, she opens the door to Louise's room and calls *Abuela*, picking up the mirror, balmy morning Marie greets Louise with a smile. Good morning my angel, she pauses . . . morning, I am not touched by the time she says wistfully, but yesterday in the garden, I felt the spring all around me. Not touched by time, what a luxury Marie says, no clocks, no schedules, just the bliss . . . . Louise interrupted, of nothingness. I am sorry *Abuela* that was unkind for me to say, it is hard to understand how your spirit is dwelling in the hand mirror, in a circumstance I cannot comprehend. You are not a ghost, I am correct in that assumption I know. Yes, my angel I am not a ghost than what . . . . Maria there are things we do not understand and never will, my faith tells me when I have fulfilled what the Holy Mother wants she will take me in her arms to Heaven, when I do not know only that it will happen, and my spirit will be at rest. I wish I had that faith to believe, to believe in anything. Maria, you know who you are now, believe in yourself and together we will see what the Holy Mother has for us, Louise says. I guess you are right *Abuela*; it is difficult for me to be patient. Louise smiles my angel I have had practice, both women laugh.

Abuela, I found a small box in the attic, Marie fingers the delicate silver chain around her neck, what was in it angel Louise asks. Marie places the metal box on the dressing table opens it and removes the envelope that contains Charles's commitment papers. *Abuela* do you remember when you said Charles left one day and never returned, yes, I remember. It is because Tillie had him sent to a Sanatorium; he was there nine years before he died of Heart Disease. Sanatorium, Louise repeated, a place for crazy people, she put him in a place for crazy people. Maria he was not crazy Louise is crying, he was so broken,. I know Marie says, but he was sick in addition, *Abuela*, he was dependent on opium, and it was killing him. Yes, I could see it was, I asked him every day, sometime pleading with him not to go to "The Seven Moons," you knew about" The Seven Moons" but how, how could you know

Abuela, Charles told me, he told me everything, we talked for hours at a time. Did he say to you that he was going to tell Rosie about you and Charles Marcus? Marie was visibly upset now, she was only fifteen a child. No, he said nothing to me, just that he thought someday, Rose should know she has a half-brother. Charles promised Tillie to wait until Rose was twenty-one she will be older and can understand a little better. But, he has become obsessed with telling her and, will listen to no one, even the lawyer Mr. Burton Sr. tries speaking to him but it is of no use. Tillie decides for Rose to have him committed to a sanatorium in Boston. How do you know this, I also found a small journal that belongs to Tillie, she writes about why she felt this was the only way to protect Rose from her father. She wants Rosie to be free from the burden of the family secrets a while longer, to be young and, carefree at least until she finished college. *Abuela* I could understand, Tillie was protecting Rose just as Rose protected me. What I do not understand is Charles's obsession to tell Rose about Charles Marcus, how he can hurt his daughter like that when she is so young why not wait as he promised? Louise was silent, I am sorry you had to hear this, yet you need to know the truth Marie says as I do. You are right to reveal this news to me, Charles was wrong, he could have hurt Rose, Tillie was protecting her child from pain, as any mother will, is there more Louise asks, only that I think Tillie loved Charles until the day she died. Yes, I know Louise says.

Abuela I want to call the lawyer to find out if Meadow Brook is still opened and is there information on Charles confinement if he found out about the ranch if your family still owns it. Yes, please

Louise comments do you think my family still lives on our ranch. We will find out soon enough, be back shortly Marie says as she closes the door behind her.

Down in the library she calls the lawyer at his home number. The telephone is ringing quite a few times before she hears the voice of Mr. Burton, hello may I help you. Mr. Burton this is Marie Black, my dear how nice of you to call, sir I did as you suggested and went to the city archives. Yes, what did you find out? Nothing there were only two files and both were practically empty, there is more information in Rose's safe on the Black family and the Barton family folder had just a few papers nothing of relevance. I asked the archivist if anyone could remove the papers. Miss Kenny said they could not, but I have my doubts. I seem to agree with you, Louise thinks it was Charlotte, no, the lawyer replies if it were anyone it was Tillie's father, he had more to lose if the scandal is made public. I have good news for you though, what it is, Marie inquiries, Louise's brother Miguel's family still own and live on the ranch. Miguel and his wife Gabriella are dead, but they have three sons and two daughters all alive with their family living and running the ranch together. Louise will be excited to hear the news that her family is still well and living on her beloved ranch. What are you going to do and when will you leave for Mexico the lawyer asks. I am not sure, but will you have your office write to the Gutierrez family informing them, Tomas's daughter would like to meet them. Of course, my dear I will have my office draft a letter and send it out within the week. Thank you, I have two other requests of your office, certainly my dear what can I do to help you, Will your office handle the sale of Rosie's house, as soon as

Louise and I are ready, I want to leave for Mexico, when the house is sold you can just send me the check. That is not a problem for my office, we will be happy to handle the sale for you. You said two matters dear, yes I did, Marie hesitates a minute, I went up to the attic last night and found a small metal box hidden in an old steamer trunk in it was a leather journal that belonged to Tillie. She did not seem to write in it every day, just events and days that were relevant to her. I have a clearer picture of her how she felt, and the love she had for Rosie. You are right about mistakes, many happen out of love for others. Yes, Marie, it does not excuse them but gives understanding as to why they occur. There was something else in the box, what Mr. Burton inquires, an envelope containing Charles's commitment papers to Meadow Brook Sanitarium with the name of your father and a psychiatrist Dr. J Henry as witnesses. I would like an explanation as to why nothing was said about this, where you hoping I would not find out. No, Marie that is not the reason the lawyer answered then what was it Marie has an edge to her voice. I was going to disclose the matter to you, I have all the papers here at my home, and I wanted to wait a bit you have so much to try to understand. I was planning to meet you and Louise explaining to you both about the reason Charles was committed. I am truly sorry you found out this way, the lawyer apologized. Do you know if Meadow Brook is open Marie asks, yes it is still in operation Mr. Burton answers her. I think I will pay them a visit to see if there is any useful information about Charles confinement, they can disclose to me. Good idea I found some letters Charles wrote, along with other documents concerning his commitment. When you return from Boston call me, and we will arrange for me to visit. By that time I will have all the real estate papers drawn up and ready, maybe even an answer from Louise's family, the three of us can sit and discuss these matters what your next course of action will be. I will call in a few days when I return Marie replies see you then. Yes, dear hear from you soon. Marie hangs up the phone and leaves the library saying, I guess Boston is my next stop.

Marie decides to go up in the attic again but stops to tell Louise the good news that her family owns and is still living on the ranch. How is that for good news *Abuela*, Marie exclaims, I am so happy, so happy, the family is alive and well Louise answers. I knew in my heart Miguel, and, Gabriella had gone to heaven to be with God, but three sons and two daughters how wondrous that is, and living on the ranch, how many children do they have Louise questions. Mr. Burton did not say, but I am sure we will find out soon as I asked him to have the office send the family a letter stating I am Tomas's daughter and want to visit them . . . . What about me Louise interjects . . . . , and I have something valuable that belongs at the ranch I would like to return Marie finishes. I am sorry angel to interrupt you, I am so excited, about this news, I know Marie says, it is fine only I am not going to tell the family that it is you, I am going to return to the ranch, I do not quite think they will understand yet. Hum, good idea, I think you are right, not yet Louise replies. *Abuela* I am going up to the attic do you want to come along, maybe there are things you recognize and want me to keep. Louise hesitates then answers. Marie cautiously climbs the steep attic stairs turning on the dim light bulbs as goes up carefully holding the silver mirror close to her body. At the top, she places the mirror on a shelf propping it against a wall, so

Louise has a clear view of the room. Where should I begin *Abuela* Marie asks, it is extremely messy and dirty here maybe the drawers in that chest over in the corner Louise tells Marie. As good a place as any, Marie walks over to an old chest and pulls out the top drawer but only finds clothes neatly folded, pulling out the rest of the drawers she see they too are filled with clothing. Well nothing here Marie says as she turns around Louise is weeping, what is wrong *Abuela*, turning her gaze in the direction Louise is looking, she sees a baby's cradle filled with infant clothes, quilts and baby toys. Oh, she whispers, picking up the silver mirror, *Abuela* let's go back downstairs there is nothing up here that you need to see, yes Louise murmurs, Marie turns off the lights and closes and locks the door.

Marie and Louise together go down to the kitchen where Marie fixes herself lunch. I want to go through my belongings this afternoon *Abuela* and sort out what I want to take to Mexico with me, everything else I will give away or have the lawyer sell. Marie invites Louise to help with this task and takes her upstairs to her bedroom where the two women chitchat like best friends at a sleep over. The silver mirror propped against the pillows on the bed so Louise can see around the room as Marie places things in piles of what to take, not to take and I am not sure. By the time, Marie has made order out of chaos and decides on what to take with her, evening is creeping over the Connecticut Hills. Finished, Marie exclaims as she looks over her handy work, everything she will never need again neatly packed away in boxes for The City Mission to pick up. The rest of her belongings she will pack in suitcases and load into the car when she and Louise leave. Let us have dinner Marie says I am starving as she picks up the mirror and heads downstairs to the kitchen. Angel, are you sure, about what you are doing Louise inquires as she watches Marie make dinner for herself. Yes, *Abuela* sure it is time for a change there is nothing holding me here, and I am excited for my future. Louise smiles at her great-granddaughter, I am excited too, she says. Tomorrow I am going to Boston, when I return I will call Mr. Burton, by that time he should have all the paperwork ready for handling the sale of the house and maybe an answer from your family. We can then set a date to leave, how does that sound Marie says, yes Louise answers I would like that very much.

Boston;

Marie decides to leave in the morning early to avoid as much traffic congestion as she can. Meadow Brook Hospital is in the suburbs of Boston just outside the city proper Marie checks her route figuring in about three hours driving time give or take. With that done she goes to Louise's room, *Abuela*, I am ready to leave now I will be home soon, I love you no worrying, please she gently kisses the mirror, and lays it on the dressing table. Proceeding down the staircase, she picks up her overnight bag and walks out the front door into the sunshine, placing the case in the trunk of the car Marie pulls out of the driveway heading towards Boston, soon she and Louise will be on their way to Mexico and a new life there. She cannot help humming to herself as the warm sun shines through the windows of the car.

The sign says "Meadow Brook Psychiatric Hospital" Marie drives the car through the heavy ornate iron gates she shutters the warmth she felt from the sun is replaced by a cold chill. She proceeds down the beautiful tree lined road surrounded by manicured lawns and colorful flowerbeds. She did not know what to expect on her drive up from Connecticut, but this she could not have imagined A Psychiatric Hospital encircled by such a beautiful park like setting, yet this chill she feels. Maneuvering the final turn in the road Marie slams on the breaks of the car. Looming before her is an old towering red brick structure reminiscent of a Gothic Horror Novel, as described in one of "Poe's" stories, high gables decorated with ornate iron rails reach their spiky fingers to the sky. Crows soar in circles on the wind currents above the building calling to an invisible force as if waiting for instructions to swoop down unsuspectingly. Marie looks up at the rows of enormous barred windows that coil around the structure like a giant snake staring, unseeing, blind to the outside world. Marie parks her car in a space marked visitors only, climbs the old stone steps to the enormous steel doors, and rings the buzzer. A voice inquires as to Maries business, she answers she has an appointment with the assistant director. The doors open with a mechanical groaning sound Marie a bit hesitant steps inside to a large reception room she hears the heavy doors object as they now slowly close sending a jolt up her spine. How may I help you a young woman neatly dressed in a dark suit, asks from behind her desk? As Marie walks over to the receptionist, she cannot help but notice the cold starkness of the room, her high heels click on the black and white tile floor as she moves. I have an appointment to meet with the Assistant Director at eleven thirty Marie answers. Yes! That will be Ms. Jackson, let me notify her you are here your name please, Marie Black. Why not take a seat by the window, the receptionist points, to a row of uncomfortable looking molded grey plastic chairs at the far end of the room. Ms. Jackson will be with you shortly. The clicking of Marie's high heels start again as she proceeds to one of the chairs to take a seat the metallic sound seems to echo throughout the whole space. Sitting down Marie feels, she has stepped into a time warp, and a frightening one at that, her hands feel like ice and every nerve in her body is on razors edge. Looking around she sees the walls are painted a grey green any adornment hanging on them is in the form of signs giving information. Marie feels dwarfed by their sheer height, hanging from the ceilings are large industrial fixtures with grey metal covers forcing the light downward through steel cages. The impression given here is one of an institution managed efficiently with no attempt at softening the feel of misery and desperation.

A door opens at the far end of the room Marie stands as she watches a woman walk toward her. Ms. Jackson is short in stature and rather over weight; her hair is pulled back from her face in an unbecoming French twist, exposing her heavy features. She wears a dark flowered dress that moves as she walks, giving the impression of a garden swaying in a breeze. I am Ms. Jackson she says as she extends her hand, her eyes focusing on Marie, and I presume you are Miss Black, yes Marie answers. Well then come to my office and you can tell me how I may help you, her voice has a condescending quality about it. As Ms. Jackson turns the air is filled with a choking scent of flowers emitted from the perfume she is wearing, Marie's stomach is in her throat, she swallows hard trying not to gag. Why did I wear these shoes Marie thinks hearing them click across the floor as she follows the Assistant Director? Ms. Jackson looks down at the source of the noise, poor choice of footwear she comments, you should be wearing shoes like mine pointing down at her flat rubber soled walking shoes, sturdy and quiet. This woman has a way of talking down to people trying to make Marie feel like a naughty child, this will not do Marie thinks to herself.

Come in and sit down Ms. Jackson points to a grey plastic chair similar to those in the reception room, her eyes again focus on Marie. Why are you here she says in a curt tone of voice, Marie recognizes the strategy she has used it many time with her own students. All business, Marie answers with her own unyielding voice squaring her shoulders back and sitting straight in her chair. I am here regarding my great-grandfather Charles Black Junior any information you can give me on his stay here from June 6, 1934 when he was committed until his death on October 13, 1943 would be appreciated. Do you have proof of your relationship to Mr. Black, Ms. Jackson asks. Marie smiles and places a brown manila envelope on the desk, here are all the papers you will need to prove my relationship to my great-grandfather she replies, in the no nonsense voice of a teacher. As Ms. Jackson begins to search through the documents taking her eyes off Marie, she has a chance to look around the room and sees it is just a smaller version of the reception room with the exception of a large ornate dark wooden desk that seems out of place in this austere room. On the wall behind Ms. Jackson, is a ceiling to floor bookcase, filled with books on the treatment of Psychiatric Disorders with some spilling over in neat piles on the floor. Diplomas and Certifications hang on the other walls yet nothing else, not a painting, a picture, or a vase of flowers, not even a rug on the tile floor. I am admiring your desk Marie comments as Ms. Jackson looks up. My predecessor left it here when he retired without taking a breath she states, your papers seem to prove you are whom you say you are, only I hope you understand I can give out no information on our patient Charles Black I am bound by doctor patient confidentiality.

My great-grandfather has been dead fifty-six years, the law of the Commonwealth of Massachusetts states you can release information if the patient is dead with no time constraint. Permission from the executor of the family's estate must be obtained, and if you look close, a letter to that fact is there on your desk drawn up by the family lawyer, Marie declares. If Ms. Jackson wants to play tit for tat Marie is surely willing too. Sorry I must have overlooked the authorization letter, scanning it quickly Marie could see the lines on the woman's face tighten as she looks up her eyes become narrow slits directed on Marie. Please come with me, our receptionist has the information you are looking for and will direct you to a room where you may look at the papers she will makes copies for you if you like, the originals must not leave this facility. Following, Ms. Jackson her heels clicking on the tiles Marie smiles with a new confidence. Take Miss Black to the small meeting room where she can look over the files of Charles Black Junior make any copies she requests. Yes, Ms. Jackson the receptionist replies, Marie watches the Assistant Director waddle off without a good-by. Following the young woman to a small meeting room, she finds all the files neatly piled on a table. Whatever you need let me know I will be at my desk. Thank you Marie replies as the receptionist closes the door behind her, sitting down on one of the plastic chairs, Marie opens the first file and says to herself, Ms. Jackson plays the games well.

Meadowbrook Sanitarium: June. 16, 1934

The heavy steel door slams with the sound of its finality, a tall gaunt man in white straitjacket walks slowly along the chilly sterile corridor, escorted by two hospital orderlies. Screams and haunting laughter, the faces with eyes that see into an abyss peering from behind barred doors, babbling words that say nothing, are all a part of the chaos that assaults Charles like a hammer with merciless accuracy. The men walk on, Charles in a silent daze unaware of the world he will now endure. Here is your room one orderly tells Charles while the other opens the door, Charles hesitates, and tries to pull away as if just awakening from a nightmare unsure of where he is, fear grips his mind and he struggles to get free. The orderlies drag Charles in the room and force him on the bed, when you decide to cooperate we will be back to take the jacket off. The heavy door closes with a dull thud Charles can hear the men laughing as they walk down the hall. Louise he whispers help me, help me as he tries to reach out to the vision of his wife he holds in his mind's eye. Sobs and an uncontrollable anger overwhelm him and Charles lashes out screaming and throwing his confined body against the walls of his room over, and again, he has to hurt, he must feel pain, but there is nothing. Charles sits on the floor of his padded room and feels the walls closing in on him burying him in this hell.

Doctor Henry comes into Charles room with two orderlies, Mr. Black I have been told you are not cooperating now look at you laying here on the floor and Oh! My, you have soiled yourself a grown man what a shame. The orderlies stand Charles up he is trembling and sweating profusely. It is starting Doctor Henry informs the orderlies, take him to the showers and clean him up then bring him back to his room and secure him to the bed I will be back later to see him and give the nurse instructions as to medication and treatment I see fit to administer at this time. Now Mr. Black I want you to go with the nice men they are going to give you a warm shower and clean you up then put you back in bed and tuck you in so you will not fall on the floor again how does that sound? Charles does not respond to the doctor. Should we feed him one orderly inquires, No! See if you can get some water down him and put a diaper on him it will be cleaner to change, Doctor Henry instructs as he leaves the room. The two men take Charles to the shower room where they take off the straitjacket and his filthy clothes stripping him naked then they drag him into one of the shower stalls and turn on the cold water. Charles bolts upright as the icy water stings his body like a thousand needles. The orderlies' laugh they watch Charles shivering as the freezing water cascades over him, here one of the men hands Charles a brush clean yourself you pig, but he just stands there shaking. Dammit! the other says, as he grabs the brush pulls Charles from the shower and starts to scrub him, Charles cries out which angers the orderly, and he pushes Charles back under the freezing water, this will teach you not to make a mess. Charles can no longer stand and starts to slide down the tile wall, turning off the water the men drag Charles from the shower stall wrap him in a towel and take him to his room. Charles still wet and shivering as the orderlies put a hospital gown on him and try to lay him down, but his body becomes ridged and his arms are flailing in every direction, hearing the commotion a nurse comes in the room and calls for two more men to come and assist in restraining the patient. Before Charles can struggle again he finds himself on the bed being diapered, his hands and feet are then secured to the sides of the hospital bed, and a restraint blanket is fastened in place Charles's confinement to his bed is complete and he is left alone with his demons.

Charles gazes up at the ceiling and focuses on a single light bulb illuminating his room. The light gets more intense until it surrounds Charles in its fiery brightness impossible to closes his eyes, he can only stare feeling it sear his eyes blinding him to everything except the horror within its sphere. Dark hideous faces shriek his name trying to devour him in their huge jaws Charles tries to escape, but he is held fast in the confines of this tomb. Creatures crawl out of the abyss deep within the jowls of the faces and fall on Charles slithering and crawling trying to tear and consume his flesh. He is screaming, howling only no one is there to save him. Charles is aware at times of shadows hovering over him white clad Spector's communicating among themselves in a language he cannot understand, moving in slow motion around and around until they are gone.

Doctor Henry instructs the orderlies to place Charles in an ice bath to shock him back to reality from the world of hallucinations that are swallowing him alive. He feels the icy water prick his skin, at first he tries to escape the cold only to find him ensnared in its clutches. However, Charles begins to relax the cold water affirming he is alive.

Well Charles how are we doing today better I hope, Doctor Henry has come to check Charles condition, you have had a miserable three days he informs Charles as he instructs the nurse with him to take the patients vital signs. I am leaving orders for you to start having three full meals daily, you must be hungry and we want to build you up so you can start joining the other patients in the dayroom, I am sure you will like that Charles, but he says nothing. Remember Charles we do not tolerate disobedience here as you already know. Nurse, please instruct the orderly to make sure our patient eats every bit of his meals we want him nice and strong, with that Doctor Henry and the nurse leave Charles's room.

Days appear to be weeks' time is standing still in Charles mind, he is as a man in a daze unable to comprehend what has happened to him following instructions he is given yet at times, not sure, where he is.

Doctor Henry does not consider Charles a threat to himself or a noncompliant patient any longer he can now spend time in the dayroom with the other patients. Only Charles sits silently by a barred window alone never looking at the other men, some approach him, babbling in his face the nonsense flowing through their minds, Charles does not react, and they generally tire of his non-response and leave him to his solitary drifting. This day starts out as any other Charles is sitting at his customary place looking out the window when one of the orderlies comes up to him and says "Charles you have a visitor," He looks up to see his lawyer Mr. Burton walking towards him, Charles dear boy he exclaims, putting his hand on Charles shoulder. The orderly pulls up a chair for the Lawyer and states have a pleasant visit Charles and to Mr. Burton says let me know when you are ready to leave, then walks across the dayroom and stands near the door. Mr. Burton is trying to look relaxed in the midst of chaos; two patients are screaming and flailing at each other, with two orderlies trying to separate them, cause other men to become agitated. One starts to bang his head on the floor while another starts to rock violently back and forth slapping at his face and laughing, Charles is impervious to the madness. Finally looking directly at the lawyer he states, "When can I leave," in a quiet determined voice, Mr. Burton clears his throat Charles that is not my decision to make. I am sure, when you are strong enough, Doctor Henry will consult with Matilda, and the two will make the necessary arrangements for you to leave. Charles looks at the man he has known his whole life and says, "I will die here then." Charles do not say such a thing, I am sure Tillie will want you home, as soon as you are healthy and sound again. Mr. Burton knew that Charles was right, unless Tillie has a change of heart Charles will never be released from this nightmare he has been plunged into. Charles think about getting well, and about becoming a loving husband to Matilda and a caring father to Rose, they both love and need you in their lives. I know you have suffered much over the loss of Louise, only why must you destroy everything good in your life. All have suffered tragedy you are not the only one, why are you crushing those around you who love you. What has Rose ever done to deserve to have a father who is never there for her, a shadow lurking in the darkness on the fringes of her life? I am sorry to be speaking to you like this, but Charles, think on what you have not on what you have lost. I will be visiting you every month now, and when you are ready Matilda, and I will visit and talk about your release, how does that sound. Charles is quiet, the lawyer stands and places his hand again on Charles shoulder, I have known you since you were a baby Charles, I have watched you grow to become a man. I also feel the loss of Louise and see the heartache it has brought to your life, but I am Charles interrupts, you know nothing of my life, don't you see Louise is alive, Charles, no, her spirit is alive, Yes, in your heart, and she will always be alive there. Charles grabs the lawyers sleeve, his grip is like a vice, Charles, Mr. Burton says as he tries to free himself, go to the house, and ask Tillie to let you into my bedroom Louise is in the silver hand mirror on the dressing table. Tillie knows she is there, do this one last thing for me Charles pleads, alright dear boy I will go, and ask Tillie, I promise, now calm down, I must leave now visiting time is over. I will be back soon, is there anything I can bring you on my next visit, Charles looks at the lawyer and sadly says just tell me Louise is safe.

Mr. Burton asks to see Doctor Henry before he leaves but, the doctor is with a patient and cannot be disturbed. Mr. Burton asks the receptionist to have Doctor Henry call him in reference to the patient Charles Black and leaves the Asylum. On the drives back to Hartford, the lawyer decides to visit Tillie, and request to see Charles's room.

Charles's days are a nightmare in boredom routine is standard with no deviation from the unchanging rules permitted, or harsh punishment is soon to follow. He can hear the screams of some men as they are stripped of their clothes and thrown in shower stalls. Sprayed down with icy water or immersed in a tub of frigid water restrained, so no movement is possible, and left for hours alone. He has been subject to both "Therapies" as the orderlies call the torture, and has learned to walk the thin line that has been drawn trying not to traverse on either side. He sits quietly at his window and looks through the iron bars at the freedom he no longer has and waits, but for what he is no longer sure. Nights locked in his room he relives the horror of Louise's death and his powerlessness over God to stop it. Why did God allow him to taste such a deep eternal love only to snatch it away so soon, so cruelly? The night sounds around Charles wash down the halls like giant waves obliterating silence leaving only the agonizing screams of mad men confined in their minds.

Charles notices that some morning's men are missing to return days later head bandaged shuffling quiet not making a sound looking through eyes that are now dead, he wants to ask the orderly what has happened to them but is afraid, so he sits and watches and waits.

When Mr. Burton visits, he brings candy or cookies, news and a few letters from Rosie, Charles seem disinterested since Mr.

Burton told Charles Tillie would not let him in his room because she had it cleaned, and emptied, and now locked. Charles believes Tillie destroyed the mirror and any vestiges of Louise that were left, she is gone, and he is alone. Why do you come Charles inquires of his lawyer, I am sure you have more important matters to care for, like clients you can actually help. My are we a bit irritable today Charles the lawyer remarks, I come here because I gave you my word, your family have been my clients for an exceedingly long time and Charles I still represent Tillie and Rose and want the best for your family and you. Then get me released Charles demands, you know I cannot do that Charles. Matilda went to, and filed papers to have you formally committed for your natural lifespan declaring mental incompetence, and drug addiction. Why couldn't you stop her, I tried Charles," however" Tillie's father hired the best attorneys, and with affidavits from the staff here and Doctor Henry's reports the judge ruled in Tillie's favor. I did all I could do, why when I brought Matilda for a visit after two years and she begged you to promise on your word not to tell Rose about Louise and Charles Marcus until Rose turned twenty one, why could you not try to understand Tillie's reasons and cooperate the lawyer states. I want my daughter to know about her brother Charles stubbornly replies, so because you want your own way you are willing to hurt Rose and Matilda to say nothing of what you have done to yourself. My telling Rose she has a brother will not hurt her I would not do that." My word man "Mr. Burton sighs, can you not understand if you tell Rose she has a half-brother, then you must tell her about Louise, and the horrible day she died, and why you sent your only son away to be raised in Mexico by his grandparents. She will ask why you married her mother so soon after Louise's death. What will you say Charles, that you loved Matilda or it was because Charlotte wanted wealth and status in the community, and Tillie brought all that to the marriage, the lawyer was visibly distressed, sitting in a chair opposite Charles, he runs his fingers through his silver hair. Why doesn't Rose visit me Charles wants to know, she writes me letters, I am allowed to keep them but she does not come? A court order forbids Rose from seeing you until she is twenty-one; she will then make her own decision. Tillie thought of everything, no Charles her father and his lawyer did. They were protecting Rose just as you safeguarded Marcus by sending him to Mexico, remember part of this story involves her father and "The Seven Moons" why not protect Rose as you protected Marcus from Charlotte. I cannot understand Charles, Rose is your flesh and blood; she is not Louise's flesh and blood Charles says in defiance. My God man how can you say that, she is your daughter and a beautiful accomplished young woman, when she graduates college she is planning to be an art teacher or do you care. I think Charles, Matilda is right all that opium has affected your mind and has turned you into someone we do not know. Mr. Burton stands and shakes his head, I will see you next month Charles, looking down at this man and seeing him for the first time as the weak, selfish individual he is. Walking away Mr. Burton stops and turns to face Charles, in a few years Rose will be twenty-one, and she will come to see you if she pleases. I will be with her to give her the support she will needs at that time.

Back in her hotel room, Marie put the stack of documents from the hospital on the desk near the bed. Kicking off her shoes she picks up the menu and calls room service to order dinner sent up, she has just enough time to shower before the food arrives.

An hour later Marie is sitting on the bed, dinner in hand reading Charles Medical reports. One file catches Marie's eye it is the log of all of Charles's visitors from September 1934 until his death in October 1943, it seems his only visitor is his lawyer. Tillie's name appears only twice on the list in nine years, yet she never divorces him, love or hate I wonder which? Marie then sees on May 1, 1940 Charles has a new visitor; Rosie on her twenty-first birthday went to visit her father. Tillie appears as good as her word; she said she would tell Rose everything when she felt she was old enough to understand. What was that first visit was like between father and daughter.

Every month as promised Mr. Burton visits, and as the years drag on, he watches Charles decline. His hair turning white although still full as when he was younger, his tall frame, and angular with a tremor now he must be helped to his customary chair by the window. Only Charles eyes once lifeless from his drug use have become black penetrating orbs seemingly aware of every movement, missing nothing. And every month the same question when is Rose coming and the same answer when she is twenty-one, she will come when she is twenty-one. The lawyer brings necessities and always some exceptional goodie that Charles likes. Tillie sees to it Charles has all that he needs and then some yet she never visits or writes, when Mr. Burton inquires why, she answers, it's better this way and changes the subject. A few times the lawyer has asked Tillie if he could see Charles room, she declines but says when Charles dies, both he and Rose can enter the room, not until then. Mr. Burton must be satisfied to wait. Over the years both Matilda's parent die, she is heir to their estate yet decides to remain in Charles's family's home and asks Mr. Burton to handle all the legal matters in selling her parents' home and establishing a trust for Rose with the proceeds. All other assets will be offered for sale, and the money's she will use to live on, also instructing in her will that any money's remaining after her death be equally shared by her daughter Rose and her husband Charles to meet any needs he may have if still alive.

As Rose reaches, her twenty-first birthday war is again raging in Europe and only England is valiantly standing against the Nazi's onslaught. Rose and Tillie volunteer in the war effort and join the Red Cross wrapping bandages and filling boxes with medical supplies then shipped to England. Working together mother and daughter feel a particular bond in sharing something greater than just them. Rose will graduate from College in June and has a position as an art teacher in a local private girl's academy. Tillie is happy for her daughter, she has become a vibrant young woman achieving her goals and looking forward to her future with the optimism of youth. She knows in a few weeks Rose by law be able to visit her father, and Rose has already told her she is eager to do so. Tillie makes the decision to visit Charles at Meadowbrook and calls the lawyer to request she accompany him on his next visit. Matilda I will be driving this Saturday, are you sure about this the lawyer asks, positive Tillie responds I want to see Charles before Rose does to soften the shock of seeing her father for the first time in all these years. You know he is going to tell her; yes, I am sure he is but I want to see him and ask him to be loving and kind to Rose to take his time in the telling. He has been waiting for Rose all these years I hope as you, time has softened his heart, I know seeing you will be emotional for him please prepare yourself the lawyer informs Tillie. I am not afraid of his outbursts she says, not only that Matilda, Charles is ill and looks older than his forty-seven years you might not recognize him as he has changed in appearance dramatically. Thank you Tillie says you have been kind to Rose and myself I appreciate you telling me this, and I will prepare myself, now what time Saturday shall I expect you.

The ride to Meadowbrook is pleasant Mr. Burton and Tillie make small talk discussing Roses new teaching position at The Francis Academy for Girls, in the fall and Mr. Burton's son Isaac attending Harvard School of Law, neither mentioned Charles. Driving along the road to the Main Hospital building Tillie is silent looking out the window trying to gather her thoughts and steal her for what was to come seeing Charles after so many years. Parking the car, the lawyer turns and says are you sure, yes Tillie replies I am sure.

Tillie blocks everything from her mind and looks straight ahead as the two walk through the halls to the dayroom she is determined to let either sight or sound deter her from her purpose in seeing her husband. An orderly opens the door to the large room and points to where Charles is sitting, the lawyer smiles and thanks him, Tillie walks slowly towards Charles as he looks up she grabs the lawyers hand and stops, taking a deep breath she whispers his name and walks closer. Charles the lawyer calls in a forced cheerfulness, look whom I have brought to visit you, Charles's dark eyes concentrate on his wife. Hello Charles Tillie says as she sits in a chair across from her husband trying to hold in the dismay she feels in seeing the once tall handsome man she married reduced to this old shriveled corpse sitting across from her. Do you know who I am Charles she asks, his eyes burning deep into her soul, why did you come, he says, looking at Mr. Burton, Charles asks where is Rose, you said you would bring Rose, why didn't you bring Rose, what is Tillie doing here, why did you bring Tillie and not Rose. It is fine Charles I received special permission to bring Rose next week on her birthday. We will have a party, and celebrate with cake, and, ice cream, and presents. Will she be here Charles asks, nodding toward Tillie, no Charles I will not be here it will be just you and Rose, and you can observe her birthday together with Mr. Burton of course. Tillie reaches for Charles's hand, and hold firm has he tries to pull it away, Charles I am here to talk to you about Rose, I am telling her he says, I know you are, and I hope she is old enough to understand, I am not here to stop you. I am here to ask you to use wisdom, to tell her about love, how you loved Louise and when she died you loved your son; Marcus, Charles interrupts, yes Marcus, you loved Charles Marcus so much you sent him to his Grandparents in Mexico to live. That love sometimes does not have a happy ending, but no matter what has happened you have always loved her. Please, Charles that is all I came to say that you tell your daughter you love her. Charles pulls his hand from Tillie's, looking out the window he whispers I don't know Rose, no you do not know her Tillie responds. When Rose was, growing up you were too busy in your own world of pity to find time for her. Matilda Mr. Burton scolds, I am sorry Charles, that's long past, no you are right Charles answers, you are right, But I do not know how to love Rose, Charles, she is your daughter Mr. Burton says, yes he answers, but she is not Louise's daughter. Tillie jolts back crying out as if she was slapped hard across the face, her eyes fill with tears. Enough Charles the lawyer snaps, Tillie stands tears flowing from her eyes, your cruelty knows no bounds does it, she says I guess there is quite a bit of your mother in you isn't there Charles. Tillie sighs I would like to leave now she informs Mr. Burton. Yes, my dear come along, the lawyer looks at Charles in disgust. If I were you, I should think on what Matilda said today. I will bring Rose next visit, and I am warning you Charles any show" of unkindness or cruelty on your part" we will leave. I will make sure you never see your daughter again am I making myself clear. Charles nods and returns to looking out the window.

Tillie's decision is now firmly resolved, she does not confide in the lawyer, he might want to dissuade her, and she will have none of that.

When Tillie arrives home Molly is getting dinner ready, will you stay to dinner Tillie invites the lawyer, no dear but thank you for asking, I must stop at the office before going home and Abigail will be expecting me shortly after that, I understand Tillie says and thank you for accompanying me today. I am sorry it went badly; no, I think I just expected too much, I thought Charles could find it in his heart to love Rose. I know he could never love me, but his daughter, I don't know how he cannot know how to love his own daughter, is there not a small flicker deep within his heart for her. Is he so self-centered and selfish he can only think of himself. Tillie seems to be talking more to herself than the lawyer. Matilda dear I promise you I will not let Charles hurt Rose next week, and I will speak to Charles before I bring Rose into the room and warn him about his behavior Mr. Burton says, thank you again I know I can count on you.

The week speeds by and before Tillie can seem to take a breath it is Friday and Rose is turning the car into the driveway. Tillie watches from the living room window as Rosie full of energy hops out of the auto and run up the drive waving as she sees her mother at the window. Tillie opens the door and hugs her daughter as if she has been away for months, not just two weeks. Oh, it is so good to be home the campus is in a frenzied Rosie says as she and Tillie walk into the house. Everyone is packing up and getting ready to leave, and the only talk is of the war, all the students feel we will be in it soon, and many of the boys are joining up now, what you think mom will we be going to war. I think it is nice to have you home, sorry mom, it is just so much is happening, yes and tomorrow is your twenty-first birthday too such excitement. Dinner is almost ready why not go to your room and freshen up, we can spend a quiet evening at home together and I thought Sunday we can go to a lovely restaurant and a movie the film "Rebecca" based on the book by "Daphne de Maurier" is playing at the Royal they say it is superb motion picture. That sounds grand mom Rose replies as she runs up the stairs to her room to tidy up before dinner.

Rose chats non-stop throughout dinner, and Tillie loves every minute of it, with Rose away at college, the house is quiet even after four years Tillie has not gotten used to the silence. Rose dear Tillie interrupts her daughter, do you have any plans for this summer, I know you must prepare for your teaching position at The Francis Academy might there be a week or two we can spend together, I was thinking of the Cape. Let me check in with the school and see what schedule they have for the new teachers, you know meetings and such. But, Mom I think it will be fun, Tillie smiles, let me know when you will be free, and I will make the arrangements you are right it will be fun.

Rose leaves the dining room going upstairs to shower and change into comfortable clothes for the evening. Rose dear, when you have finished, please come to the living room we can have desert and talk, how is that Tillie says. I will only be a bit Mom Rose answers Tillie from the upstairs hall. Tillie requests Molly serve dessert in the living room and then not to disturb them for the rest of the evening, her resolve is still firm.

Within the hour, Rose has bounced into the living room dressed in her pajamas and fuzzy slippers, reaching for a piece of cake she exclaims, what shall we talk about Mom I have so much to tell you. Tillie stops her daughter and says me first, there is something important I must discuss with you, it is about Dad isn't it, yes, and Tillie replies it's about Dad.

Dad is going to talk to you tomorrow about some things in his life that both he and I want you to know now that you are older.

I thought it might be easier for you to hear some of it from me. Your side Rose says, well yes I guess you can say that, my side. I went to see your father last visiting day along with Mr. Burton, why Mom? Your father is extremely frail and has aged from his illness I guess I wanted to prepare you for when you see him, Mom he is only a year older than you, yes Rose but your father has had a terribly hard life with much loss and disappointment. Mom what are you trying to tell me is Dad dying, oh no dear no Dad is not dying, than what Mom tomorrow I will be twenty-one for nine years I have not been able to see Dad only write to him, why was I not able to visit him I think it is time I knew. Yes, Rose it is time, dear you see before your father and I were married Tillie pauses he had a wife. What! Rose exclaims, please dear let me finish, your father and I were engaged to be married, I graduated from college, and my parents took me on The Grand Tour their gift to me before the wedding. Your father went to serve in the army and was an Attache to General Pershing in Mexico. There, he met and married a Mexican woman her name is Louise. But he was engaged to you, Tillie reaches across and holds Roses hands in hers feeling their warmth, yes I know dear. Yet they married, and when Louise was seven months pregnant, Charles brought her to Hartford to meet his Mother, and Father. They were very angry and felt humiliated by your Fathers betrayal. Did you know, did someone write, and tell you, Mom you must have been so terribly hurt Rose says? No, dear I did not know, do not forget I was with your Grandparents touring Europe. I sent postcards, letters, and received only correspondences from Charlotte, saying all was well, and Charles will coming home from Mexico soon we can then start to plan our wedding. In March Louise gave birth to a healthy baby boy, you see dear you have half-brother his name is Charles Marcus, Rose covers her mouth with her hands as if to stifle a scream, I love you and wish there was some way to make this easier for you, Tillie tells her daughter. Where are they now Rose murmurs, Louise died giving life to Baby Marcus and your Father decided to send his son to be raised with Louise's parents in Mexico, Why Rose questions that you will have to ask your Father, after that he got sicker and sicker. Mom if you knew all this why did you marry Dad, I did not know and did not return from my trip until May everything was over by then we were still engaged, Charles and his family pretended as if nothing happened we were married that June. When did you finally find out Rose wants to know, it wasn't until after you were born, and your father was ill, one day I opened the safe to put your birth certificate away when I found their marriage license, Marcus birth certificate, and Louise's death certificate I confronted him, and he told me the truth. Why didn't you divorce him Rose asks her Mother, Oh? Rose the scandal, I would not have cared, mom yes you would Tillie answers you must have a reason to end a marriage dear. All the reasons would make our family the object of gossip I could not have that for you. Your father promised not to tell you until you were twenty-one and your Grandfather protected, and supported our family with exceptional care. Did Dad love you, now, I am really not sure, I think he only loved Louise and no one else, and me Rose asks sadly, I think He wants to try I don't know if he understands how? Do you love him, when we first married, I loved your father with all my heart and would have done anything to please him, now I love him but, not with my whole heart any longer. Rose get up and hugs her Mother, then sits down next to her, can I tell you something Mom, of course anything dear. I wondered when I was little why Dad was always away on business or up in his room sleeping and could not be disturbed as I got older I would hear him leave at night and at times come home early in the morning or not at all for days. I asked Grandfather once, he only said Dad worked very hard, and I was lucky to have a father so diligent when it came to business. He was only trying . . . . Rose interrupts her Mother; yes, I know to protect me only from what, so right before Dad was sent to Meadowbrook I was about fifteen I followed him one night, now it was Tillie's turn to cry out cupping her hands over her mouth. Dad went down a very dark ally in this awful part of the city and into a place called "The Seven Moons" I was terrified and ran all the way home. I asked some friends if they ever heard of it one said it was a bad place where people smoked opium, and, injected other drugs into their veins. Tillie whispers you knew, all this time you knew, yes Mom I knew and I know that is why you had Dad committed it was to protect me, Tillie starts to sob her body collapsing deep into the sofa Rose wraps her mother in her arms and lets her cry.

The next day Mr. Burton arrives at 10 a.m. prompt Tillie opens the door come in she says Rose will be but a minute. On top of a large table in the foyer, he sees a box with a birthday cake inside Molly baked for the occasion, brightly wrapped presents Rose wants to give to her father and a bag filled with assorted cookies. How every nice the lawyer comments to Tillie, yes I wish to make the day as pleasant as possible for Rose. Tillie leans against the table for support and says I told Rose last night, I thought you may the lawyer replies everything, not all the ugly details but mostly everything only Rose had a surprise for me, she knew of her father's addiction. Oh! Dear no, how, the lawyer asks, Rose followed Charles one night and saw him go into "The Seven Moons," some of her friends told her what the place was when she asked them. Mr. Burton shakes his head all these secrets and lies for all these years and for what before Tillie can answer Rose comes down the stairs. Hello Mr. Burton are we ready she says with a smile, I am ready if you are he replies, did mom tell you we talked last night and she told me about some things in dad's life to try to prepare me for today. Yes, she did, and that I knew dad was an addict, yes she told me that too. Rose looks at the mother and blows her a kiss turning back to the lawyer she says, we better be leaving I do not want to keep dad waiting.

For the second time in a month, the lawyer has driven down the long sad road leading to Meadowbrook Asylum with the women in Charles's life. Rose is extremely quiet, her hands tightly clasped in her lap, the bravado she showed in front of her mother gone. Replaced by an anxiety at seeing her father after nine years, how are you holding up my dear Mr. Burton inquires, I feel nervous, I am not sure what I should say. The lawyer pats her on the hand if you think another time will be better, we certainly can turn around. I will make your excuses to your father, Oh! No! I want to see my father I did not think I would be so nervous, I guess I just am not sure what to expect. Completely understandable dear, I will go first to let Charles know you are here, and will be at your side the whole time, when you feel it is time for you to leave simply let me know. Feeling a bit better now, I guess so Rose answers as she looks up at the towering archaic building in front of her as the car pulls into a parking spot marked "visitors."

Rose dear I know the building looks intimidating, but it was built many years ago when this style of architecture was in fashion, please do not let it scare you. It doesn't Mr. Burton, I went to the college library and found some photos of Meadowbrook in an encyclopedia before I came home, it's not the building but what is inside that I am sure will frighten me. I know my dear I wish there was some way I can make it easier for you, your being here with me Mr. Burton is giving me strength and don't forget I have mom's courage too. Stepping through the huge doors, they enter a vast reception area that reminds Rose a bit of Grand Central Station in New York City with its cavernous space that echo's every sound. The lawyer gives their names to an unhappy looking woman seated behind a large desk, she inquires what is in the boxes as the lawyer informs her they have special permission to have a small birthday party today. She checks her list again gives an abrupt nod and buzzes open the steel doors.

Rose now steps into another world one Tillie can only hope she is somewhat prepared for. Holding tight on to the cake box and walking close to Mr. Burton, Rose walks down the corridor to the dayroom to meet her father. As promised, Mr. Burton enters the room first to speak to Charles and finds him in his usual chair by the window. Charles looks up and says Rose is here, yes Charles she is here, do you remember what we spoke about when I was here last about you showing your daughter love, and kindness. Yes, Charles answers, then I will bring her in, just remember if you are cruel to her, we will leave, and you will never see her again. I know Charles replies, please I want to see Rose.

The lawyer enters the hall to find Rose conversing with one of the patients as if they were old friends although neither understands what the other is saying. Ready Rose, yes, turning back to the patient she said it was so nice chatting with you, I hope we can do it again sometime, the old man smiling walks down the hall with the orderly to his room.

Rose holding on to the lawyers hand walks through the door into the dayroom as they approach his chair Rose in a soft voice says father, Charles turns from the window and see his daughter for the first time in nine years. Rose, yes father it's me it's Rose, she hands the cake box she is still clutching to Mr. Burton and reaches out to hug her father, only Charles pulls away, but recovers and says stand in the light of the window so I can get a proper look at you, Ah! That's better my you are quite the lady now, very grown up. I am twenty-one today yes I know Charles replies, we brought a cake and some presents so you can help me celebrate if you would like. That will be nice Charles says, his tone of voice is wooden without any emotion. Father I have missed you and, pray for you every night, thank you Charles answers for praying, but I do not think you missed me, you have your mother and I am sure you have many friends. Rose is unsure as to how to answer when Mr. Burton responds, Charles that does not stop Rose from missing her father. You are right Charles says, looking back at Rose, I am sorry I have been ill and must live here, but your mother thinks it is for the best. Yes, father I know, now why don't we have some cake, Molly baked it, look how lovely the orderly fixed a table for us. Now lets over to the table and have our cake and open the presents I brought for you. Charles is unsteady he is helped to the table by an orderly, and slowly sits down. How about a nice round of Happy Birthday for the young lady the orderly say loudly and everyone in the dayroom starts to sing their version of the birthday song. Rose stands up, and bows to the room saying thank you and now cake for everyone. The orderly cuts small pieces of cake for the patients which they all enjoy, many just scooping the whole piece into their mouth with their fingers. There wasn't that nice Rose says father why not open your presents. Charles looks at his daughter and says it's not my birthday, no it's not it's mine, and I brought presents to give to you. You are like your mother Charles tells Rose, and before he can say another word, she replies why thank you I am proud to be like mom. I have to tell you something, I want to go back to my chair so I can tell you, I cannot tell you sitting here. Mr. Burton asks the orderly to help Charles back to his chair by the window and whispers to Rose how are you holding up my dear, fine she answers, you know what is coming next, signal me when you are ready to leave, Rose smiled and nodded as she walks to when her father is sitting.

Rose sits next to the lawyer, and he places his hand over Roses' smiling at her for assurance. Well father I know you want to tell me something extremely important and have had to wait such a long time, I am here now father a ready to listen. Charles looks at his daughter unable for a moment to speak, Rose, yes father, Rose, I want to tell you, you have a half-brother, his name is Charles Marcus and, He lives in Mexico Rose says, how do you know, mom told me last night. Charles clenches his hands on the arm of the chair, she had no right, Rose interrupts father I was told because mom wanted to make this day easier for me, she said you would answer any questions I have and not to be fearful to ask you. Charles looks confused all these years he has rehearsed what he would say to Rose, now it seems it has already been said without his knowledge, she had no right he says again. Please father talk to me, I know you were married before you married mom. Tell me about Louise, Charles brightens she was beautiful, and we were going to live in Mexico, and I was going to learn the horse breeding business from her father. We were happy, but she died didn't she father, yes, and it is my fault. Why do you say that Rose asks Charles, I should have never brought her here to Connecticut we should have stayed in Mexico, then why did you bring Louise here? I wanted our child to be an American, and I thought if my mother met Louise, she would love her as I did. She hated her, and when the baby was born, she would not help, by the time I got back to the house with the doctor Louise was dying. Rose with tears in her eyes reached out to touch her father but again he drew away, I am sorry father that Louise died, but was the baby healthy, yes, he was, but Louise was dead, I had nothing. No father you had your son, why did you send him away, I had to, I had to protect him from Charlotte, he had to have a chance to be raised in love, he had to leave and the safest place was with his Grand-parents in Mexico. Is he still there, have you ever contacted him or Louise's parents, Charles looks at the lawyer and Mr. Burton answers looking at Rose, your father has not wanted to have contact with his son, I have periodically, been in touch with Louise's family, and Marcus is quite well, Charles utters thank you. Rose's emotions boil, she angrily says, if you loved this woman so then why did you marry my mother just two months after she died. Why did mom have to find out about Louise herself, why didn't you have the courage to tell her you were married before and had a child, can you answer those questions for me, can you father. Charles is shaken and, starts to tremble, but Rose is relentless, answer me father. Charles looks down at his hands when your mother came home from Europe I was going to break off the engagement and tell her everything; "however" my mother said no the scandal would destroy both families, so I kept silent and were married as planned. So no scandal, everything hidden, perfect for the world to see is that right father, Charles is silent. Didn't you forget something in your story father what about "The Seven Moons." Charles looks up at Mr. Burton his pallor a ghost grey, she knows the lawyer says, Tillie Charles asks, no father, not mom I followed you one night when I was about fifteen, and saw you go inside, my friends told me what the place was an opium den, you were an addict. I was told you were sick, and had to come here only I knew better why father, I could not live without the drugs, the pain was to great they helped me live without Louise by my side. What about the pain you caused mom and I doesn't that count, Charles looks at his daughter I love Louise, do you love mom, and me Rose asks, her father is silent. Rose looks at Mr. Burton I think it is time for us to leave Charles expresses Mr. Burton as he and Rose stand up to depart, will you come again Charles enquires of his daughter, yes father I will, it may be difficult at times, but I will do my best. Rose, Louise was alive she was trapped in the silver hand mirror in my room, I spoke to her always, Rose looks at the lawyer, and he shakes his head. She is gone now Tillie destroyed the mirror, and Louise is gone. Rose reaches out to touch her father's shoulder only pulls her hand back and says instead good-bye father I will try to see you next month, but Charles is staring out the window already lost in his thoughts. Rose and the lawyer walk to the car in silence.

Marie is only now beginning to understand the sadness Rosie hid so well beneath her cheerful exterior. On further examination, Marie sees that every month without fail Rosie visits her father and is with him on the day he dies. I wish Rose kept a diary, a journal, something where she recorded her thoughts, but Marie knows Rosie never did, she would always say today is a new day, a fresh beginning so why write down the past when a new horizon awaited. Looking at the clock Marie sees it was past one a.m. wanting to get an early start in the morning she knows it was time to go to sleep, turning out the light she whispers good-night Rosie and falls asleep.

The trip back to Connecticut was unremarkable the usual traffic and congestion on I 95was light and by mid-afternoon Marie was pulling the car into the driveway. She is eager to see Louise, and tell her what she found out about Charles, and his life at Meadowbrook. Marie drops her overnight case on the couch in the living room along with the copies the receptionist made for her of Charles records, calling *Abuela* I am home, she quickly sorts through the mail finding a letter from the lawyer, and runs up the stairs.

Abuela, Marie calls as she opens the door to Louise's room, there is a letter here from Mr. Burton's law offices she says as she picks up the mirror. *Abuela* are you there, yes! My angel Louise answers I am here. Marie props the mirror against a stand she has set up on the dressing table, so it stays upright. I think this is the letter we have been waiting for from your family, her hands are shaking, and her voice cracks with excitement. Well what are we waiting for Louise says open it, Marie rips open the envelope and finds two letters inside one on Law Office Stationary says ;

Ms. Marie Black;

I have enclosed the reply from Hilly Guiterrez and The Guiterrez Family to your request to visit them in the near future.

Sincerely;
Isaac Burton Esq.

A Family in Mexico

The early spring day is warm in the bright blue sky; although early, the *hacienda* is a whirr of activity. Every morning the men of the family meet at the main house to discuss plans for the day over breakfast. Three generations gather around a large table in the dining room reviewing work schedules, breeding charts and the ranch maintenance. At the head of the table sits Hilly Gutierrez, eighty-four years old, patriarch of the family to his right sits his younger brother Emilio seventy-seven. The sisters Pillar and, Flora are busy getting ready for their busy day. They will catch up on any important business at the evening meal when the family meets again. After breakfast, everyone leaves to go about the business of running one of the largest and most successful horse breeding ranches in Mexico. The brothers walk slowly out to the veranda; Emilio likes to spend the morning in the coral with the horses. Hilly will sit in his favorite chair and, wait for his granddaughters Elena and, Deanna to arrive from their home built close to the main house to start their days work in the office of the house. As the family grew members, who wanted constructed their homes on the ranch property. Over the years, a group of dwellings grew up around the central *hacienda* so there was always the commotion of family nearby and Hilly loved it.

Good morning, he calls as he sees his two granddaughters walking through the gate, each a mirrored reflection of the other. Buenos, *Abuelo* they say with a smile, are you ready for a hard day at work the old man replies his eyes with a good-natured twinkle. The two women walk up to Hilly giving him a peck on either cheek, *Abuelo*, you are such a tough boss Elena informs him with a laugh, as they walk to the house to start their accounting and secretarial duties in the office.

Hilly sits in the sun feeling its warmth on his old bones and thinks of his past, and its former glories. Signore Gutierrez, Hilly wakes with a start, I am sorry to bother you, I have a registered letter you must sign for, the mail carrier says apologetically. It takes Hilly a moment to shake the sleep from his body, letter he repeats, yes Senor you have a registered letter, please sign here the young man says pointing to the place he wants Hilly to write on the receipt. Who is writing me and registered no less, Hilly signs the delivery receipt then returns to his chair letter in hand. Looking at the return address, he sees the name, Isaac Burton Esq. I thought the old man dead he says aloud, no this is the son he was a child when his father came to bring Marcus and *Tia* Louise home. What can he want; Hilly with a quiver in his hand opens the letter?

Dear Senor Geraldo Gutierrez;

I am writing to you in behalf of my client, Ms. Marie Louise Black (your great-grandniece). Miss Rose Black has recently died; upon her death, my client has become aware of your family and its relationship to her. As you can expect Ms. Black

168

was quite stunned, by this news. However, she is extremely eager to meet you and asks permission to come to Guadalajara for a visit.

I would appreciate your consideration of this matter. Please inform me of your decision as soon as possible.

Sincerely;
Mr. Isaac Burton Esq.

Hilly studies the letter again to be sure he is reading it correctly, fingering the paper almost in a caress. Tomas's daughter wants to come home to meet her family Hilly whispers to himself. Well Rosetta you have kept your secret all these years only now it has died with you and Tomas's Maria wants to come home to the country where she belongs. Hilly knows the question must be discussed tonight with the family at the evening meal but as far has he is concerned Maria will come home and welcomed with opened arms. Maria he says weeping her name holding the letter close to his heart the timeworn gentleman waiting to share his good news with the family falls asleep under the warmth of the sun.

Hey! Old man, have you slept all day, shouts Emilio as he slowly walks to the veranda where his brother is just waking from his nap. Who are you calling old Hilly replies, stifling a yawn Emilio puts his arm around his brother, and the two men walk into the house? I have news Hilly tells Emilio have good news.

As the family gathers around the huge table in the dining room, for the evening meal Hilly is at the head Emilio to his right, Flora to his left and next to her their youngest sister Pillar. Hilly feels a strong sense of pride in this family; each member has worked hard, and overcame hardships relying on one another, as a family must. Now he can share with them his good news that one that was lost to them is coming home. As Hilly stands, he casts an eye over their faces I have an announcement to make he says then abruptly stops. Where is Ramon, why is he not at dinner? Anger tinged his voice, Ramon his youngest grandson is wild, and Hilly has little patient with his reckless behavior. Elena tells her grandfather that Tio Ramon is in the city and has not returned. The old man looks at his son Pietro; you must do something about Ramon, yes but what *Padre*. Ramon is thirty years old a grown man. I cannot spank him as you would a naughty child. No, you cannot, but it is past time that Ramon settles down, after all, he has a son of his own, and what is he teaching the boy. When he returns, Pietro, you and I will meet with him and have a talk. Hilly does not give his son a chance to respond, now to my news he takes the registered letter from his vest pocket. Today I have received this registered letter from the law firm of Isaac Burton, is that not the lawyer of . . . . yes, yes Hilly says not letting his brother Emilio finish, both his sisters make the sign of the cross. What is it the rest of the family asks; is it sad news, who is this lawyer? Enough, Hilly bangs on the table rattling the dinnerware, to get the family's attention. Buenos he says the news is good the lawyer has written me letting me know Tomas's daughter Maria would like our permission to come and get to know her father's family. Everyone is speaking at once, stop, Hilly waves the letter in the air, Emilio, looking at his brother, is Rose dead he inquires, yes Hilly replies then shaking his head says she must come home. Hilly then looks at his sister Flora, Louise is dead, Marcus is dead, Tomas and now Rose, Flora makes the sign of the cross and asks her brother is it over Hilly is it finally ended? Si sister it is over then she must come home Flora replies. Hilly then looks at his youngest sister Pillar still wearing the large wooden Crucifix around her neck that was a part the habit she wore as a nun in the convent of Our Blessed Mother, well sister what do you say. Pillar smiles and in a soft voice utters it is a sign from Our Blessed Mother, Hilly bring the child home. With that, the rest of the family all speaks at once, their questions flying around the table.

Hilly ignores the queries and gets up from the table; he motions to his granddaughters and asks them to follow him into the office. Leaving the questions for Emilio and his sisters to answer, they close the door.

Marie picks up the second letter, Louise asks her to read it aloud.

Dear Mr. Burton;

Tell the child to come home we are all waiting.

Sincerely;
The Guiterrez Family

Marie starts to cry, between sobs she whispers, I am not alone I have a family, and they want to see me. Louise looks at her great-granddaughter, and sees in her the generations of her family, her mother's faith, her father's kindness, the son she could not raise and grandson she never knew all before her in the eyes of this astonishing woman who is part of her beloved Familia. Do not cry my angel this is good news, yes *Abuela* extremely good news, we are going home now, home Louise whispers to herself. Tomorrow I want to call Mr. Burton to ask if all the paperwork for the sale of the house is in order, we can then map out a travel route, set a date, and get ready to leave. Louise looks a bit worried and asks Marie how are we to travel, by train. No, no *Abuela* we will travel by car, I will drive, I thought of flying, flying oh, please I do not think that is a good idea, not to worry flying is out of the question, and so" is the train". The safest, and most practical thing to do is for me to drive, when we do arrive in Mexico I will need a car. Louise is calmer knowing they will travel by car but, how will you bring all of your things with you, will the automobile hold everything. *Abuela* you are a worrywart, I made arrangements to have my things shipped when I am ready for them. Mr. Burton has arranged an account for me in the EL Nationale Bank of Guadalajara all of my funds will be transferred there after we arrive, and when the house is sold the money will be deposited in my account automatically. How can this be Louise questions, it is very difficult to explain, I know remember when you and Charles were traveling, and he sent a telegram to Mr. Burton informing him when you were arriving, yes, well it is something like that a telegram Louise says sounding confused. *Abuela* instead of words being sent it is numbers and those numbers inform the bank how much money will be in my account. But where is the money Louise still confused asks, please not to worry it is truly mystifying but when I need the money it will be there waiting for me. *Abuela* I want to change my clothes and unpack, then we will go sit in the garden I think now is the time to tell me how you met Charles" I want to know before we talk about what I found out about his stay at Meadow Brook". Yes, angel you are right now is the time and the garden the perfect place. In an hour, Marie with Louise in hand were sitting in the cool shade of one of the garden trees. Louise is holding the mirror so Louise can see and enjoy the beautiful flowers I have always loved sitting here even when I was a child this section of the garden was always magical. I would dream of fairies and elves all living under the flowers, and in the trees, Marie confided to Louise. Enough of that Marie said now how did you meet my great-grandfather

How Charles and Louise Meet:

The battle to capture Poncho Villa was a war of skirmishes between the men of Gen. Pershing's Command and the Villistas' men under the command of Poncho Villa. In March, the First Aero Squadron equipped with six Curtiss JN-3 began to conduct aerial reconnaissance to seek out Villa's base camp. They found it at Casas Grande in Chihuahua. Supplying the troops was difficult because of a dispute the American Army has with the Carranza government. Now the military must employ a truck-convoy to deliver the supplies to the men in the field. This is the first use of non-rail motor vehicles by the military and provides a record used as the country entered WWI. Skirmish after skirmish Villa and his men avoid capture. On May 14, George Patton's eighth Cavalry near Chihuahua raid the ranch of Julio Cardenas a prominent leader in the Villista Army. With 15 soldiers and 3 Dodge armored Motorcars, Patton pulls off the first armored vehicle attack, killing Cardenas and two other men Villa is not at the ranch. The Army in many areas where roads are non-existent has the Signal Corps run telegraph wires to keep the lines of communication flowing.

Charles a junior attaché to Pershing is assigned to a group of Cavalrymen as second in command of the expedition to get fresh horses to replace mounts killed in action. Senor Gutierrez has been selling quality horses to the army at FT. Bliss for years. General Pershing knows and trusts Senor Gutierrez as a decent man and an excellent breeder of horseflesh from previous dealing. Marcus Gutierrez agrees to join the Army at a friend's ranch in Zacatecas with 50 fresh horses.

In the early morning of May 1916, a truck-train with a company of men set out from Del Parral Mexico with Charles second in command. The journey for both groups of men is about one hundred fifty miles it will take Marcus five days maybe shorter as he has traveled this route many times on his way to Fort Bliss. For Charles and the men it will take three days by truck, all together the Army Company will be gone only ten days with time to rest the horses in Zacatecas before loading them onto the trucks back to Del Parral.

Charles is pleased to be away from their base camp, it's monotony of life, and the frustration of not capturing Villa, raid after a raid with no results. Bumping along desert roads in the heat keeping a constant lookout for Villista extremely pleased to attack, and capture their armored trucks, Charles feels a thrill at the danger he and his men might experience, his heart races, and his face flushed, maybe, just maybe he could be Charlie the Magnificent once again.

The men gripe at the frustration they feel as they traversed the empty desert over near non-existing roads. Charles now is seeing the beauty of this land torn by rebellion.

The three days pass quickly with no sign of Villa and his Villistas as the truck-train drives through the town of Zacatecas on its way to the Esteban ranch. Citizens come out of their stores and, homes to watch and wonder what is happening. Father Joseph stops the first truck asking the commanding officer where the vehicle is heading his black Cassock blowing in the strong breeze making him look like an enormous black bird readying for flight. Speaking perfect English, the Priest tells the officer that the Esteban Ranch is about five miles to the southeast and, assures them Senor Esteban is expecting them. Thanking the priest, the men move on as Charles looks back Father Joseph cassock flying around him disappears into the church.

Within the hour the truck-train and its men move through the main gates of The Esteban Horse Ranch, they drive on for miles before seeing large out buildings with sizable corals, men and horses are everywhere all going about the day-to-day tasks of running this large breeding ranch. Some men cease their work to watch the trucks go by most ignore the column and, continued with their business undisturbed by the American Army. The main *Hacienda* is a well-built adobe design, not unlike most homes in Mexico Charles has seen. Senor Esteban greets the men with a shiny gold tooth smile and a Buenos Nada. Esteban with significant pride welcomes Charles and the First Lieutenant into his home. The rest of the men and trucks are taken to a large bunkhouse where they will settle for their stay. All hospitality is exhibited to the soldiers, and they are impressed.

One of the servants accompanies Charles and, his commanding officer to their room and, informs them dinner will be in an hour, enough time to clean up from the days ride and rest. Both men looking around seem astonished by the luxury in this area Senor Esteban is a rich man and loves to put his money on display. Overstuffed mattresses are on elaborately carved beds. Colorful quilts and shawls have been set at the end of each bed along with comfortable chairs and a large desk all make the room feel relaxed. Both men fall onto the beds and are snoring in minutes. Later a knock wakes them from their peaceful nap, and they are taken to the dining room for dinner.

As they enter the dining room, Senor Esteban gets up and greets them with a handshake and his glittering smile. I hope your room is adequate, Marcus asked me to treat you well as if I would not. Sit here he says pulling out one of the overstuffed chairs. The table is so filled with food and drink one cannot see the top. The men reach for the food as Senor Esteban bows his head and starts to say a blessing, hands in midair both men bow their heads and mumble a few words. Esteban looks up we must always thank Our Dear Lady for her blessings on our home and all who live and work here. Now gentlemen please eat and tell me what is happening up north. This kind of campaign he told Charles and his commanding officer is not good for business. Not all Mexicans see Poncho Villa as a hero. Well most of the civilians we meet are protecting Villa, hiding him and his men, feeding them, and helping Villa avoid capture, Charles responds. Peasants, what do they know Villa gives them a crust of bread, and he is their Savior? AH, he says in disgust throwing up his arms, come Esteban says getting up from the table I need a drink and a good cigar. The men follow their host into a large sitting room with a table at one-end durable leather chairs and sofas fill the rest with the space, this is a man's room, where the head of the house comes to rest from the cares of the day.

Tequila, Yes! Esteban asks not giving the men time to answer he hands them a shot glass filled with a clear slightly amber liquid, on a tray there are lemons and three saltcellars. Lifting their glasses, Esteban toasts, Saludo to Mexico, the two soldiers respond to The United States. Esteban laughs ah! Yes, to The United States, with a slight edge to his voice, we must not forget our neighbor to the north.

Marcus will arrive tomorrow afternoon Esteban says, Miguel his sons will be with him along with some of his most trusted men. There has not been fighting this far south, but Marcus will not allow his beloved horses befalling thieves. General Pershing has exceptionally high praise for Senor Gutierrez and admires the quality of his horses, states Charles. The Army has sent us a far distance to secure his horses, the commanding officer comments. Can you tell us, what is different between his horse stock and yours? Esteban smiles, he is an honorable man, his breeding stock is of champion background, he will breed only the best horses and takes pride in what he sells. Some ranchers are not so dedicated in their business dealings they do not have the luxury of that kind of honesty. You seem to have done well, what we have seen of your ranch looks remarkably profitable the officer says. Esteban replies yes, I have my ways of doing business there is a harsh tone to his voice. Charles changes the subject quickly by commenting on how much he thinks Mexico is such a beautiful country, with it wide open spaces so different from where he lives in the United States. Esteban calms down and asks the men about their home, Charles tells him about Hartford Connecticut, and his life there, Esteban seems genuinely interested. The Commander remains still looking bored he makes his excuses and leaves the room to go to bed.

Charles tells Esteban he would like to check on his men before he turns in and the two walk out into the warm desert night.

Charles wakes up to the morning sun coming through the open windows promising a sweltering rest of the day. He is up early, dressed, and ready for Esteban as they have planned to ride out and, meet Signore Guiterrez to help him and his men drive in the horses. Charles is excited at the idea of getting away from the frustration of just waiting around if only for an hour or so. He has cleared it with his commanding officer who like the rest of the men seem content to relax before the long journey back to Del Parrel with fifty horses.

Buenos Dias Charles greets Esteban as he enters the dining room, good morning Signore Charles, now sit down, eat I do not want you to ride out into the desert on an empty stomach, Esteban smiles his gold tooth smile. There is no reason Charles trusts this far from honorable man, by his own admission, except, he likes him and, feels in Esteban, you see him up front, nothing is hidden. When Charles finishes eating, the men walk to a stable where their horses are saddled waiting for them. Charles's Army mount is grazing in one of the corals with the rest of the horses, inclined to relax after the long three days journey. The stallion Esteban provides Charles is a magnificent animal as he mounts Charles pats the horse's neck and takes control of the reigns. The two men move out into the desert heat already starting to ripple over the landscape.

Maria Guiterrez convinces her husband Marcus that since he is delivering fifty horses to the American Army and meeting them at the Esteban Ranch a short ride from Fresnillo where her sister Juanita and her family live this is a excellent time for a visit. It is hard to deny Maria when she has her mind set and, it is set on this visit even though the trip will be difficult and dirty there is also a deadline to meet, there will be no time for dawdling. Louise and I are not dawdlers, Maria informs her husband your daughter rides, as well as her brother, and as for me, I will ride in the supply wagon with the cook the dispute is over as she prepares for the journey. A week on the trail does not diminish Maria or Louise's passion for their visit. Both look as fresh and radiant, as when they rode from home, Maria was correct their presence on this trip has kept everyone spirits up making the days seem to go faster. Marcus is proud of the two women in his life and today as they are nearing the Esteban Ranch he sits high on his horse a man satisfied with his life.

Ahead the men can see riders approaching, Marcus tells his men to slow down and raise their pistolas, he orders Louise to go back to the wagon and, stay near her mother, Marcus is taking no chances these riders could be Villanista's and he is ready for a fight. Miguel with pistola and rifle drawn flank his father, turning back to make sure Maria and Louise are safe Marcus nods his head in approval seeing both women along with the cook have rifles at the ready.

As the riders approach closer, tension fills the men no one moves a muscle except for tightening their trigger finger. Then Marcus hears the distinctive laugh of Esteban as he shouts to them, Guiterrez do you have so many amigos that you can kill one? Marcus shakes his head at his friend's folly and signals for his men to lay down their rifles.

I have come to help deliver your horses; the Army is waiting at my ranch for you, Esteban tells Marcus as he tips his sombrero to his old friend. Charles positions his horse close to Marcus, Senor Guiterrez I am Second Lieutenant Charles Black of the United States Army extending his hand. Marcus greets him warmly and introduces his son Miguel, the horses are moving past the men about 200 yards to the left picking up speed as if they can smell the fresh hay and water waiting up ahead. Esteban motions for his men to help with the horses, all the ranch hands, are now riding together like a seamlessly choreographed dance moving to silent music. Louise now rides to her father's side, Senor Esteban she smiles in greeting, Ah! Senorita Louise I did not know you were coming with your father. Marcus answers, Signora Guiterrez and our daughter will be visiting family in Fresnillo for the time I am away as I have some business I must attend to in Nieves. Then we must go back to the ranch quickly so the women can freshen up, you all must be hungry. Charles cannot seem to take his eyes from Louise. Esteban inaudibly utters Lieutenant Black to get Charles's attention we must leave now to start back to the ranch. Louise remains silent, wondering who this handsome American Soldier is as she rides next to her father and brother toward her destiny.

Charles knows that meeting Louise alone is out of the question; Mexican culture forbids a young unmarried woman to be alone with a man without a chaperone. Charles must ask Esteban how to accomplish this task without giving offense to Louise's family. He father Marcus and, brother are formidable men and will not look kindly on any breach of etiquette, concerning Louise.

Conversation at the dinner table is lively Marcus and, Miguel have much to share about the trip. The Lieutenant inquires if they saw any Villinesta further to the south, but there was no news to report, the only scare was when Esteban and Charles road out to meet them, and they laugh when recalling the scene. Maria and Louise are quiet during the meal, mostly speaking to each other. Occasionally, Louise looks up in the direction of Charles studying his face.

After dinner, the men retreat to the lounge for drinks and cigars, Maria and Louise withdraw to their rooms for the night

Charles waits until Marcus and his son retire, he, and Esteban are alone before he broaches the subject of speaking to Louise. Ha! Ha! Esteban laughs I saw Louise casting glances your way at dinner, extremely dangerous Senor extremely dangerous. Then tell me what I must do to be able to talk to her what should I ask her father? Please Esteban, will you help, Charles implores.

Wait Senor, there are customs that must be followed Senorita is unmarried and is in her father's care until the time she chooses a husband. The mans' family must approach the woman's family for permission to see the Senorita and your family are in America, is there some way around that Charles enquires, I can act as your Padrino, Padrino what is that Charles wants to know, your Godfather Esteban answers. I am not catholic Esteban shakes his head in disbelief at Charles lack of understanding of Mexican customs. As your Padrino, which I might add, is a tremendous honor, I am to advise you in matters of courtship and of our customs. Louise will choose a Madrina or Godmother who will accompany her and give her wise counsel. A Senorita can choose her own husband but only if her father approves of her choice and he and his family are above reproach. Therefore, you see Senor Charles your way in this situation will not be easy. Esteban can you be my voice, Charles hesitates, I want you as my Padrino, and you will be my family here in Mexico. You still do not seem to understand our Senorita's do not keep company alone with a man, only with the intention of marriage and, when families are in talks together then they will have a chaperone when they do meet. Senor you are here with General Pershing, not with the purpose to marry, after you catch Poncho Villa, you will be gone. I cannot disgrace the Gutierrez family and myself, seeing a young unmarried woman is a serious matter nothing to take lightly. I will not do the favor you ask, Esteban gets up to leave the room, if you will not help me then I will ask Senor Gutierrez, I promise you Esteban my intentions are honorable. Esteban stops tell me does your honor lie in marriage, yes! Charles answers, how can this be, you do not know Louise or her family, you talk of honor, but I think it is

American opportunity you speak of, and that is a far cry from what we as Mexicans hold as decent and honorable. If I speak on your behalf Esteban says, and the answer is no, then I swear I will not bother her or the family again Charles answers. Esteban takes in a deep breath and, answers I will speak to Marcus tomorrow after breakfast. I am going to sleep now, and you should do the same, Esteban leaves the room not at all happy with the task facing him in the morning.

Marcus's goal was to spend one day at the Esteban Ranch after delivering the horses to the military and being paid. He will then take Maria and Louise to his sister-in-laws for their promised visit, before riding with his son to Nieves to look at some breeding stock, hoping to be gone about a week plenty of time for a nice visit for the women.

In the early morning, Marcus and Miguel along with Esteban go to the Corals to meet Charles, and his Commanding Officer where they will examine the horses and pay Marcus the agreed amount in American money. He wants to go to Zacatecas and, replenish the provisions for his trip to Nieves, he will take Esteban, Miguel can stay behind with his mother and sister to tie up loose ends should there be any. Esteban is holding a small celebration in the evening to a business transaction well done, Marcus is ready to relax and enjoy dear friends, tasty food and, good music before leaving and he was sure Maria and Louise will delight in a little gaiety after the long days on the road.

Esteban says he wants to talk with Marcus before they leave for town. The two friends sit in Esteban's office a quiet room at the rear of the house. Esteban seems nervous which his friend finds a bit odd as Esteban is not a nervous man. What do you think of the American Officers he asks, Marcus pauses I have not seriously thought much of them, they are likeable enough, seem to know their way around Caballos why? The young one Senor Black, what is this Esteban: tell me. Senor Charles requests that I act as his Padrino, to ask your permission to speak to Louise, and, visit with her at your sister-in-law Juanita's with a chaperone of course. The silence is deafening in the room Esteban looks at his friend waiting. So this is why you were nervous Marcus replies in a firm, but even tone of voice, Esteban shakes his head, well I will think on it and, speak to Maria and Louise but tell your young Lieutenant not to get his hopes up there is no future here for him. However since, you are acting as his Padrino, I am by tradition bound to consider this matter with my wife and daughter in question. Without further discussion, Marcus gets up and leaves the room finding Miguel waiting for him already to ride to town to obtain their needed supplies. *Padre* I thought to ride with you since all seems well here. The wagon is already out front when are we leaving, Miguel enquiries, soon I must speak to your mother, Marcus answers, is Senor Esteban ready? I am not sure he is coming with us, go ask, I will be with you shortly Marcus informs his son as walks away to locate Maria.

Marcus finds his wife sitting in the garden praying her rosary. Mia Amor Marcus quietly says to Maria, he does not wish to interrupt her when she is praying; she looks up at him with a smile that conveys the love she has had for him all these years. Sitting down next to her on the bench he takes her hand in his, is something wrong she asks, no Mia Amor he says as he bends to kiss her on the cheek, then what, I thought you left by this time, where is Louise he inquires, I believe in her room. Marcus what is it; Maria now getting anxious is something amiss? Amor; Esteban has spoken on behalf of Lieutenant Black as his Patrino, he seeks our permission to see Louise with the intent of marriage. What was your response to Esteban, I said I would discuss the matter with you, and Louise, as tradition requires but for him to tell the Lieutenant not to get his hopes up. Will you please speak to Louise, as we are honor bound to do so, when I return we will discuss this matter further, and before we give our answer, I will talk to the Lieutenant and Esteban alone? He has respected our customs, but we know nothing of this man or his family we must be assured his intention is marriage, and he must understand we will accept nothing less as our culture demands, I will not allow him to bring shame on our family. Until these questions have an answer, I cannot give my permission.

Marcus and Miguel have been gone for about an hour before Maria searches out her daughter. She waits while in the garden to ask Our Lady of Guadalupe for her guidance before speaking to Louise about Senor Black, also to gather her thoughts on the matter that has seemingly come up unexpectedly. She will hear what Louise feels before she voices her thoughts a wiser path to take she believes. Knocking on the door of her daughters' room, she calls to Louise. It is mama *amour*; I have come for a talk with you. Louise opens the door, mama she stretches come in, were you asleep Maria inquires, no, no just relaxing I want to be fresh for the fiesta tonight it is extremely kind of Senor Esteban to have this celebration in our honor. Yes, Maria replies, now sit I have something to discuss with you before your father returns from town. Louise makes herself comfortable on the edge of the bed while Maria pulls up a chair close to her daughter, what is it mama, Maria fold her hands in her lap and clears her throat. Mama is something wrong . . . . Maria shakes her head, Senor Esteban acting as Padrino for Senor Black has spoken to your father about visiting you while we are staying at *Tia* Juanita's. There she said the words breathing a sigh of relief. Tell me your feelings in the matter Maria inquires of her daughter. Louise smile, I think I knew Senor Charles would ask I just knew it. Louise, her mother remarks, a bit critical what do mean you knew and using his Christian name is not at all proper. Louise what has come over you, nothing I am sorry Mama it is not proper to refer to Senor Black by his Christian name, please forgive me. Yes, yes, but you are fortunate papa was not *present* at your outburst he is not as tolerant as I am. Well does this mean you are agreeable to Senor Black request, yes I am Mama. Louise I should not have to remind you that Senor Black's intentions must be marriage or you will be disgraced, and this can turn out badly for all of us. I know Mama, only there is something deep within saying he is the one, he is your future. Maria feels uneasy as Louise speaks to her this way, and says I am praying to our Beloved Lady for guidance and, will see if one of Senor Esteban's men can drive to the church where I can light a candle, maybe I will light two candles. When your Father returns we will speak together again, then he will meet with Senor Esteban and, Senor Black no decision will be made until we have thought fully and learn more about him and his family maybe a ring of promise from Lieutenant Black. But Mama, that is too much a ring of promise we are leaving in the morning Louise exclaimed, her voice cracking now with emotion. Maria raises her hand to silence her daughter I have a plan I will suggest to your father since this decision is vital we should stay a few more days and, leave with the Army as we all are going in the same direction anyway. Traveling further north it might be wise to have the Army escort us to your Tia's and Senor Black will know the way. Mama, you are incredible, Papa has not said yes yet, but it is beneficial to have a plan in case, Louise hugs her mother as Maria leaves the room to find Esteban and conveyance to church. She does not feel as sure as Louise does about this courtship, she utters the words aloud courtship, marriage, Maria's thoughts journey back to when she was a young woman, Louise will at least know her young man, spend time with him not alone yet that is something she never had. Her father arraigned her marriage to Marcus and, she only saw him twice before the wedding ceremony. Maria remembers being terrified while her Mama was saying a prayer of protection and, guidance over her, she was trembling with fear, and before she knew it, she was at the church standing alongside Marcus a married woman. She has a good life and, loves Marcus with all her heart it took time, one day out of nowhere, she knew she loved this man with every fiber of her being and nothing he can ever do will change that. As she thought of her life with Marcus, a dark shadow pulled at her spirit and unease filled her heart.

It was late afternoon when Marcus and Miguel return from Zacatecas with the supplies. Miguel took the wagon into one of the barns to park safely for the night. He will then water and feed the horses bedding them down. Marcus enters the house to find Marie he knows the answer she will give him, walking through the large sitting room he finds Esteban relaxing and having a drink, Tequila, he offers Marcus a glass, but he places it down on a table nearby no I think not. I am looking for Marie, and I do not think her smelling Tequila on my breath is a good thing. I understand Esteban answers, I would like to speak to you, and Senor Black Marcus states as soon as possible do you know where he is, I think at the corals I will send someone to find him. I think my office is a good place for our meeting, yes Marcus replies I will meet you there shortly, I believe I know what Maria is going to say, however, I will see her first Marcus turns and, finishes walking to His and Maria's room. Marcus finds his wife in their room standing quietly looking out the window. I have just returned from church she says not turning around, Marcus smiles, I prayed and lit two candles, two candles he questions, why two? I feel in my heart one is for our Louise and the other for Senor Charles. Hum Marcus replies it's Senor Charles now is it, yes, then Louise is in favor of Lieutenant Blacks attentions Maria nods still looking out the window. Marcus walks to his wife and puts his arms around her she rests her head against his chest and sighs. I will ask for . . . . Maria interrupts" a ring of promise" you know my every thought Marcus replies holding Maria a bit tighter to his chest. I think I will write to my friend Gen. Pershing on this matter, yes a letter I will write a letter before any decisions are made or rings given. Let us stay longer leave with the army it will be more suitable if we do, Maria says. Yes, you are right Mia Amore, Maria turns putting her arms around Marcus and starts to sob.

Marcus enters Esteban's office and finds the men waiting, his friend motions him to a chair, and he quickly sits down. On Esteban's desk is a tray with glasses a saltcellar, a plate with sliced lemons and a bottle of Tequila. Esteban does not offer anyone a drink, the Tequila is for a later time if all goes well with this discussion. As Charles Patrino Esteban begins with formally asking Marcus for his permission to allow Charles to speak to and visit Louise with the commitment of marriage in the future. Marcus is silent for a moment then discloses that he has not made up his mind. Esteban squirms in his chair and looks uncomfortable, Esteban I must ask Senor Black questions regarding his intentions toward my daughter, Charles interrupts, I assure you Sir my intentions are honorable. Marcus is annoyed at Charles's seemingly rude behavior. You Senor speak of honor, yet I know nothing of American honor, or you. Charles tries to speak again, but Marcus gestures to silence him. In our country, he continues a father protects his daughter until the time of her marriage, he meets the future husband's family, he makes sure they are respectable, and their son has the means to take care of a wife and children that he is a decent man with a prosperous future. My, daughter can select the man she would like to marry, but the marriage can take place only with my permission. When I speak I do speak of marriage, there are places in this country as in all countries where a man can casually be with a woman. My family is not that place, and my daughter is not that woman. Marcus's irritation at Charles seems cooled as he sits back in his chair. Senor Gutierrez, I am sorry I interrupted you before may I speak Marcus nods. Sir I know by all propriety this seems strange, and you have every right to question my intentions toward your daughter. As you have said, your duty as a father is to protect her from harm my intent is not to harm Louise but take her as my wife and be the best husband and provider I can, and I assure you I will love Louise until the day I die and beyond. Esteban has been silent all this time not sure of what his role is anymore since Senor Charles is now speaking for himself and does not need his help. Marcus probes Charles further, sir this love you speak of, tell me how do you know it is true and not lust you feel for my daughter, she is uncommonly beautiful, and we have had to ward off unwanted attentions from others who were let me say not so marriage minded. Do you love your wife Charles questions Marcus, Esteban gulps in the air and a squeaking sound bursts from his mouth, he can only muster a faint Senor? Marcus ignores him and answers. I love my wife very much, when did you know you loved her Charles asks, in my day a marriage was arranged by the families the bride and groom had nothing to say, I was allowed two visits before the wedding Marcus answered. That is not what I asked you I wanted to know, yes, yes . . . . When did I know I loved her? By our second meeting, what I felt for her I had never experienced before, and that love is stronger now as the years have passed. Then I rest my case Charles replies. Where do you intend to take my daughter to live America? No, with your permission Sir, I will seek our future here in Mexico, and I was wondering if you would teach me the horse breeding business. I can learn much from you and Louise will be close by her family. Tell me Marcus asks Charles, what will your family think about this marriage and you remaining here in Mexico? They will be happy for me and stand behind my decision with their full support Charles replies. Yes, but I do not know that or do I know them or you for that matter, yet I must give you my answer immediately,

No I need more time to think on this. If I agree and I say if, there is one custom I request you fulfill, anything Charles answers thinking he might prevail, I ask you to give Louise a "ring of promise" to seal your commitment to marry within six months. Charles smiles and looks at Esteban will you help me pick out the ring for Louise. We will go into town tomorrow and pick out a beautiful one for her Esteban responds and sighs with relief. There is no hurry to buy a ring, not for some time, I will Charles replies tomorrow I will. All this talk of commitment and marriage has been overwhelming, and Esteban realizes this might be the reason he never married, just too complicated for his liking. Drinks are now poured, and glasses raised to the future, then is the answer yes Charles asks and more serious did Louise say yes, she is willing to enter into marriage with me? Louise's answer is yes Marcus replies but remember the final decision is mine, and I have not made up my mind there are questions to be answered and much to prove in the next few months. You will see Charles says I will work hard to show you I am the right husband for Louise. I will honor the trust you have granted me in loving and caring for her forever. Yes, yes, Esteban says love and trust are all good, I think now we must get ready for tonight it seems we have much to celebrate. Charlie the magnificent stands up, smiles, squares his shoulders back, and walks out the door to his room.

The fiesta in the evening will be an enormous success if Esteban has anything to say his house staff, spend many hours in the preparation. The gardens are decorated with banners and candles light up the night, tables laden with food are set on the veranda, Pollo spiced with hot adobo sauce, Birria a spicy stew made with lamb, sends its fragrance streaming into the air, soft Tortilla's sit in stacks covered nearby. Chili Rellenos filled with meat deep-fried and covered with cheese line platters like green and brown soldiers. Meatballs covered with Mole Sauce together with Guacamole and Biillo bread shaped like bobbins, coarse and crispy crowd baskets ready for the taking. There is another large table filled with fruits of every variety, Cajeta, burnt milk, Flan, and Alfajor a candy made for festive occasions. Sharing these large table bottles of tequila, surrounded by plates of lemons, and limes along with saltcellars, there is Sangrita served along with the Tequila made from orange juice, grenadine, Chile powder, and tomato juice. Large pitchers of Sangria and gleaming glasses twinkle in the candle light. In one corner of the veranda is a large fire of wood coals on which the cook is roasting Alcarbon (lamb and goat meat), the guests are surrounded by the spicy smells of Serrano Peppers, Hot Chilies, and Cooked Garlic Sauce that delight their senses. Esteban is puffed up like a bullfrog as he greets everyone entering the garden and veranda. Charles sees Marcus and his son Miguel talking to Esteban's ranch Foreman, but he does not see Maria or more importantly Louise. As he walks over to the men Marcus smiles, you have my permission to speak to her she will be here soon her mother will chaperone. Miguel says nothing and walks away. A Mariachi Band begins to play softly strolling along the paths. Charles looks up and sees Louise and her mother arriving, he stands still like a sculpture unable to move. Louise's dark is held back with a beautiful tortoise shell comb allowing the candle light to fall softly on her beautiful face. A white blouse delicately exposes her smooth shoulders, and a tooled black leather belt with leaves and flowers cinches her small waist a ruffled long skirt the color of the sunrise and a yellow shawl give her the appearance of a heavenly being come down to earth.

Esteban nudges Charles, well what are you waiting for he laughs, Charles hesitates a minute then moves forward to Louise and offers her his arm they sit on a bench close by among the flowers and speak comfortably together as if they have known each their whole lives, Maria sits on the bench also but at a discreet distance. The Lieutenant is unaware of Charles request to court Louise, when he questions Esteban as to what is going on Esteban smiles his glittering smile, places arm around the Lieutenants shoulders, and escorts him to the table holding the Tequila.

The journey to Fresnillo is without incident Louise rides alongside her father, brother, and Charles. The company is relaxed and happy arriving at Maria sisters home after only a few hours. Juanita is thrilled at seeing her family and has everything prepared for their visit. She is surprised at their escort she was not expecting to entertain the United States Army. The commanding officer decides his men, and horses will set up camp close to the river, spend the night, and leave at dawn. The soldiers are happy with the decision as the next two days will be hard traveling to reach Del Parrel on the date given for their return to camp. Juanita invites the Commanding Officer and Charles for dinner later that evening. Charles and Louise smile to each other not wanting to part for long, Maria and Marcus keep a watchful eye. Let us move out the commander orders, the men, and horses head to the river to set up camp, Charles rides off with his company and Louise goes with her family. Juanita gives her sister a questioning look as she is aware of what has just transpired between Charles and Louise. Maria quietly says we will talk later and the women proceed into the house. Marcus and Miguel go to the barn to feed and bed down the horses for the night, the wagon is brought close by and covered.

Maria is barely settled in her room when Juanita is knocking on the door, come in Maria exclaims knowing her sister will now probe her for information about Louise and Charles's actions earlier. Maria loves her sister dearly, but she knows Juanita takes her position as the oldest in the family extremely serious. Tell me what this is all about, I do not like how Louise, and that American are acting, there will be gossip, she will be disgraced, what are you thinking my sister to allow such behavior Juanita exclaims as she enters the room. Now, now dear sister take a deep breath and I will explain, I am waiting Juanita is visibly upset. Maria pauses for just a minute to gather her thoughts well, Juanita, Senor Charles has asked through his Patrino Esteban, Oh! Madre, Madre Juanita exclaims making the sign of the cross. Esteban is a rogue, he owns no honest bone in his whole body, a Patrino, he cannot be any man's Patrino. The Godfather is a wise, honorable man a man of respect. Please dear sister calm down and let me explain, Maria places her arm around Juanita, sit, and I will finish as I said before Esteban acting as Senor Charles Patrino has asked to court Louise with the intent of marriage, What! The family is disgraced how can you and Marcus let this happen . . . . disgraced. Nothing has happened, let me finish, Senor Charles has honored our tradition, and we are duty bound to consider his proposal you know that. Juanita is short and dumpy woman, giving the impression she lives and eats well, now from all the excitement she has started to perspire freely, between wringing her hands and trying to wipe her brow her clothes have become damp and clinging extenuating her ample bosom. Holy Madre listen Maria says as she tries again to explain to her sister. Marcus has not given his permission, there is still much to learn about Senor Charles and his family. How do you expect to do that, Marcus will write a letter to his friend General Pershing, Senor Charles is his aid, and ask questions before any answer is given on this matter. Then we will demand he give Louise a Ring of Promise, he will have six months to prove to Marcus he is worthy of marrying our daughter, only then and with Marcus's permission can he give Louise a Ring of Intent afterwards they will be formally engaged, and the wedding plans can be made. Is Louise acceptable to the arraignment Juanita wiping her brow again, asks her sister? Yes, Maria answers and one more thing, will you be Louise's Madrina and chaperone her meetings with Senor Charles if the answer is yes, guide her and give her your wise advice. Juanita looks at her sister astonished, you and Marcus approve of even considering this matter shaking her head. It is what Louise wants, Maria answers. Our children should not always get their own way, and it is a parent's duty to say no Juanita comments. Sister, Marcus will have the final decision, and Senor Charles has promised to honor it, now will you be Louise's Madrina. Juanita pushes a wet strand of hair from her face, yes, I to seem to have no choice as you know I cannot refuse this honor by tradition. Thank you Maria whispers as she goes to hug her soggy sister.

Early the next morning Marcus leaves with Miguel for Nieves to inspect the breeding stock they want to purchase. The First Lieutenant, Charles and the men depart the same time. They will all ride together until Nieves then the Army will travel further north to Del Parrel. Charles and Louise say their good-byes and he ask Marcus for permission to come back spend two days at Tia's home visiting Louise before the family leaves for Guadalajara, Marcus agrees. Charles has leave time that he has not taken since his deployment to Mexico and feels now is an excellent time to use some of it. Both Charles and Louise know if given permission their visits together will be short, scheduled around Charles time away from the Army yet they both are excited at the prospect of being together even for brief occasions, and under the watchful eyes of *Tia* Juanita. Who is scrutinizing them now for the smallest impropriety like a hawk ready to swoop down and rescue Louise from the hands of this American Soldier whom she see no prospect in at all. The women stand on the veranda and wave good-bye, on Louise's left hand is a beautiful Turquoise Ring of Promise with silver filigree work as delicate as gossamer lace enfolding the exquisite oval stone. Charles was so nervous giving it to her with the whole family looking on, Marcus agreed to the ring, only with the assurance if his decision is no Louise is to return it, *Tia* Juanita is not happy. To Louise the ring symbolizes a bond of love and commitment Charles has made to her. She will hold this love in her heart with the knowledge it will be eternal.

Nieves;

197

Marcus and his son reach Nieves mid-morning and ride directly to the corals where the horse auction is being held. Marcus knows the mare's he will bid on, the two men find seats near the front of the room, Marcus is hoping the horses come up early in the selection. Papa I will see in what order the horses will be lined up for auction Miguel says as he gets up from his seat and walks toward the barns. Marcus speaks to old friends and colleagues as they all wait for the Auctioneer come in and mount the platform. Miguel is coming back from the barns with a smile on his face, Marcus looks up, you look pleased with yourself he comments to his son. Papa come to the barns with me Senor Diaz wants to have a word with you. The auction will be starting soon, Marcus stays seated. Papa Miguel whispers in his father's ear, Diaz wants you to make an offer on the two mares; he prefers them not to go through the strain of the auction if he can help it. Marcus all but jumps out of his seat, father, and son head for the barn to make a deal to purchase the horses.

In less than an hour, Marcus and Miguel are sitting in a Cantina ordering their mid-day meal. Marcus is pleased with the deal he has struck with the horse breeder Diaz and wants to applaud his good fortune with a hardy meal.

Marcus looks up as he recognizes the deep commanding voice of General Pershing," well as I live and breathe" Senor Guiterrez Pershing exclaims as he and his staff walk over to Marcus and his son. Miguel you are looking more like your father every time I meet you. "Before Marcus can say anything Pershing tells his men to find a table he will be with them in a minute pulls out a chair and sits down." Marcus cannot believe his good fortune, Miguel orders the General Tequila, and while they wait for the drinks, the men make small talk. Marcus telling the General bout the two Mares' he has just purchased and the general commenting on his excellent business sense. I am waiting for my men to return to Del Parrel with your excellent quality horses Pershing remarks. This is the opening in the conversation Marcus has been waiting for. The Commanding Officer and Second Lieutenant Black left this morning from Fresnillo with 50 of my best horse stock. Fresnillo? I thought you met my men at Esteban's ranch in Zacatecas, yes, but with all the uncertainty along the roads your officers agreed to escort us to Fresnillo as my wife Maria and daughter Louise are going to visit family there, and it was along the way. Yes, good decision happy they could oblige. How is your wife haven't seen her in about a year is that correct, and your daughter Louise is it she must be quite a lady now? They are both well Marcus answers, Miguel sits quietly with a frown knowing what his father will say next. Senor Pershing may I ask you something, certainly Pershing replies, what is it. About Senor Black, what about him, has he offended you in any way? I will have his stripes if he has the General bellows. Sir may I speak to you as a father, one of the generals men walk over to the table, General Sir will you be long? In minute Pershing replies dismissing the Officer with a wave of his hand, now how can I help you? Marcus proceeds to explain to the General what has transpired over the past few days, Charles request to court Louise, his selection of Senor Esteban as Patrino all with keeping in their traditions and the decision Marcus must now make. How can I assist you Pershing inquiries? Senor Black and his family do you know them. Is Senor Black a respectable, honorable man, is his family of a good reputation? I must make the right choice for my daughter or we will be disgraced, you know I am bound to consider his request. General Pershing has been sitting contemplating his reply to Marcus. I am not happy with the conduct of Lieutenant Black, as a rule I do not encourage my men consorting with the civilian population in most cases it leads to trouble. However if as you say he has followed your custom, and conducted himself as an Officer of the United States Army with dignity and honor. I will say to you he has an impeccable Military record, and was chosen at my request to serve as one of my Junior Attachés in Washington and in Mexico. He is a New Englander from Connecticut one of our first Colonies, his family is an old one whose sons have served with courage in the defense of our country and Lieutenant Black is following in those footsteps, all else, I do not know. You have a hard choice to make Senor I do not envy you the task. Marcus sits still for a moment, Thank you Sir he says as the General gets up to leave, he assures Marcus he will talk to the Lieutenant on his return to Del Parrel and stress the gravity of his request and he, General Pershing has given a favourable report as to his character. If he is not serious in his intent, he will not only dishonor your family but also his reputation in regards to his service in the United States Military I will see to it the General states. Pershing bids both men a farewell and goes to his own table. Miguel looks at his father, well Papa he questions. I have much to think on Marcus replies.

Marcus decides for the two of them to stay only overnight he has paid for the horses up keep for the night and feels a fresh start in the morning will do them all good. He wants to be back in

Fresnello before Charles's visit. Nieves is busy filled with horse trader and buyers alike and most are friends of Marcus and Miguel they will spend the time catching up with other breeders, talking shop. Both men love horses so spending time with friends will be informative for both and Marcus can relax and enjoy some time free before making any judgments as to Charles and Louise future.

Before departing, General Pershing reassured Marcus of his intentions to speak to Lieutenant Black on his return to Del Parrel, but also expresses to him that this decision is his and his alone. The two men say *adios* shaking hands warmly, and Pershing is gone.

A few days later as promised Charles arrives back at *Tia* Juanita's ranch to visit Louise, he has a sealed letter from General Pershing addressed to Louise's father. Juanita is not happy she glares at Charles as walks through the veranda into the house custom demands her hospitality but as Louise's Madrina she has no intention taking her eyes off this American for a moment. Marcus excuses himself to read the letter General Pershing has sent while Juanita has the housekeeper ready a room for Charles. Louise is happy to see Charles and the two go sit out on the veranda with Juanita close behind.

In their room Marcus finds Maria trying to take a brief siesta, General Pershing has sent me a letter he tells her, sitting on the bed next to his wife he opens the envelope. What does it say Maria inquiries, the General writes he has spoken to Lieutenant Black and informed him that he will not look kindly on any behavior that does not become an officer of the United States Army in this matter. Our family is honorable if his intentions toward Louise cast any shame on her reputation the General will use his authority to end the Lieutenant's career in disgrace. He also said again the final decision in this matter is mine, and mine alone. Maria lays her head on her husband's shoulder, what shall we do? Marcus kisses her lightly on the cheek watch, and wait during the next six months any actions not suitable on Charles part he must leave, and never see Louise again, and she must return his ring. I will speak to him now and tell him I will hold him to the highest standard, are you sure, this is the right thing to do Maria murmurs. No, Marcus answers, kissing her again on the cheek, he leaves the room to find Charles and tell him of his decision for now. Charles and Louise spend most of their time together they seem to have known each other always, finishing each other's sentences, learning about one another and finding out there is little difference in what they like and want in life. All thought Charles is quiet and reserved and Louise out going with the knack of making people feel at ease they appear to be a perfect match. The two days pass quickly with *Tia* Juanita on active patrol never leaving the two alone for more than a few moments yet there is a serene composure about the couple as though they have hidden knowledge that they are fated to be together, and no power on earth will change their path. The two days pass quickly Charles must return to duty at Del Parrel and Louise will leave with her family for Guadalajara. The couple is aware they will not meet for at least a month when Charles will hopefully be able to take a week's leave and travel the two hundred miles from Del Parrel to Louise's side at her family's ranch. He also knows the journey will fraught with danger until Poncho Villa is in captured or killed, yet he does not question his commitment to Louise he knows in his heart, she is the one, and they will be together forever. Saying good-bye is difficult for Louise, and she cries silently as Charles with Marcus's permission holds her close his strength and faith in their future calms her as he whispers his undying love, and devotion to her, and reassures her nothing in heaven or on earth can stop him from seeing her in a month. I will write you every day dear one of my love for you Charles says, and you must do the same, Yes I will but a month is so long Louise replies. No, I promise it will pass quickly and before you know it we will be together, please no more weeping I don't want to leave seeing you crying Charles pleads with Louise as he dries her tears.

Every month without fail, Charles makes the long dangerous journey from Del Parrel to Guadalajara to see Louise stopping always to see his Patrino Esteban for advice and encouragement. Most times Esteban will accompany Charles to his friend's ranch to make sure all is going well with the courtship, and Marcus is still open to the idea of marriage. Esteban has taken his role as godfather very serious much to the surprise of Guiterrez family.

Poncho Villa still eludes capture and the war is going badly for the Americans by November of 1916 there is talk the American Expeditionary Force will depart as early as January 1917. The war in Europe is raging becoming a quagmire in the trenches, President Wilson has pledged to keep American out of Europe's war, but Pershing believes that is impossible and although publically he claims success in Mexico, privately he is furious at Wilson for tying his hands making it impossible for him to accomplish his mission.

With the talk of Pershing's departure, November also marks the end of the six months of Charles period of consideration as to whether he has followed traditions courting Louise, and deemed an honorable man. Esteban now as custom demands will approach Louise's father Marcus, and formally as Charles's Patrino ask for her hand in marriage if the answer is yes a ring of commitment is given, and the engagement formally starts. The decision Marcus has put off for six months is finally facing him, Louise has been unusually cooperative and loving towards him with her yes Papa and right away Papa, she cannot fool him he knows what she is doing. Maria his wife is quiet with a worried look on her face they have discussed this situation at length many times. He has listened to her fears his being mostly the same, Charles is a upstanding man, he has conformed to tradition followed all the customs and rules of courtship he has treated Louise with love and respect. He has promised to stay in Mexico to learn the ranching business so Louise can be near the family and Charles has no drawbacks in marrying in the Catholic Church, and raising their children in the Catholic faith a plus in Marcus's eyes. However, he is an American and still unfamiliar with their ways then overtime will he become homesick, and want to return to his own country taking Louise with him and this worries Marcus. Today is the day no more waiting Charles and Esteban will be arriving early, and Esteban acting as Patrino on Charles behalf will ask for Louise's hand in marriage and Marcus must give his answer.

Louise up for hours is anxiously waiting for Charles's arrival and can barely sit still at the breakfast table. Maria requests she please calm down, worry lines etched in her brow, and she speaks a bit crossly to her daughter. My, *amour* Marcus reaches across the table and takes his wife's hand in his, all will be well *amour*, not to worry all will be well, she smiles at him and nods. They are here Papa Louise says, as she gets up from the table and walks quickly out to the veranda *Tia* Juanita who has been visiting her sister and advising Louise as her role as Madrina requires is close behind. Charles is smiling broadly, and quickly dismounts his horse holding open his arms as Louise runs to greet him. Juanita declares" Iya Basta" (that is enough) coming between the couple, Esteban dressed in his best with immense dignity aware of the role he will play today dismounts his horse and greets Juanita with a bow as he says *"Hola,"* she is unimpressed and ushers everyone into the house. Rooms have been made ready for the men's arrival, and they hurry to freshen up after their long ride, today is a crucial day, and both Charles and his Patrino want to look their best. Charles enters the large receiving room where the family has gathered to wait Marcus's decision, and to discuss preparations for either a wedding or a departure. Louise get up from a chair and stands close to Charles, *Tia* Juanita walks over to Louise, and stands next to her making sure there is the proper distance between the couple. Where is your Patrino, Marcus asks Charles, but before he can answer Esteban enters the room with a flourish. At your service Senor he states to Marcus, Esteban is clean, and shiny not a trace of dust from the road can be seen on his clothes. The silver buttons on his jacket and trousers are gleaming, and his boots are spotless never one to miss a chance to show off his wealth Esteban is a picture of a man dressed for an occasion. Standing next to Charles he clears his throat, Senor Gutierrez he begins a bit shaky at first, clearing his throat again he declares "I Senor Esteban

Arturo Perez, acting as Patrino for Lieutenant Charles Black of the United States Army." Esteban I know who you are, Marcus interrupts can we get to the point, yes, yes Esteban says Charles Black, Esteban, Marcus exclaims the point. The point is I have come to ask for the hand of your daughter Louise in marriage, I did not know you wanted to marry my daughter Louise, Marcus replies with a smile totally enjoying Esteban's discomfort. Not me I do not want to marry your daughter, I do not want to marry any one Esteban is visibly flustered. Papa Louise scolds let the Patrino finish, Esteban thanks her and continues as I was saying I have come to ask in behalf of Lieutenant Black for Louise's hand in marriage, Esteban breaths a sign of relief. Marcus takes his time in answering as the silence hangs heavy in the air, Papa, Louise questions her father, Marcus holds up his hand as to stop her from saying more. Motioning to wife, Maria walks and pauses next to her husband I have thought on this matter for many hours, my wife, and I have considered the idea of our daughter marrying someone, not of our culture Marcus is looking directly at Esteban and Juanita as custom demands. Maria has prayed, and pleaded with our Holy Mother for direction, a father wants what is best for his daughter when deciding on the man she wants to marry. Is he honorable, trustworthy, and man of integrity, will he love, and commit his life to her, provide for her, and their family, is he kind, and gentle, and will the two live their lives growing old together. Marcus takes his wife's hand, Maria smiles up at him. Most important does his daughter love the man she will marry times have changed no longer does a father choose a husband for his daughter, the daughter chooses, and the father must approve or disapprove. Now with the discussion I have made I must pray my daughter's love and commitment for Charles and his for her will endure, and grow stronger over the years lasting into eternity. Papa, thank you Papa, Marcus holds out his arms to his daughter only Louise has quickly turned to Charles, and they embrace. Esteban struts over to Marcus and pats him on the back saying yes, good decision, do not be so appreciative you still have much work ahead before the wedding Marcus answers. You must counsel the bridegroom in our customs and the ways of marriage in our culture and since you are not married or ever likely to be married you have much to do. Charles holding Louise's hand walks over to her parents he shakes Marcus's hand with a firm grip I promise I will love Louise, and make her happy always through to eternity and nothing will ever part us he declares looking directly at Marcus and Maria. Juanita stands next to her sister with an unhappy look on her face shaking her head. Marcus asks Esteban if he has the ring of commitment as everyone in the room turns to watch him fumble in his vest pocket. Do you have it Charles questions his Patrino, you didn't leave it behind at your ranch, no, no here I have it as he takes a small white box from his pocket. The ring is a perfect match to Louise's ring of Promise a beautiful silver filigree band set with three flawless oval turquoise stones both rings after their marriage will be worn together on her left hand. Charles slips the ring of Commitment on Louise's right hand and kisses her gently. Maria hugs her daughter and smiles as she comments on the beauty of the ring now gracing Louise's hand. Look *Tia* is not this the most beautiful ring you have ever seen, Louise holds out her hand to her aunt, Juanita takes it in hers yes, dear one the most beautiful, Juanita looks at her sister Maria her eyes full of sadness. The couple stand together receiving congratulation from the family members present, Louise thinks of her brother Peter and wishes he could be here to see how happy she is at this moment though she feels he is watching from heaven. Miguel approaches his sister quietly, and kisses her on the cheek he shakes Charles's hand yet says nothing to the couple. Sadness is etched in deep lines on his forehead, Louise holds on to his hand tightly, and whispers please brother be happy for me, Miguel touches her face gently and walks away.

A small celebration dinner is arranged for the evening with only the immediate family in attendance with the exception of Esteban. The family has decided to forgo a large celebration as is customary by tradition. Charles must leave in the morning early to return to Del Parrel if the talk is true he says he will be mustering out of the army between January and February, which is only a few months away. After that, there will plenty of time to celebrate and plan the wedding. Esteban and Juanita as godparents to the engaged couple have a place of significant importance in the couples lives, they will help and guide them through-out the engagement help plan the wedding, stand next to them in the church and be there to advise them during their married life. With this responsibility, Esteban feels it appropriate to interrupt dinner at various intervals to toast the couple's good fortune until finally Juanita sits him down saying enough for now, with the comfortable conversation of family resuming around the table now that Esteban is silenced, though he sits sulking feeling Juanita has over stepped her role as Madrina.

The night is warm with a full moon lighting up the sky, after dinner Charles and Louise walk outside amid the desert flowers lost in each other's company, looking out over the garden Louise see her parents walking hand in hand and her brother Miguel and his wife Gabriella sitting close together on a garden bench. This time, this moment as no other Louise feels a touch of the eternal, then it is shattered Esteban and Juanita come into the garden discussing in loud voices what role each will play in the wedding preparations as each try to out do the other. Louise looks at Charles and smiles I think our godparents will now be quarreling over who will be in control, I believe you are right Charles answers, my money is on *Tia* Juanita he says with a laugh in his voice as he kisses Louise on the cheek.

Arriving back at camp in Del Parrel Charles finds the camp in a flurry of activity, there will be one more push to capture Villa at Chihuahua further north on December 25. However, the Army is under strict orders that a full withdrawal will begin January 17, and by February 7, 1917 all military personnel will depart the country and be stationed at Fort Bliss. Charles goes into Army headquarters to report for duty and finds his orders waiting for him. Charles will remain in Mexico after General Pershing and his staff leave, to tie up miscellaneous paperwork, also to make sure, nothing can be used by the Villistas is left behind. He will then report to Fort Bliss, and there he will muster out of the military. Charles is excited by his orders he will not see Louise until February as all leaves have been cancelled, but in less than three months, they will be together forever, he hurries to his tent and writes her the fantastic news.

The raid at Chihuahua is ill fated from the beginning Villa and his men are nowhere to be found, and General Pershing is enraged at the army's lack of success. He knows with the war raging in Europe his future lies there not in the debacle that this campaign has become. He orders the full withdrawal of all forces under his command to commence immediately. On February 7, 1917 at the head of the expeditionary force, General Pershing and his men marched into El Paso Texas to cheering throngs of people. Within a week, Charles and the small group of men in charge of final clean-up operations leave Mexico and arrive at Fort Bliss their work complete as far as Charles is concerned all he wants to do is get out of the Army and return to Louise. Only he finds himself in a quagmire of paperwork, the war in Europe is stalemated in France, divisions are being formed, and trained all over the country. Soon President Wilson will have no choice but to declare war. Charles wants no part of war with Germany or the Army he feels he has fulfilled his family's military tradition of service to the country and wants to move on with his life. The Commanding Officer at Fort Bliss is requesting all men re-enlist, but Charles remains adamant although the pressure from Headquarters is becoming hard to endure. However, Charles is firm he will not enlist no matter what the Commanding Officer states or how long his paperwork is delayed Charles wants out. On April 6, 1917 the United States declares war on Germany, General Pershing received orders to organize a division with him in command to fight along-side the Allies in France, Lieutenant George Patton's name is included Second Lieutenant Charles Black's is not. Charles has been away from Louise three months, and although she writes him almost every day he feels lonely and despondent all he wants is to be rid of the responsibilities of the Army and on his way back to Guadalajara and Louise finally on March 15 1917 Charles's discharge papers come through channels he is now a civilian.

Charles knows traveling back to Guadalajara will be dangerous Mexico is still in political unrest President Carranza, Zapata, and Poncho Villa are in a deadlock with each man's loyalists fighting for control of the country. Charles is determined to get to Louise, and he feels in civilian clothes he has a decent chance to get to Esteban's ranch from there the two can ride to the Guiterrez ranch in a few days. It seem Esteban knows everyone in the country if not personally then a friend of a friend or family member, it is one of the reasons Charles likes Esteban. With his gregarious nature, and ability somehow get you to do what he wants and all with a smile. Charles knows he is the exact opposite and wishes deep down he were more like Esteban and Charlie the magnificent less like Charles, no matter, his first stop is Zacatecas and Esteban.

When Charles reaches Zacatecas, he rides around the outskirts of the town to avoid any trouble, Esteban's ranch is only a mile away Charles will feel out of harm's way once he rides through the gates and hears his friends hardy laugh. Charles is right Esteban's housekeeper (ama de llaves) is happy to see him; she says Esteban is in one of the corals with the ranch hands training some horses. Charles's room is always at the ready, and he goes to freshen up before going to the corals in search of Esteban, he feels at home here, more than any time in his life he is among friends and is comfortable in their company. As Charles leaves to find Esteban the housekeeper smiles, happy to be back he says to her, are you hungry, come to the kitchen, and I will feed you, thank you. I want to find my Patrino first to see how he is she laughs, and motions to Charles to vamooses, and heads towards the kitchen to prepare the main meal for the day. Charles hears Esteban before he sees him, his hardy laugh and robust voice carry through the desert on the waves of heat and could reach Mexico City if he shouted. Esteban hugs Charles and slaps him on the back *Hola*, welcome we have been expecting you, how was your journey, safe I hope, yes Charles answers good, good his Patrino says. How did you know I was on my ways here, Esteban half smiles, I have ways, don't tell me Charles replies I do not want to know. Come putting his arm around his Godson the two friends walk to the house.

All of Charles favorite food is served at the dinner table or maybe he thinks to himself all Mexican food is his favorite as he enjoys every dish so much tastier than the bland New England fair his mother serves at home. Tonight warm thick corn sopa is served with Chorizo sausage seasoned with chilies and spices, crispy Bolillo the two men eat with gusto without pausing to talk until the second course is laid on the table. Tostadas piled high with meat, beans, roasted lamb cook to a turn, and Tamales warm snug in their corn-husk cocoons. Tequila flows non-stop to quench the men's thirst, full, and happy the two retire to the reception room for more tequila and a decent cigar. I have been asking some friends about the planning of the wedding you know our responsibilities. That is a good idea Charles tell Esteban since you have never been married, tell me have you ever been a Patrino. Esteban clears his throat well not really he answers, not really what does that mean, Esteban again clears his throat I was a Patrino to a friend of mine.

Then you know what is required of you Charles replies, well not really, what not really Charles wants to know, where you a Patrino or not? My friend married a dancer, and I was godparent to the both of them, in church Charles asks, his family did not approve, well where then, in front of a judge Esteban answers. Wonderful how long was the couple engaged Charles want to know, three days Esteban discloses. What! Charles exclaims, do not to worry the bride's family plans everything you only have to agree, to what Charles is shaken by his Patrino's lack of experience, to everything, whatever Louise and her family want is fine with you. Tell Louise her dress is beautiful, compliment her mother on the food she has chosen and always praise Marcus on what a generous father he is, there finished; No not finished, what do I provide for the bride and toward the wedding, the groom must pay for something, nothing is Esteban's answer the groom pays for nothing. That cannot be true you must be have gotten the information wrong, I did not Esteban replies a bit sullen at his godson's lack of confidence in his efforts, he hesitates wait you are right I did forget something, I thought you might have Charles replies, can you please inform me now before you memory fails again. Fine, the groom pays for the honeymoon, he must have a Casa to take his bride to but since you will be living with Louise's family until you learn the horse breeding business you have time for that, and he must present the bride with *"trece monedas de oro"* on the day of the wedding. Explain, Charles speaks a bit critically to Esteban, thirteen gold coins that are blessed by the priest he answers. What is the custom behind the coins Charles wants to know? By giving the bride the gold coins you are showing her you have unquestionable trust, and confidence in her, and by her accepting the gold coins, she is vowing her utmost devotion to you, feel better, not really, Charles voices concern; you have thirteen gold coins, now Esteban voices concern. I have the coins Charles replies it just appears to easy. What is wrong with Americans must everything be difficult Juanita, and I will have things in control just do as I instruct and all will be well, the only thing you must remember is to say yes, the thirteen gold coins, and the honeymoon of course. Charles looks at his Patrino puffed up like a bullfrog full of confidence, and says well godfather you have gotten me this far I presume you can get me the rest of the way.

The Wedding

From the time Charles arrives in Guadalajara late in March, his life becomes a flurry of activity wedding preparations are in full gear. *Tia* Juanita has assumed control of the Brides trousseau, wedding gown, and all the church arrangements. She is as a commanding general deploying her troops, and no one has the courage to say no to her. The best seamstress in the area has volunteered to make Louise's dress form the finest lace with a veil as delicate as a spider web. The church arrangements are made for June 1, with a high mass being observed, and dedicated to Our Lady of Guadalupe before the wedding ceremony, the church will be filled with flowers of every kind with strict orders from *Tia* no red roses anywhere. Tia's mission is now to harass Esteban as Charles is busy working alongside Marcus, Miguel and the ranch hands learning the horse breeding business. Charles is laboring long hours, and Marcus is pleased at his progress as Esteban predicted all Charles has been doing is saying yes, he will not be able to see Louise 's wedding gown until the ceremony but reassures her it must be beautiful, and she will be the loveliest bride ever, there that accomplished with little or no difficulty. Charles has asked Louise where she wishes to go on their honeymoon and she has decided a small village on the coast of Mexico Puerto Vallarta will be the perfect place for the two of them to be together. Charles quickly rescues his Patrino from the clutches of *Tia* as she has been badgering him about the status of the honeymoon along with keeping him apprised of any *haciendas* nearby by for sale. She seems to turn a deaf ear when Esteban reminds her that Charles and Louise will be living with Marcus, and Maria "until Charles" learns the ranching business. Her comment to that is a married couple must live on their own without the interference of family.

That woman is the reason I never married Esteban informs Charles a hurricane on two legs as he shakes his head. Louise has decided on where we will spend our honeymoon, Ah! *Maravilloso* Juanita will finally stop hounding me about it, what has been decided, and I hope you said yes to everything as I advised you, now where are you going? Louise has decided on the small fishing village of Puerto Vallarta on the coast Charles informs his Patrino. Vallarta, Esteban replies there is nothing there and, off the coast is the Islas of Marias and the Federal Penal Colony, it is beautiful very quiet and secluded but nothing. Have you been there Charles inquires of Esteban, I visited a friend a few times on the Islas Marias, the prison colony Charles asks, not to worry he was innocent, Charles does not probe any further. How do I go about, getting there, where will we stay are there hotels and restaurants Charles wants to know, I will hire a carriage, and driver to take you, the roads are excellent, and a ride along the coast is very beautiful, leave everything to me. I will rent a villa on the beach, and a woman to cook, and clean during the day. When all the arrangements are made we will go and see then you can pay, do you think it will be expensive Charles asks, no not really his Patrino answers. By the way, you do have the thirteen pieces of gold I hope it will be a matter of time before Juanita will ask, yes Charles answers, good you are learning, yes good answer. I will inform *Tia* and start to make inquiries pronto. Thank you Charles says "by the way, is your friend still on the Islas Marias, Oh! No, Esteban answers he escaped years ago, happy to hear it Charles utters as the two men part company. Esteban is now on his new quest for the perfect honeymoon villa, and Charles back to the corrals to work alongside Marcus and Miguel, and their beloved horses.

The evening meal is alive with conversation about the wedding plans, Maria is getting the guest list ready and is worried she will leave someone out that would be unforgivable. Juanita again is unhappy now with the location of the honeymoon, why did you pick Puerto Vallarta she questions Charles, there is nothing there just a small fishing village, Mexico City now there is where the honeymoon will be. Esteban tries to interrupt but is quickly silenced Vallarta, no place for a decent honeymoon what will people say. Louise speaks up *Tia* I want to go to Puerto Vallarta it is my idea, whatever for Juanita demands before Louise can answer, she says I know He does not have the money for a honeymoon in Mexico City, just as I thought. Charles is holding back his anger and is about ready to explode when Louise takes his hand and smiles *Tia* she says, but is interrupted by her father. Juanita I know you are taking your role as Madrina extremely serious but, I will not have you insult Louise's choice of honeymoon or the ability of my soon to be son-in-law to pay, and not in my own home. Juanita gets up from the table in a huff, please dear sister sit, and finish your meal Maria coaxes gently,

you are a very good Madrina, and I could not handle all the
preparations for the wedding without you, Louise chimes in yes,
Tia, please do not be angry there is so much to do. Louise gets up
from the table going to Juanita giving her a hug and a kiss on the
cheek Familia she whispers in her ear, and both women return to
their seats. After the meal Louise, Maria and Juanita retire to the
reception room to further encourage *Tia* that her role of Madrina
is vital to the success of the wedding. The men go into Marcus's
office for drinks and cigars as there is business to discuss. Marcus
with Miguel standing next to him waits until Charles and Esteban
become settled with drinks and a cigar before beginning. Charles
soon you will be marrying Louise and will be a part of our family
this is a large prosperous ranch, and there are legal matters that
I must take care of before the marriage Marcus pauses a minute
to enjoy his cigar. There better, as I was saying in my will the
business and all the land were equally shared between my three
children, now that Peter is dead Miguel and Louise inherit evenly.
This house belongs to Maria on her death it is inherited by our
oldest grandson, what I am getting at is if Louise should die before
you her share of the land and business goes to her children if there
are no children, heaven forbid Esteban interrupts. Yes, heaven
forbid Marcus replies Louise's share returns to Miguel. Marcus
looks up at his surviving son, Miguel understands that this land
is never to be sold to outsiders, and must remain in the family.
Miguel places his hand on his father's shoulder, and nods in
understanding. This is not customary, Esteban comments, when a
woman marries all of her money, and land belongs to her husband,
and he manages her possessions as he sees fit. Not in this case,
Marcus responds, the land is in our blood, and stays in our blood.

That is the way it will be, well as Charles's Patrino I will have to reflect on this matter, Esteban's air of importance is rocketing to the surface. Esteban, Charles motioning to his godfather to silence him, turning to Marcus and Miguel he says I agree with the conditions of your will I think it is sound logic. You are right the land is in your blood, and I can only hope someday it will be in mine too.

It is the night before the wedding ceremony, traditionally the bride is concealed from view in her room with only her mother, and Madrina permitted to see her. However, the flurry of last minute activity has prevented any visits from either woman, and Louise can barely contain her excitement, as she makes sure her trousseau has been packed for the honeymoon, going over the list at least ten times to check all is in order. Her wedding dress and veil laid out lovingly with her shoes and lacy undergarments nearby. Louise has chosen to wear a small cross around her neck on a delicate filigree chain and with no other jewelry. Maria agrees with her daughter's choice in the simple beauty and knows Charles will have only eyes for her and no one else. She will wear a similar cross and chain as will Gabriella Miguel's wife in remembrance of Pedro whom Maria knows is smiling down from heaven. Maria along with Palomar the housekeeper has worked for the past weeks shopping, organizing, decorating and cooking all in preparation for this day. Early morning the staff Maria has hired will finish with the decorations, and setting out tables, enormous cook fires will be lit for the lamb, and pig that will be roasted over the wood coals. A large underground pit has been dug filled with charcoal, a goat has been wrapped in banana leaves and is slowly roasting over the hot coals all night. It will not be until Maria is satisfied that everything is under control that she and Juanita will spend the night with Louise in her room instructing her on married life. Maria is looking forward to this intimate time with her daughter, realizing by tomorrow night Louise's life will be forever changed.

The men are on the veranda drinking, and remembering old times each with a more fanciful story of past conquests and victories won by their prowess alone. As Maria passes by she sees Charles laughing at their sagas as hears bits and pieces of their claims and smiles to herself, men she whispers and goes about her business. She has already warned Marcus, and Esteban that they will be up early tomorrow with much to do and no excuses about tonight will be tolerated. Maria can hear their laughter and the cheerful music being played by the Mariachi and feels good in her heart as she sets out to look for her sister Juanita, finding her in her room putting on her nightdress. I will bathe change into my night attire Maria informs her sister while you set out your clothing for tomorrow and meet you in a half hour in Louise's room, will you have time to set out your clothes also for tomorrow Juanita asks her sister. Palomar has readied my clothes earlier so we could make sure everything is in order, I must hurry while there is still hot water Maria rushes from the room and down the hall to the bath.

Right on time Juanita is waiting for her in front of Louise's bedroom. She knows it is not her place to enter the room before Maria, and if Juanita has one quality it is she follows tradition. Are you ready sister she asks Maria as she opens the door allowing her sister to enter first. Louise is sitting on her bed in a soft blue nightdress Mama, *Tia* I have been waiting so long Maria warmly hugs her daughter, I know we have had much to check on to make sure tomorrow is a perfect day for you. I know it will be mama, Louise pats the bed sit mama by me here Louise says as Juanita plunks down in the large chair by the window. Are you nervous *hija* Maria inquires holding Louise's hand, of course she is nervous Juanita answers. I was terrified, and mother was of no help, she told me to do what my husband says and be quiet it would be over quickly. Juanita, please, well that is what she said, I know but times have changed, Louise and Charles are in love, what does that have to do with anything Juanita mumbles. Louise chimes in mama is right *Tia* times have changed, there are book written on such things, Louise, Maria says in a shocked voice Juanita makes the sign of the cross Madre Mia she cries. I am a little nervous, but I know all about sex, *Tia* yelps, like a frightened puppy, stop I cannot hear such sinful talk, Shush Maria admonishes her sister as *Tia* covers her ears. Where did you learn such things Maria questions Louise, Oh mama all the girls know, we would talk about it at University. You see I told you not to send Louise to school, it corrupts young women's minds, shush Maria says to Juanita again. Mama it is nothing just talk, but Louise that talk as you say, is not proper for a young woman I am disappointed in you. Please do not be mama, not tonight, not now, well maybe you are right, Juanita feels Louise's morals have been compromised, have you confessed these sins to the Priest, you must confess before you are married, tomorrow before mass, I will tell the priest you must have absolution. *Tia* do not worry I confessed to the priest a long time now, thank you Madre, Oh thank you Juanita says in near tears, she has started to perspire profusely as she always does when upset. I must go to my room, tomorrow at church before mass I will light a candle now I am too upset and must rest, walking out the door she turns, and I will say a Rosary for you before I go to sleep if I can sleep ever again.

Do not be angry mama, no hija I cannot be angry ever with you come lie down and we can talk Maria covers her daughter with the quilt and climbs in bed next to her.

Mama when did you know you loved Papa, Maria giggles like a young girl. I was so terrified to marry I only saw you father three times before the wedding, and as *Tia* said our mother was of no help to ease my fears, at the church I was shaking so much that the pedals from my flowers were falling onto the floor. Mama how sad, no Papa was kind and gentle, he made me laugh and put me at ease, I knew even then I was a lucky woman. One day I do not remember how long we were married only a short time. I watched him ride in from the desert, and I knew "I love this man with all my heart and forever". Oh mama that is how I feel about Charles, the exact minute I saw him I fell in love and knew I would love him forever and ever and he loves me and nothing bad can ever happen to change that love. Maria kissed Louise's cheek I know hija I know. Now tell me are you nervous about what will happen tomorrow night, just a little mama I do not want to disappoint Charles, and I am worried about the pain some of the girls say it is very bad. So now you see why gossiping about a subject you know nothing about is silly. Let your love for your husband take over your heart and relax I will pack for you a small bottle of tequila with some herbs to help put you at ease. Mama I have never seen a man naked before, Maria giggled again, they are so funny looking all big and, swollen ready for conquest. Funny she says I think they are looking for love, and to be love just as we are. Never judge particularly in the bedroom, a man's pride is a fragile thing if it is destroyed especially by his wife he becomes lower than a beast. When Charles is with me, I can feel his pride, his strength, and love, I think Mama he needs someone to believe in him and I do Mama I do. Maria holds her daughter tight to her heart rocking her as if a babe stroking her hair.

Maria wakes with a start as she hears the birds singing; quietly she slips out of Louise's room and hurries down the hall to dress as she opens the door to her room she finds Marcus dressed and ready for the day. Good morning, sleepy head he says and you were worried I would not get up in time he laughs giving Maria a kiss on the cheek and whispers *amour*. I will go to the coral and make sure the two carriages are decorated properly, and the horses are fed, curried, and dressed. What time must we leave for the church, no later than eleven Maria answers, good I will instruct the drivers to be in front at ten-forty-five, I will not have the horses waiting in the sun for too long? Is Louise awake, no, there is time, let her sleep Maria replies, yes you are right Marcus says as he leaves the room. Maria is dressed, and right behind her husband rushing to the kitchen, she need not worry Palomar has everything under control the kitchen is her domain, and she runs it with an iron hand. Maria finds the staff she has hired bustling between the kitchen, and the gardens carrying large trays of dishes, and glasses. So many tables have been set up all covered with white clothes, two large vases of flowers are adorning each signifying the union of the couple, the effect is a sea of white dazzling to the eye, banners and colored lights hang from every tree, even the cactus has been ever so gently decorated with lights. The huge wood fires are lit lambs, and pigs slowly roasting over the coals. As Maria returns to the house, she suddenly has a frantic thought Marcus said the two carriages did he forget the buckboard for Palomar and the ranch hands to ride to the church in, and the extra horses for him, and Miguel to ride home on, Maria runs to find Marcus.

Louise is up now soaking in a warm bath humming to herself, she is surprised how calm she feels, and a little hungry as she can smell the aroma of the meat roasting over the coals mingling with the smell of honey cakes in the oven. Her tummy gives a loud growl, quiet she says looking at her stomach the next time you eat you will be married. May I come in Oh! Mama you look beautiful Louise exclaims as Maria enters she and Marcus have both changed into their wedding attire. Now she has come to help her daughter into her bridal gown, Louise gets out of the tub and wraps herself in a towel, let me see mama turn around, you look so lovely. Maria has chosen a rich teal dress, with a deep purple underskirt. Her black hair is braided, and softly coiled around the back of her head tiny silver clips hold it in place, a silver cross, and small silver earrings finish her look. She will wear no mantilla, but a deep purple shawl that she will use to cover her head in church. Juanita bursts into the room as Maria is helping Louise into her lacy underclothes I thought I would be too late to help. I did not sleep a wink last night as I said I would not. Good-morning *Tia* Louise greets her with a smile, Mama was just starting to help me dress Maria turns and there in front of her is her sister in brilliant color. Juanita's dress is black lace as befits a widow, but that has never deterred her, the under skirt of her dress is bright orange and her shawl is yellow trimmed with silver threads, a silver belt tries to cinch in her thick waist. Heavy silver chains drape her neck and an ivory rosary with a large crucifix hang over her ample bosom into which she shoved a large orange flower that looks as though it is blooming between two mountain ranges. Long silver and turquoise earring dangle from her ears, yellow, orange, green and silver bracelets adorn her arms a silver, and turquoise enormous hair comb holds her black mantilla in place a yellow rose is tucked behind her ear the Madrina is ready. You look Umm lovely sister dear Maria says as she helps Louise into her petticoat can you please hand me Louise's shoes, delicate satin slippers slide easily onto her feet. Louise wears her dark hair pulled back from her face cascading down her back in small ringlets. Tiny white seed pearls are scattered through her curls giving the effect of glistening snowflakes. The two women are careful putting Louise's bridal gown over her head so not a hair is out of place, the lace gown fits over her Bodice hugging every curve at the waist it billows out as if clouds have fallen from the sky. *Tia* puts on the small silver cross and, the final touch is the white mantilla delicate as a spider web held in place by an intricately carved tortoise shell comb. There Maria says as she holds her daughter at arm's length to get a good look at her handy work. Tears well up in her eyes as she sees Louise no longer a child but a beautiful woman ready to embark on this new journey. You are beautiful she whispers, now no crying Juanita says her voice cracking as she too tries to hold back her own tears, we must leave for the church the carriages are waiting we cannot be late. Juanita walks toward the door when Maria asks her to please go ahead and inform Marcus they will be out momentarily Juanita starts to question Maria about the delay, when she remembers smiles and leaves the room. Maria holds Louise's hands and begins the mother's prayer for protection and guidance for her daughter throughout her life, Louise bows her head to receive her mother's blessing, Maria kisses Louise before the two women step out to their future.

Juanita is already seated in the first carriage when Louise and Maria walk on to the veranda Marcus has been waiting patiently trying to ignore his sister-in-laws constant chatter when he looks up and sees Louise standing before him, he is overcome and cannot speak to her beauty it is beyond his words. Marcus helps Louise and Maria into the carriage, then sits next to his daughter lovingly taking her hand in his and murmurs "today I give my heart away" but Louise is listening to her Madrina as she is giving last minute instruction as what to do when they arrive at the church, and she does not hear her father. The two carriages leave and pull onto the road heading to the church, Charles and Esteban left earlier along with the buckboard filled with Polamor and the ranch hands Maria has left nothing to chance.

As the bridal party drives into town Louise is overwhelmed at the sight, colored banners stretch from one side of the street to the other creating a beautiful arch for the carriages to drive under. All the stores are decorated with flowers, and white ribbons are tied everywhere, people are in the street waving as they walk to the church for the ceremony. Oh! Papa Louise exclaims how beautiful I never expected anything so grand, nonsense Juanita interrupts your father is a *Dueno*, the town could do no less. The carriages arrive at the front of the church Miguel, Gabriella, and their two boys get out of the second carriage, and come over to Louise. Brother and sister embrace as Miguel touches Louise's face whispering in her ear, she nods and smiles at him as he and his family enter the church escorting Maria and Juanita to their seats.

Are you ready Marcus asks his daughter, you know we can always go back home, oh? Papa stop fooling, Charles is waiting, Marcus takes Louise's arm, and the two enter through the huge doors of the church. It takes Louise a minute for her eyes to adjust from the bright sun light to the dim candle lit church but only a minute as she sees Charles and Esteban waiting for her at the main altar. The music starts Louise and her father walk down the aisle. Marcus feels a slight tremor in his daughters hand and watches a some pedals fall from one white rose in her bouquet of flowers onto the floor.

Charles is smiling as he sees his bride coming toward him, he is aware of nothing else but Louise as she comes ever closer. Esteban gives him a gentle nudge moving him to stand next to Louise on the steps of the altar as his Patrino and *Tia* stand next to the bridal couple. As part of the ceremony, Marcus places Louise's hand in Charles and steps back to sit next to his wife. As the couple exchange vowels the priest asks for the 13 gold coins, Esteban is carrying them in a velvet pouch, he has counted and buffed them so much they sparkle as a sunbeam, counting them out he hands the coins to Charles being careful none should fall to the ground. This is Esteban's big moment, he has spent the morning washing, combing, and primping. He has not a hair out of place, and his boots are spit polished as all eyes in the church are on him now it would not do to fumble. The priest takes the coins from Charles blessing each, and everyone, he then asks Louise if she accepts the coins as a sign of her utmost devotion to her husband and of his trust and confidence in her. Taking the coins Louise smiles at Charles and says Si. *Tia* takes the coins from the bride and hands them over to Maria. Now she takes from a small silver purse hanging from her belt an ivory rosary both she, and Esteban will lasso (El Lazo) the rosary around Charles and Louise's hands signifying an unbreakable bond of love and trust. Charles feels the warmth of Louise's hand in his together connected through eternity, never separated. As the priest pronounces them husband and wife Charles feels a sharp stabbing to his heart as he looks at his beautiful Louise, lasting, but a second they kiss to seal their union. Everyone is laughing congratulation the couple and throwing small red beads for luck as they walk down the aisle of the church to the front doors. More red beads are thrown as the couple walks out into the blazing sun. Esteban claims the brides first kiss as a married woman and then claims a wedding kiss from Juanita as she puts up a not to vigorous protest to the delight of the crowd. Papa I want to walk down the street, and under the beautiful arch to greet the people who have come out to see me can the carriage meet us at the end of town. Marcus informs the drivers, and the wedding party with Louise and Charles in front begin to walk down the main street receiving the blessing and well wishes of the shopkeepers and friends who have lined the street. Charles has never seen anything like this certainly not in Connecticut he is touched at the out pouring of genuine good will that is being express by people who at this time are perfect strangers to him. Do you know all of these people he asks of Louise she smiles at him since I have been a little girl, what do the red beads everyone is throwing mean he asks, she stops and turns to her husband holding both his hands in hers they mean good luck. Then we will have all the good luck in the world he says and kisses her on the cheek. The ride back to the ranch was full of laughter everyone was ready to celebrate as the carriages arrived at the *hacienda*. Charles and Louise can hear the mariachi band playing, children laughing, and their guest waiting their arrival. Entering the garden, the guests give them a rousing cheer, the band plays louder, and the children all run to the Pinata wanting to be the first to swing the stick at it blind folded. Esteban and *Tia* try organizing the guest into a heart shaped group around the Bride and Groom as they are taking the stage for their first dance together as man and wife. Marcus comments to Maria on what a happy couple they make and how proud he is to be Maria's husband. I am thinking back to our wedding, not as grand as this he whispers, you were so beautiful, and I was so nervous. I did not know you were nervous you seemed so calm and sure of yourself she says Ha ha, he laughs my heart was beating so hard I thought I would fall. Marcus places his arm around Maria's waste and swirls her onto the dance floor.

Esteban has taken charge of the piñata as the children swing unsuccessfully at it, he has lined them up so each will have a turn as he struts around like a rooster gathering his chicks. Finally, a bigger boy with one fell swoop hits it, and the piñata burst open revealing the sweets and candies inside to the delight of all the guests as the children run around filling their pockets. Maria and Juanita are the perfect hosts making sure food is plentiful tequila, and sangria flow as freely as a waterfall. Esteban stands and announces it is time for the dollar dance, and a white board is brought front and center as the music begins. Charles is unsure what is required of him as Esteban pushes him into the arms of one of the female guests and tells him to dance. Each guest pins money to the board, for the honor of dancing with either the bride or groom this includes the children also. A small girl pins up her dollar and asks Charles for a dance. He bows and says I am honored she giggles, and he picks her up in his arms and spins her onto the dance floor. Charles is laughing as he dances with most of the female guest even *Tia* Juanita pays for a dance with the groom. Charles and Louise smile and wave as they pass by each other music riding on the air around them.

Esteban finally grabs Charles from the dance floor and tells him to go change he and Louise will be leaving within the hour for their honeymoon. The carriage and the driver are already waiting for them, and their luggage has been loaded aboard. Where is Louise Charles asks, she is changing hurry. Charles rushes down the hall to the room he and Esteban have been sharing, and quickly changes, finishing he steps out into the hall to find Louise waiting. Well hello Mrs. Black he says funny meeting you here as he takes her into his arms holding her close, he can feel the warmth of her lips as he kisses her and feels her body yielding against his. Let us leave now Louise murmurs are you sure, we can go into your room no one will know. Someone will miss us and start looking, yes you are right probably Juanita, and what a surprise she will have. Louise laughs *Tia* will never sleep again, come let us say our good-byes, and by sunset we will be in our villa alone, just the two of us. Charles kisses Louise as the two walk hand and hand back to the reception. The guests all wish the couple good luck and there is much hugging, kissing, and backslapping. Maria holds her daughter tightly to her heart not wanting to let her go, and whispers look in your small bag I put something to relax you tonight in it, thank you, I love you Mama today has been perfect, Louise replies kissing her mother on the cheek. *Tia* Juanita is fussing as usual making sure everything is in order, and nothing is left behind, come *Tia* Louise holds out her arms to her Madrina, thank you she says, you and mama, Oh! it has been so wonderful the most remarkable wedding ever. Juanita blushes just a bit, then says not to loud, remember tonight just do what you are told, close your eyes, and it will be over quickly, yes *Tia* Louise answers with a smile I promise. The guest watch as the couple gets into the carriage all the single women gather in excitement as Louise turns and throws her bouquet right in Juanita's arms to the disappointment of the younger women. Esteban slightly tipsy pats her on the bottom saying nice catch old girl Juanita in shock pushes him away, fool she exclaims as she stands close to Maria watching the carriage pull away onto the road. Marcus and the guest return to the party but Maria linger until the carriage is no longer in view. Come dear sister Juanita takes Maria's hand, Louise as all the women before her belongs with her husband and must obey and care for him always. I know it is a hard thing to let your daughter go, but you must as our mama did when we married. Now your guests are waiting, and it would not do to let them see you crying. Juanita wipes her sisters tears, and the two slowly walk back to the celebration.

The Death of Charles

The sun is starting to set casting rays of pink light through the branches of the trees illuminating the garden in its enchantment when Louise finishes her story. *Abuela* how romantic, thank you for telling me I now see a another side of Charles, yet how much he loved you, that is how as much he hated Tillie, and in the end he destroyed himself. I know my angel, hate has a life of its own, and when we feed it the hate will grow and devour us. But, my angel I loved him so, he is and always will be my life, *Abuela* I wonder if love has changed over the years, no, never. Love is love and never changes. I am not sure of this *Abuela*, what do you mean, well today a woman has her own life, and her husband, and children if she chooses to have them are part of her life. What! If she chooses to have them, yes many women today decide not to marry or if she does she, and her husband come to a decision not to have children, how sad. No! *Abuela* we have options now and are not forced by custom into unwanted marriages. We try to choose what is best for us; please don't forget I am not married. Did you choose not to marry Louise inquires, I am not sure if I chose or just didn't meet the right person, but the issue at hand is a woman can make her own decisions, and that is a very big step in our rights. Rights Louise says unsure of what her great-granddaughter is expressing,

Abuela I think on our trip to Mexico we will have time to discuss the woman's rights issues until then let's go in I am starving. Marie with Louise walk through the garden in to the house aware of only the fragrances of the night. After dinner, Marie takes Louise to her room kissing her reflection and saying good night. She has decided to leaf through the papers she has brought home from Meadow Brook to get an idea of how to make clear to Louise how Charles died, yet not go into a detailed description that she feels will not help only hurt Louise. There are errands Marie must attend to in the morning then call Mr. Burton to make sure the papers are ready giving him authorization to sell the house on her behalf. She also wants to make sure he has established a bank account in Guadalajara" in her name" as she want s the lawyer's office to transfer the funds of her inheritance from Rose there. Tomorrow will be a busy day Marie says to herself. I think the best time to talk to Louise about Charles is in the evening, in the garden amongst the beauty and delicate scent of the night.

Marie arrived home late afternoon and went directly to Louise's room, *Abuela* she called to Louise not wanting to startle her Great-grandmother by just picking up the mirror. How was your day Louise inquires smiling at Marie, funny I miss you when you are not in the house, can you tell when I am not here Marie asks. Yes, Louise answers I feel empty like something is missing, I felt it every time Charles went out and then one day he never came back, I was alone and terrified. You told me Tillie at times would come in the room and speak with you. She did, not long visits, but she came, she told me why Charles was not here that he was ill and could not come home. When Rose was older, and she went to visit, her father Tillie would tell me how Charles was doing and when Rose found Marcus she would read his letters and even show me the pictures he sent. I did not know that, I thought she cleaned out the room and locked it. Louise looks at Marie puzzled, Tillie never touched anything, the room is just like it was the day I died, although I could hear her lock the door when she left. Then one day she came, and told me Charles had died, she was very gentle in the telling. I let out a sob she tried to touch my face and said not to cry, yet before she told me I knew he was dead something vanished from my heart. I saw in her eyes tears, you see angel we both loved Charles. Tillie said she wanted Rose to meet me, and know I was here if she wanted to come to visit Tillie would not stop her. I know Rosie visited you, and when Tillie went to live on Cape Cod she moved into this room Marie said. *Abuela* did she ever tell you why and why she never brought my father to you, I don't understand. She only said it was better if she stayed in this room now, as for Tomas he would never know about me, but she would always tell me what he was doing and would show me pictures of him as he grew birthdays and school pictures, when he graduated university and his wedding picture. "When you were born Rose was so happy" she said, she was a grandmother, but she wasn't Marie interrupted, it did not matter she was, and I was a great-grandmother. She showed me your newborn baby picture, and she said you looked just like me I thought so to. We spoke late into the night I have never seen Rose so happy, there were just the two of us now in the house, Tomas had moved away teaching in another part of the state, but Rose always told me all his news and would show me the pictures he would send. Rose was happiest when you all came for a visit she said the house was filled with laughter as it should be. *Abuela* lets go into the garden I want to tell you about my day, oh yes, I love the garden Louise answers. Walking along the path among the flowers to Marie's favorite bench, she tells Louise when she called Mr. Burton's office the secretary told her all the papers were ready for her to sign and the account established in Guadalajara. So, *Abuela* I decided to go to the office sign the papers and put the house on the market, what good news angel I thought so Marie says. Does this mean we will be leaving soon Louise asks yes, just a few more details, and we will be on our way I also bought a new car today? A new car Louise exclaims is your old car broken, no *Abuela* my old car is not broken, we will be driving a great distance I don't want to take any chances of something happening, please stop worrying everything will be fine. Marie sits down on the bench *Abuela* I went through the papers I brought home from Meadow Brook, you told me Tillie informed you the day Charles died did Rosie ever tell you how he died? Louise looks sad, no Angel she never mentioned her father's death to me, than you don't know Rose was with him when he died, no but how do you know this, it is recorded in the paperwork Marie answers. Then he did not die alone Louise utters quietly, no *Abuela* his daughter was there with him he was not alone.

As she promised nearly every month, Rose visits her father at Meadow Brook. These are busy times for her Rose now has a position at The Francis Academy for Girls teaching art. The war is raging on two fronts and, many of her college friends who were in such a hurry to enlist are dead now killed on islands no one has ever heard of, or in small towns" in Europe". She and her mother volunteer their time at the Red Cross doing whatever is needed to help the war effort, Tillie rolls bandages packs boxes with the personal items the soldiers need and always makes sure there is extra gum, chocolates and cigarettes. Rose particularly enjoys visiting the wounded men in the hospital where she reads, writes letters, and generally spends hours with them trying to cheer them up just a little. The house has changed also her father's room is locked, and Tillie has gotten rid of some of the heavy ornate furniture that was through-out the house and has requested her daughters opinion on color and decorating ideas. The house seems a happier place Tillie has made a point to make new friends and acquaintances trying to shed her past unhappiness, she only occasionally asks Rose how Charles is doing when she returns from her visits. Rose has invited her mother to come with her to see her father, but Tillie always graciously declines saying, "daddy wants to see you, not me". With her mother's encouragement, Rose has made inquiries about her brother Marcus through Mr. Burton and is now in contact with her half-brother and his wife. They are writing to each other about every two weeks with news on family matters and idle chit-chat getting to know each other and learning about their lives. Rose has sent a photo of herself to her brother, and Marcus has done the same, she sees in his dark brooding eyes and handsome good looks her father, when he was young. She has asked Marcus if he would like her to send a photo of their father, but he refuses saying he has his mothers and fathers wedding picture, and that is enough. Rose wants to visit Mexico, but with the war widespread, though-out the world she knows that will have to wait as travel to Mexico is not encouraged. Germany and the Mexican government are on to friendly terms for the likes of the politicians in Washington. On this visit to Meadow Brook Rose brings new photos of Marcus and his wife Sophie in his letter he writes she is going to have a baby, and the family is very excited. Rose hopes this will cheer her father though she doubts it, he barely looked at the other pictures of Marcus she has brought, but he insists she reads the letters. Today as Rose walks down the corridors of the asylum there is a lightness to her step the cool autumn breezes seem to clean the air, and she is going to be an aunt. Rose opens the door to the reception room and sees her father in his usual place by the window she smiles and acknowledges some of the patients that she is used to seeing on her visits as she walks by. Hello father Rose says as Charles turns to look at her, Rose sits down and starts to take her father's hand in hers only he pulls away, I brought your favorite candy, are there letters he asks, yes father and some good news too. Charles cannot seem to focus his eyes on Rose it is as if he is looking through her into another dimension yet their bright blue color has not diminished over the years. Father, Rose reaches out to touch his frail hand, and he is startled back to reality. Let's sit here quietly for a while she sees his breathing is labored, and his hands are trembling more than usual. But Charles interrupts his daughter, no read I want to hear the letters all this time, and all these visits there is no warmth in his voice for Rose. She sees in front of her a man old beyond his fifty years who cannot see or feel the love, only the despair that has lived within him feeding on his mind and body until what is before Rose now is a hollow creature living in a shadow world of past realities. As Rose begins to read Charles listens intently. He never mentions Louise why doesn't he mention his mother Charles utters. Father, Marcus, he interrupts Charles Marcus his name is Charles Marcus, well Charles Marcus then he never knew his mother, are you forgetting you sent him to live with his grandparents when he was just a baby. Why didn't they tell him about Louise, Father they did I am sure, but he is a grown man now with a wife of his own and did you hear they are going to have a baby. You are going to be a grandfather isn't that wonderful news. Marcus sent some pictures here look he is so handsome, and his wife Sophie is beautiful are they standing in front of the *hacienda*. Rose tries to show Charles the pictures only he pushes them to the floor, and turns away. Why can't you look at your son Rose says in an angry voice as she picks the photos up from the floor. Where is Louise, I want Louise, Charles cries, in disgust Rose replies she is dead and better off so. No, she alive, alive in the mirror, Charles is agitated his hands shaking. Tillie killed her she broke the mirror and put an end to her spirit. My mother killed no one if anyone killed Louise it was you and along with Louise, you destroyed everything you ever touched, ruin hangs over you like a shroud. No, Charlotte killed Louise, stop, that is just not true father; yes, she let her bleed to death on the floor. Please father calm down it is not good to get so excited, Rose wants to hear no more. She killed her because she hated her, and I did nothing Charles's voice is dark and guttural but I didn't let her kill our son, ha! I fooled her. Father look at the photos of Marcus, Rose tries to distract Charles, no he pushes Roses hand away again. My mother thought by me marrying Tillie she would be rich but no, I showed her Charles grabs Roses hand, and pulls her face close to his, she killed the only person I could ever love, so you see I had to kill her. Father, Rose tries to pull away, but Charles's grip is to strong. I waited he whispers, and one night when we came home from the country club, she was so smug talking about people who would not have given her the right time of the day if they knew her dirty little secret. "After everyone was asleep I quietly went into her room she was alone my father was sleeping in his dressing room". I took one of the pillows put it over her face and pushed down hard. She woke up, but I was too strong mother knew it was me as I was suffocating the very breath from her and laughing until she was no more. I was Charlie the magnificent again, and Charlotte could not stop me. Charles is squeezing Roses hand laughing a cruel laugh with her free hand Rose motions for an orderly. Her father's laugh has turned into hysterical screaming I did it for you I did it for you, Louise. He slumps to the floor his hands reaching out to a vision only he can see, Louise he whispers, Louise. Father Rose cries trying to hold Charles in her arms to be thrust away. Louise darling Charles utters smiling we are together for eternity, the orderly quickly arrives but there is nothing he can do, Charles is dead. Rose kneels next to her father's body to stunned and, unable to shed a tear.

The silence of the night wraps around the two women like a cloak *Abuela* Charles's last words were calling for you Maries says looking at Louise, but she says nothing *Abuela*, Marie speaks with a question in her voice are you all right, he pushes his own daughter away, he was dying, and he pushes her away. Rose how I wished I had known your hurt. That is why she never spoke of her father, Charles how you could have been so cruel? Louise seems to be speaking directly to him, Marie interrupts he was a very sick man *Abuela* obsessed with what he thought was love for you because of that fixation he could love no one else. His daughter,

Louise put her hand to her face as if to shield herself from the pain, *Abuela*, I am not sure I should have told you this, I am sorry I hurt you. He killed his mother because of me (killer asesino) Louise cries out in anger her eyes wide with fury. Hurt you could never hurt me my Angel Louise cries trying to control her emotions. It is Rose that was hurt growing up with-out a father, and Tillie that was hurt living with-out love how they must have hated me. No *Abuela* it was not hate if it was they could have destroyed the mirror, yet Tillie brought Rose, and Rose on her death-bed told me never to destroy the mirror her way of telling me about you. Maybe hurt and fear not understanding no matter how hard they tried Charles could not love them; it was not hate for you. But fear also, of facing the truth that a bit of Charlotte and Charles exists still in Rose, and in me. Louise is quiet as she looks at her great-granddaughter, you see *Abuela* that is one reason I want to leave this house, and its sadness start a new life with no secrets no lies there has been enough. And me Angel what about me.

Journey of the Soul

The bell chimes and Marie opens the front to door to let in her closest friend the family lawyer Mr. Burton are you ready the old lawyer asks no, only I am going anyway. You can always change your mind, I know, all night fear gripped me, holding me in its clutches, willing me to stay showing me every reason not to go. Then I thought of Rosie, her love and sacrifice for my father, and me what it cost her to keep the terrible secrets she was burdened with and I know I cannot stay. The lawyer puts his arm around Marie, you are making the right choice, start a new life, spread your wings and see how far they will take you I know Rose would be proud of you. No need to worry about the sale of the house and furniture my office will take care of everything and keep you posted. I made an extra set of keys for you one for the house and one for the car just in case. Her old friend smiles I am not sure in case of what however, I thought just in case. Marie gives him a kiss on the cheek, thank you, she looks warmly at the lawyer, since Rosie died "you have taken the place of family" in my life, I will miss you, what will I do with-out you the Isaac Burton takes her hand live, he says, live. Now you must be on your way. Where is Louise, here I am she calls out from the front seat of the car. The lawyer opens the door to see the beautiful blanket Louise bought as a gift for Charles's father all those years ago folded neatly on the seat, and on top is a large wooden box strapped down filled with soft cotton, and there secured with ribbons is the silver hand mirror with Louise's face beaming out. My, my looks as if you are ready for your journey home old friend, Isaac Senior says, dear amigo I do not know where this journey will lead me, but I am ready Louise replies, looking at her old ally seeing tears in his eyes. Please do not cry for me I am happy to be going home and to have Maria be the one to take me. I know we will meet again someday until then keep me in your memory, tears run down the old gentleman's face and with a choked voice says I can never forget you ever "Go with God," it has been an honor to know you. Marie then kisses the old man and gets behind the wheel of the car are you ready she asks Louise yes angel, and with one glance back, drives away.

Marie keeps up a nervous chatter as they travel further away from the house worrying about Louise's condition in the mirror constantly inquiring if she is all right. Look at me my angel I am strong, and I feel happy I am away from that room, from the darkness, and the sorrow from the heavy burden of death that surrounded, and called out to me each time I looked out, and saw the red roses gripping the walls. Do not worry about me I am excellent Louise says with a smile, Marie feels a bit of relief, yet she will still be watchful of her great-grandmothers life force in the mirror as they make their first stop in Lynchburg to spend the night.

As the miles pass, Marie is aware of Louise's presence getting powerful even her image in the mirror is more vibrant, her color glowing alive with confidence, she even seems to look younger. *Abuela* you look so beautiful, not that you were not before, but you look different somehow Marie says, Louise smiles at her great-granddaughter soon my angel I will be free and have a new life. You will have a new, different life too, I know only I will miss our talks and all the time we spend together. Louise looks deeply into Marie's eyes, I will never be far away from you always remember her voice takes on a serious tone for just a minute now tell me Louise says where are we changing the subject to a lighter one. Marie laughs Oh! *Abuela* we will be staying the night in a place called Little Rock in the state of Arkansas. Do I know this place I don't think so Marie answers, trains take a different route, and it was so many years ago, yes angel you are right there are many place I do not know? *Abuela* would you like me to set the mirror higher so you can see the city out the window, no Louise answers, wouldn't you like to see the motel we will be staying tonight. No, Louise answers again; Marie hears a hint of bitterness in her great-grandmothers voice. Tomorrow we will be in Texas, Louise's mood brightens, I can drive to Dallas, and we can stay the night. Why, the border and Mexico we are so close Louise insists in a passionate voice. I am sorry *Abuela*, but Laredo is just too great a distance from Little Rock for me to drive in one day, and I do not want to cross the border at night I will be exhausted. I know you are in a hurry to get home, but we are staying in Dallas.

Marie gets an early start the next day from Little Rock, she knows the drive will be long and hopes the traffic will be light as she turns the car onto route 30 that will take her the six hundred odd miles into Dallas. Louise seem happier now although she still tries to persuade Marie into driving straight through to Laredo, but Marie will not hear it. The women keep up a steady chatter as the miles pass, you know my angel the furthest north I have ever been was Fresnillo before my journey to Connecticut. Didn't you meet Charles there a few times during your courtship and isn't that where your aunt Juanita had her ranch? Yes, Louise answers seeming reluctant to talk about Charles, I think I would have liked *Tia* Juanita Marie exclaims. I know you would, and she would have taken you under her wing and fussed over you like a small calf. I should have listened more closely to what she was telling me and not be so headstrong in my wishes. Well that is in the past we will be home soon, yes *Abuela* just a few more days of driving and we will be there. Angel when we cross into Mexico that is when I want to look out the window I want to see my home country. That is a good idea, but there will be many changes, you might not recognize places you knew well before. I know Louise answers, but I want to see anyway. We will be crossing the border tomorrow if all goes well so it will not be long. The drive to Dallas is long, and tiring for Marie the traffic in and, around the city is a nightmare. Louise seems to sense Marie's frustration and stops her coaxing to go all the way to Laredo. From her position on the front seat, Louise can see the the tall buildings I do not like this place she tells Marie I feel closed in like I am back in my room with no light. Will you be all right Marie is concerned for Louise's welfare, I just do not like it here Louise replies I want to leave. We will not be staying in the city *Abuela* soon we will turn on to the road that will take us to Laredo and once I get on that road we will stop someplace for the night, yes Louise answers not just not here. Marie has to concentrate on the traffic patterns and watch for her turn off onto route 35, so there was little conversation as Marie circumnavigates the traffic, worried about not getting lost and keeping an eye on Louise as she is very agitated. Finally, after an hour and a half in traffic, Marie turns the car onto the road that will take them to Laredo and the traffic starts to thin. Louise is calmer, and Marie breathes a sigh of relief with another twenty minutes of driving they can see the landscape changing, becoming scrubby with sparse vegetation, the wind has picked up blowing tumbleweed across the road that is flat and straight. Up ahead Marie can see the lights of the town she has decided to spend the night and before long, they are in their room out of the brutal summer sun that reflects through the windshield of the car late in the day. Relaxing having dinner Marie questions Louise, *Abuela* what happened in Dallas, you were so upset, I was terrified you were going to disappear. No, my angel I will not leave you, not yet, I feel a deep sadness in my heart, but it is gone now. As I am getting closer to the land of my birth, I am feeling the pain of generations past, and I am becoming one with the people of today and sense them in my heart. I didn't know this can happen *Abuela*, I have been away a very long time there are changes in the people their thinking, and the way they live, so different. I must learn, understand so compassion can dwell in my heart as I will live among them. Except *Abuela* you are not alive, no my angel not my body but my spirit is, and it will find a home, Marie is a bit concerned by what Louise says at first but dismisses the thought as sleep overtakes her.

Marie has the car packed, and they are on the road by four a.m. it is still night Louise comments as she looks up at the clear early sky, no *Abuela* look there is the morning star the planet Venus see how bright it shines soon dawn will be breaking. It is very beautiful, when will we be in Laredo and cross the border into Mexico Marie laughs not for a while. We will be in Mexico today Louise exclaims you promised" her voice is a bit critical". Yes, in the late afternoon as long as all goes well about five p.m. I think. Good, Louise is pleased as she looks again at the morning sky. *Abuela* I am not sure how long it will take to cross the border, why should it take long I do not understand. It is different I will have to show my passport answer questions about how long I am staying and also where I am staying, and the border guards might want to search the car. You are going home, and you will be staying forever with your family Louise says indignantly why will they search your car? To make sure I am not bringing anything illegal into the country, illegal Louise says, something against the law Marie answers. I know what illegal means Louise snaps they are fools, no *Abuela* it is the law. I was thinking to avoid questions will you mind if I put the mirror in my bag along with the rest of my toiletries just to be safe. Louise is not happy with the idea but finally sees logic in it and agrees.

The highway takes them past Waco, Killeen and into Austin the capital of Texas Marie points out the different sights as they pass to Louise only she is disinterested her only question is 'when will be be in Laredo". *Abuela* when you arrive home, Louise corrects Marie, when we arrive home, well yes, when we arrived home, you know I have not told the family about you, and I am not sure what to do. Nothing Louise answers, say nothing I will tell you what to do and the time to do it, I guess you are right Marie replies

I will leave it to you. *Abuela* we are coming into San Antonio it is such a beautiful city it mixes old Mexico with modern Texas, I would so like to stop and visit some of the shops and stretch my legs along the river walk and maybe grab a bit to eat. No, Louise says in a sharp voice we must go on, Marie is upset at Louise's tone, *Abuela* I think if I want to stop for an hour, I have the right to do so since I am the one driving. Marie looks at Louise to see her eyes ablaze with anger but only for a minute though. I am sorry my angel Louise says in a soft voice of course you can stop if that is what you want. Marie looks at her great-grandmother feeling a bit uncomfortable at her reaction, she has also noticed Louise's presence has become much stronger, the force of her spirit more dominate. Maybe you are right *Abuela* it might not be a good idea to stop in San Antonio, but I must stop before we get to Laredo I want to fill up the car with gas, get something to eat, I am starving, and then I will put the mirror into my bag.

An hour outside of the border crossing Marie sees a gas station/ restaurant up ahead and pulls in to fill up, and grab a bite to eat. *Abuela* I am going to put you into my cosmetic bag then put it into my pocketbook now, so you will be with me just not conspicuous. Louise is not happy with this arrangement but closes her eyes and is quite as Marie wraps the mirror in a large white handkerchief and places it into her bag, there safe and, sound she says as she enters the restaurant.

Marie keeps up a steady conversation as she drives trying to keep both herself and Louise calm. She has kept her pocket book open as well as her cosmetic bag so Louise can hear what she is saying. *Abuela* we are in Laredo and in a few minutes we will be at the border crossing at Columbia Solidarity Bridge I am closing my cosmetic bag but will keep my pocketbook open, please say nothing, Louise is quiet.

Marie pulls up to the border crossing and waits her turn in the line of cars, stay calm she thinks to herself as her heart beats faster the closer she get to the guard. Why are you visiting Mexico he asks holding out his hand for her papers? With her hand trembling she picks up her passport and papers that lay on the front seat and hand them to the guard answering his question, I am visiting family in Guadalajara. Do you have anything to declare he asks, I don't think so, what do you mean you do not think so, Oh God Marie thinks to herself how stupid. I mean I just have my things clothes, makeup regular travel necessities nothing else. Please pull your car to the side the guard points to a parking area and turn off the engine, then please get out. Marie does as instructed praying Louise remains silent two guards now approach the car one with a dog. Marie has a lump in her throat the size of a boulder and cannot swallow. Open the trunk and please come with me one guard says while the other with the dog starts a search of her automobile. They walk into a non-nondescript concrete building with a few tables, folding chairs and old aluminum desk with a computer. Please empty the contents of your bag on that table Marie does, as she is instructed carefully removing her make-up case and laying it next to the rest of the contents. Open your wallet how much money are you bringing into the country he asks I have one thousand dollars in travelers checks and my credit cards, Marie answers. How long are you staying the guard is now looking over Marie's passport and other papers. I am not sure as I told the other guard" I am visiting family", is this your first time visiting Mexico, his voice stern, yes she answers. The guard looks at her makeup case do you have any medicine, no I don't take medicine, please open the case and empty the contents on the table he instructs. Marie carefully takes out the wrapped silver hand mirror and places it on the table face down the rest of her makeup she dumps out on the table making a clattering sound. What is this the guard points to the mirror, Marie's heart is racing and the lump in her throat threatens to strangle her, it's a hand mirror that belonged to my great-grandmother I have it wrapped so it won't be scratched or damaged in my case. The guard looks up out the window, he nods his head to the guards outside and with much ceremony stamps Marie's passport welcome to Mexico enjoy your visit.

Marie gets into her car fighting down nausea, and pulls out onto highway Mexico route-85 driving south toward Monterrey._She drives about 10 km fighting down panic and nausea before pulling over getting out of the car and losing the battle to nausea on the side of the road.

Abuela, Marie calls as she gets back into the car cleaning her face, and hands with the wipes she has in her case. Then taking the hand mirror out when she finishes are you there *Abuela*? I am fine my angel Louise says looking out at her great-granddaughter as Marie holds the mirror up in front of her face. I was so terrified Marie cries I thought they would see you, and how could I explain Marie is near hysterics her body shaking, and she is again fighting down nausea. Stop this Louise firmly commands her great-granddaughter the strength of Louise's voice stops Marie is babbling. I am sorry *Abuela* it is just, stop, Louise says again now take a deep breath. Marie does as she is told, that is better Louise says, her spirit is very strong, and Marie is overcome by it. Now prop the mirror up so I can see, and let us start driving to Monterrey. *Abuela*, says Marie I am tired, and have been driving a long way I know I will not be able to drive that far I looked on the map and there is a town not far Ciudad Sabinas Hidalgo I want to stay the night there, please. Louise looks at Marie and see the strain on her face oh my angel of course that will be a good place to spend the night we are home and that is what matters most, we are home. Marie starts the car and heads to Hidalgo with Louise keeping up a steady chatter as she now looks out the window on her native land.

Early the next morning Marie wakes and gets ready to leave, *Abuela* I was thinking after my breakfast we can drive through to San Luis Potosi and by pass Monterrey spend the night there and by the next day be at the ranch how does that sound. No, Louise says I want to stop in Monterrey, but *Abuela* if someone sees you how . . . . no one can see me Louise interrupts just my blood. Do you mean the guards couldn't see you, why didn't you tell me it might have saved a bit of worry on my part? Marie hesitates, and then says, but Mr. Burton could see you why. I am in my own country I am stronger, and I have more control, control Marie says concern in her voice. Not to worry angel you will see, now go have your breakfast I want to leave as soon as you return. Sitting in the restaurant Marie thinks about what Louise as just told her feeling somewhat unsettled yet also relieved if Louise can control who sees her then there is a less likelihood of unwanted questions.

Pulling the car onto highway M.85 Marie asks Louise, *Abuela* why is so important we stop in Monterrey, it is a beautiful place and where I purchased this rug and the silver chain you now wear around your neck it was our last train stop in Mexico. I want to see it again *Abuela* I am sure it has changed much in eighty years, I hope you are not disappointed. Within the hour, the road is congested with commuters all heading to work and Marie can see the displeasure in Louise's face. It was such a beautiful city, it still is *Abuela* just grown over the years. Look, there is Saddle Mountain in the distance Louise looks out the window, and smiles yes the mountains are still the same. Where do you want to visit, I read in the travel guide about old town I think that must have been the area you and Charles shopped. Keep driving Louise demands, I want to be away from this place. *Abuela*, Marie is distress at the great-grandmother's tone of voice. Nothing a stays the same I warned you about places you knew well that you might not recognize becoming angry solves nothing. Angry, I am angry, you say everything changes and nothing stays the same, I have not changed I am still locked in time and have not been a part of the changing world. I think it is too late, now you must be with your mother and father, Charles Marcus, and Tomas where your spirit is free to continue with your family, and Charles. No, Louise shouts rage fills her voice and her eyes flame with its fury. Marie pulls the car into a rest area and turns off the engine, I am getting out stretching my legs she informs Louise and she leaves the car and locks the door. From where Marie is now standing, she can see Saddleback Mountain with the morning suns dazzling rays reflecting on the dome of The Bishops Palace. Marie breaths deeply the fresh air as if to gather strength from the beauty of the city, before getting back into the car. I am sorry my angel Louise apologizes as soon as Maries enters the car the trip has made me very nervous, so many things changed and I cannot understand. I know *Abuela* I feel the same way and afraid too how the family will react when they see you and what will happen. I am not sure Louise says but I think in my heart they will understand, I hope so Marie replies. Now let's get started on the drive to San Luis Potosi, good idea Louise says, *Abuela*, Fresnillo it not far from San Luis after we get settled in our room maybe we can take the drive to Tia's ranch to see what it looks like now. I do not think I want to do that everything is so very different I want to remember the ranch the way I see it in my mind. Yes, you are right, I think we have had too much to deal with today we both need to rest up for tomorrow.

The highway to San Luis Potosi is crowded with traffic and Marie soon realizes staying the night in the city is a bad idea. Louise is agitated by the crowds of cars, and the noise, this cannot be San Luis, Charles, and the American Army searched for Poncho Villa here, how could this be Louise cries. *Abuela* it is still early in the day and I think I want to drive further south, what do you think? Louise says nothing for quite a while looking out the window her face has turned pale. *Abuela*, Marie calls to Louise but Louise is deep in thought, I wonder if the trains still run through the city to Laredo. I guess it still does why you ask Marie replies. Papa told us it was important to the revolution that the railroad lines through San Luis to Texas remain open and not fall into the wrong hands. Whom did your father support during the revolution? Marie inquirers, Louise does not answer. Heading south on route 80

Marie manages the heaviest congestion in the city by mid-day and becomes relaxed behind the wheel of the car as they start to leave the city behind. Louise is quiet absorbed looking out the window, Santa Anna and his Army marched this way to fight at the Alamo, look she points in the direction of the vast open country, see those soldiers out there and the wagons they must be part of the army, so many soldiers. Marie looks, I see nothing she comments, Louise points again, and look, they are marching so straight. *Abuela* I see nothing out there just open desert. No I see soldiers Louise cries so many will be dead soon we must stop and tell them. Marie keeps driving, they are there I see them Louise's voice is bitter and her face has a callousness Marie has not seen before. *Abuela* I am driving to *Zapotlanejo* it looks like a small city and we will stay at the *Hacienda Coyotes* I think we need to pamper ourselves. It is a pretty place very private and we can relax maybe take a walk around the gardens. Louise is quiet, when we arrive I will call Hilly at the ranch and tell him to expect us tomorrow by noon what do you think, yes stopping is a good idea. Well we are off to *Zapotlanejo* and the *Coyotes Hacienda* Marie shouts.

The city is beautiful with its old charm, and the exact medicine Marie needs, Louise feels relaxed, and is chatting about what she sees in town as the car drives down the narrow streets with its beautiful Spanish architecture. Marie is following the small signs advertising the "*Coyotes*" she finally sees a sign with an arrow pointing down an almost hidden driveway. *Abuela* look it is so beautiful, Louise is smiling yes angel beautiful. Say a prayer, and cross your fingers, they have a vacancy, Marie wraps the mirror and places it in her bag, ready set lets go she says getting out of the car; Louise giggles shhh Marie whispers they can still hear you as she opens the door. The clerk looks like studious young man and Marie clears her throat to get his attention from his book. May I help you he asks, I was hoping you had a cottage for the night to rent, do you have a reservation the clerk inquires, no Marie replies. Then let me see if there is something, the clerk looks through the desk book, Marie wants to scream please, please I need this room, but remains quiet as the young man thumbs through his book. Yes, we have a very small cottage at the back of the ranch, I will take it Maries declares, and pays for the night. The clerk gives Marie a map showing where the cottage is with a description of all the amenities available to guests, and she sets out to locate the cabin, after dinner a swim in the pool will be lovely she thinks to herself. Here we are Marie calls to Louise as she parks the car in front of a tiny adobe *hacienda* this is perfect *Abuela* as Marie opens the beautifully carved oak door. Though small as the clerk said, the room is picture-perfect. A single bed is located between two French doors that open to a small walled garden, the bed is piled high with pillows the color of the Mexican sky at sunset. Quilts are folded at the foot of the bed their colors, and patterns showing the quilters skills with a needle as each patch tells a part of the history of Mexico. Marie places her duffle on a nearby table and pulls the mirror from her purse, Look *Abuela* isn't it wonderful. Louise beams as Marie holds up the mirror so Louise can get a full view of the room, look at the lovely weavings on the walls Louise points out, each design has a name, I use to know them by heart, but I will remember. Marie feels rejuvenated the room with its overstuffed leather chairs and color cheerful patterns through-out send a message of warmth and relaxation. Marie and Louise stroll through the small garden, I was thinking *Abuela* after I have dinner you and I can walk on one of the trails close by and then I want to go for a swim what do you think. I believe it is a very good idea, now take me in and set me up over there in the corner on that table, no one will see me and I can look out on the land, now go take a shower

Arriving Home;

The telephone rings in the office as Hilly's two granddaughters are getting up to leave for the day. They can smell dinner being served in the dining room, and are hungry. Go Elena tells her sister I will answer the phone walking back to the office to pick up the receiver. *Hola* the Gutierrez ranch, the voice on the other end hesitates for just a bit. *Hola* may I please speak to Senor Hilly Gutierrez. My grandfather is just sitting down to dinner Elena asks, who is calling. I am sorry I just lost track of time my name Marie Black his great-niece I wanted to call and . . . . Madre, Elena says please hold the phone I will call my grandfather, just a moment. Elena places the receiver on the desk and runs from the room calling *Abuelo, Abuelo*. Hilly is getting ready to take his place at the head of the table when Elena runs into the dining room hurry *Abuelo* our Maria is on the telephone. Marie waiting for for Hilly to come to the phone is standing by the open French doors looking out over the garden breathing in the fresh evening breeze, is he there Louise wants to know her voice is concerned. Marie shakes her head no and signals Louise to remain silent. *Hola* she hears on the other end of the line, *Hola, Tio* Hilly it is Marie, Louise holds her breath. Maria, where are you Hilly asks in an excited voice. *Tio* I am in *Zapotlanejo* at the "*Hacienda*

Coyotes". You are so close the old man exclaims, is something wrong that you stopped, no Marie answers I am so terribly tired, and I think it is wise for me to rest for the night and get a fresh start in the morning. Yes, Hilly replies good idea we are still about one hundred miles away. Should I send my son Peter to meet you? Thank you *Tio* but I think my heart will lead me, I also have a clear map of the area, the old man laughs *si*, *si* you have driven so far already, what am I thinking. Be careful Guadalajara is a large city with much traffic, and many roads, my directions *Tio* take me around the city into Ameca and then home I should be at the ranch by early afternoon. Very good, very good, I am so happy, Marie can hear Elena asking her grandfather what time will she arrive, *Silencio* Hilly whispers, when she gets here. *Tio* I will see you tomorrow *Despedida* for now Marie says. Yes, *Adios* until tomorrow Hilly replies and hangs up the telephone. Our Girl will be home tomorrow what time Elena asks, but her grandfather is already in the dining room saying Maria will be arriving early afternoon tomorrow the family all starts to question him at once. Quiet and I will tell you, she is staying the night in *Zapotlanejo* at the "*Hacienda Coyotes*", she is tired and will start early in the morning. Pilar make the sign of the cross poor child such a long way to drive, we must get things ready she says looking at her sister Flora, who assures her that preparation are completed. I think she will enjoy staying in her grandfather old room yes Marcus would have liked that before Pilar can finish Hilly raises his hand now let us eat. The two sister's talk quietly together going over all the preparations once again. Peter chimes in *Padre*, I do not understand why Maria drove her car, and did not fly it makes no sense. Peter is right Emilio comments, so many days wasted on the road. I think she is planning to stay, Hilly says, to stay Emilio expresses yes his brother replies. Flora and Pilar speak at the same time, did she write you about staying here in another letter. Why did you not tell us, there is no other letter just the one I read to you Hilly answers? Then how do you know this, again both sisters speak in unison looking annoyed at each other. I just know, Maria is our blood and belongs here with her family on the land. Flora looks at her sister before speaking, Hilly she has a life in America you cannot expect her to leave what she knows to live here with strangers. Indignantly Hilly answers; we are not strangers how can you say that Flora I am ashamed. Tomas's daughter is coming home are you not happy. Hilly, *Hermano* I am happy I just do not want you hurt when she leaves. She will stay I know, Maria is coming home Hilly looks around the table, and smiles at the family she will stay.

Marie could not sleep as thoughts of meeting her family kept going through her mind, what will they be like, and more importantly what will they think of her, not to mention Louise. It was easy imagining their meeting when she was still in Connecticut loving and welcoming, however, now within hours that meeting will take place. What if the family is against her staying, and for the first time Marie sees them as individual people, with likes and dislikes and lives quite different from her own, not the fanciful group of her dreams. Marie sits in the garden listening to the night sounds praying tomorrow that she will truly be home.

Marie wakes abruptly when she hears Louise call her name, realizing she fell asleep in the garden, stretching to get the kinks out, I am here *Abuela* she answers walking into their room. Where were you Louise asks, her great-granddaughter, I was have trouble sleeping and went to sit in the garden, and I guess I fell asleep? Let me take a shower get some breakfast, and we will be on our way. How long before we arrive at the ranch Louise enquires, well it is about a hundred or so miles from here, we will be driving around Guadalajara, not through the city, then to Ameca and home. I think about three hours, I told *Tio* Hilly I would arrive early afternoon, so there is no rush that is good Louise says as she watches Marie walk into the bathroom.

As Marie expects the highway leading to Guadalajara is congested with commuter traffic, but before long, she sees the sign for route 70 Ameca and makes the turn. From what she and Louise can see of the city from a distance, they are both awestruck by its beauty. Cathedral spires soared to the heavens, next to modern day skyscrapers mixing old and new in perfect harmony. Louise is keeping up a steady conversation as she points out places she remembers from a distance, look there is the Cathedral of Guadalajara so beautiful how the gold spirals shine in the sun. When I was a child and our family would celebrate Our Lady's name day in the city I thought this was heaven and the cathedral was her home. Mama laughed, and said heaven is so much more beautiful, what is more, someday you will see. You will *Abuela* I know you will Marie says only Louise ignores the comment and keeps up her steady exchange about the city and her memories. Why *Abuela* are you not angry about the changes in this city as you have been with all the others cities we have driven through, Guadalajara cannot be same as you left it. Angel this is part of home I love this city, and it will always be in my memory as it once was. Marie makes a mental note she must come back to explore then drives on leaving the city behind. Within an hour, they are approaching Ameca we will be there soon Marie says, yes Louise answers in a whisper she is looking out the window and is especially quiet concentrating on the passing scenery only an occasional sigh escapes her lips. Please Louise requests turn onto the next road Marie obliges making a right turn onto the next street, and stops the car, there in front of them is a beautiful blue and white church so different than any Marie have seen in her travels through Mexico. Oh! Marie murmurs," The Templo De la Senora de Guadalupe" Louise says this is where I was married. *Abuela* it is so lovely can we go inside, no Louise answers I just wanted to see it again, Marie does not press the point. This church is so unusual like a church you would see in Holland, and the distinctive white adobe with blue trim is rather remarkable Marie comments. Yes, angel is all Louise says as Marie starts the car and drives away. Outside the city Marie see a narrow road with a sign stating El Sabino, and El Texcalame and turns the car heading south. The countryside now is vast rolling hills Marie can imagine her great-grandmother riding her horse *Sabio*, hair loose flying in the wind. Turn Louise directs Marie as she slams on the breaks almost passing the dirt road Louise wants her to go down. A large wooden archway proclaims The Gutierrez Ranch. Oh! *Abuela* we are here look we are here Marie shouts, Louise tries to reach out of the mirror with her hand to touch the sign. Marie is laughing and crying all at the same time *Abuela* we made it, Louise smiles her voice is soft, home, we are home. Marie drives slowly so Louise can see the gigantic centuries old trees standing alongside tall palms, and enormous yucca plants. Further, down the road green manicured lawns surround colorful flowerbeds. The *hacienda* is just up ahead Louise says, and Marie stops the car, what are you doing Louise demands, keep going, *Abuela* when we reach the house I will have to put you into my pocketbook, you know that I hope. Wait I want to see the *hacienda* first, what if the family is out front, Louise's eyes flash with anger and her voice is cold I said wait do nothing until I tell you, now drive. Within a minute, the road forks and Marie keeps to the right as she is told, the road to the left leads to the barns and stables Louise says then stops . . . . In front of them stands an enormous tree, the largest Marie has ever seen, and behind it, a low adobe wall surrounding a rambling Spanish *hacienda* the color of the setting sun in stark contrast to the dark umber of the Terra Cotta tile roof . . . . home Louise whispers and Marie stops the car. Are you ready Marie asks Louise yes, and she places the mirror into her handbag as she gets out of the car.

All fear Marie has about her welcome quickly vanishes as the family rushes out to greet her all speaking at once. Hugs and handshakes abound Marie is welcome with the joy of a returning lost child as she looks up she sees in the doorway of the *hacienda* a tall stately elderly man *Tio* she cries and runs to his open arms. Bienvenido he whispers as he hugs her close, welcome home, it has been a long journey Marie tells the old man Si, but you are safe home now where you belong the family now encircles the two as they walk inside Hilly giving orders to Eduardo and Richard to bring in the luggage from the car.

The large reception area is just as Louise has described it so many times, its comfortable leather furniture, colorful rugs scatters about on a lovely terra cotta tile floor even the old grandfather's clock chimes a welcome. Looking across the room in the corner Marie sees the altar of Our Lady of Guadalupe the silver candlesticks polished to a soft patina holding beeswax candles throwing of a soft glow. The mantilla a bit yellow now with age still covers the altar where fresh flowers have been placed at the statues feet. Marie refrains from the urge to run and to touch the mantilla as Hilly watches her smiling. Now with great dignity, he introduces Marie to the family saying I am the oldest of your great-grandfather Miguel's children, but will introduce my family last. He leads Marie to where Emilio and his children are seated this is your *Tio* Emilio he says, my brother. Emilio's warm smile and bear hug so genuine Marie laughs and hugs him right back, there are more embraces from Emilio's family. Hilly now moves to where his two sisters are seated. This is your *Tia* Flora he says as *Tia* stands also with the same inviting smile welcomes Marie. Introducing her family with the comment you will get to know us, not to worry, Marie is grateful for the kind words of understanding as she is trying remember everyone name to no avail. *Tia* Pilar is standing with outstretched arms, dressed in her nun's habit with large wooden rosary hanging around her neck, she looks a bit formidable, but her strong arms enfold Marie in a loving embrace. Pilar then makes the sign of the cross, I have been praying your journey was safe, Our Lady has answered my prayers; thank you, Marie says I have felt her presence. Pilar nods her head in agreement and smiles seemingly happy Marie is not an unbeliever. Hilly looks over to where his family is waiting apparently counting heads, where is Ramon he questions. The rest of Hilly's grandchildren close ranks around their father Peter as he answers. I am sure he is on his way I think he has some business in Guadalajara, business Hilly says, monkey business no doubt. Well Maria this is my family without Ramon, Peter steps forward with warm words of welcome apologizing for his son's absence. Somewhere in Marie's memory, the name Esteban leaps to the surface she giggles, recovering quickly as not to offend Peter, and says I am sure he is on his way as we speak. Humph, Hilly comments as the twin sisters push forward hugging and kissing Marie, Maria we spoke on the phone I am Elena, and I am Deanna, we are so happy you are here Marie likes them both already and feels they will become excellent friends. Richard and Eduardo introduce themselves and their families leaving Maries head in a jumble of names. Enough Flora and Pilar say looking to their nephews take Maria things to her room. Come child we have put you in your grandfathers old room we know he would have liked that very much. Marie hears Louise sigh, both sisters ask if Marie is okay and she quickly answers, I am fine *Tia's* just tired, of course to much excitement the two declare, as much for Marie as for the rest of the family. The *hacienda* is so beautiful Marie comments I feel I have been here before. Pilar makes the sign of the cross Madre she states, stop Flora says to her sister of course she feels that way this is home. Yes, you are right Hermana and home is forever from generation to generation. The three women reach Marie's room, and open the door we have changed many things in this room but have kept all the pictures just as they were when Marcus was alive. After he was hurt and sent Tomas your father to America with Rosita he moved back into this room, but we will talk later, rest now we will call you for dinner. Thank you, Marie says as the two sisters close the door. Marie turns to see if the door has a lock it does not and she then moves a small chair to secure the entrance, there that's better she says placing her handbag on the bed. Louise she softly calls removing the mirror from its safety inside the bag are you all right, yes I am fine, we are in . . . . I know I heard my son's room. Marie holds the mirror out in front of her so Louise can see as she walks around the room. On the far wall between windows that look out on to the garden are family photos as Marie approaches closer Louise starts to cry. The photos are of Louise and Charles Marcus each picture corresponds the baby pictures of her, and Marcus are grouped together, this arraignment is carried on throughout the changing years of their lives until it abruptly stops with a picture of Our Lady of Mexico. Mama did this so my son would not forget me Louise utters between her tears; maybe we can change rooms Marie says. No, replies Louise in a harsh voice, I will stay here, Marie and Louise walk to another part of the room where photos of Charles Marcus as a grown man cover the wall. There is teenage, graduation, birthday all the photographs marking significant milestones in his life. Every occasion is there as if waiting for his mother to look upon and meet her son. In the center of this collection framed in delicate silver, a tall handsome dark haired man stands proudly next to a beautiful young woman wearing a white lace mantilla as delicate as a spider web. Louise is sobbing uncontrollably now, and Marie's efforts to comfort her great-grandmother are of no use. Please *Abuela* the family will hear you we do not want that yet, finally Louise's sobs are quiet. I am so sorry *Abuela* that you are so hurt, no angel the wedding photo Marcus looks so much like his father, and his wife she has on my mantilla. I was looking back in time when Charles and I were married so happy standing together on the steps of the church of De la Senora de Guadalupe. Marie hears a knock on the door and tries to stuff the mirror into her purse then decides to lay it face down on a dresser, coming she calls as she moves the chair away from the door. I came to see if everything is satisfactory and you are, comfortable in your grandfather's room Hilly says when Marie opens the door. *Tio* the room is perfect and I thank you for your kindness in letting me stay here. May I come in for just a moment the old gentleman asks, ah yes, please Marie hesitates looking back at the mirror hoping Hilly does not see it. Hilly sits down in one of the comfortable chairs in the room I know Maria you have just arrived he starts, only as soon as I read Senor Burtons letter I felt in my heart you were coming home to stay, Marie tries to interrupt, but Hilly stops her, please allow me to finish. I am sorry *Tio*, Marie's fear returns thinking they do not want me. Maria I want you to know this is your home, this is where you belong I hope you will make an old man happy and live here on the land with your family. I know you have your life in America, and I am asking much of you. *Tio* I have nothing to go back to America for I was afraid the family would not want me to stay Marie replies. Hilly gets up from the chair my child he holds out his arms to Marie, I am happy now our Maria is home Familia together, he says holding her close. Rest now we will tell the family at dinner, but I think they already know. Hilly turns to leave the room and sees the mirror on the dresser *Madre Mio* he utters as he goes toward the chest. Marie stands rooted to the spot unable to move. Louise; this mirror belongs to Louise, how do you have this he asks Marie as he picks up the mirror. I was just a small boy when my grandmother gave it to her as a wedding present she spoke often of the mirror always wondering what happened to it. He fingers the silver gently touching the beautiful initials *Abuela* had it made especially for her there is none like it he expresses as he looks at Marie who seems frozen, and unable to speak. Hilly then turns the mirror over to the reflecting side, and there looking at him is Louise. Jesus Cristo he cries as Marie finally able to move lunges for the mirror before Hilly drops it onto the floor as he grabs onto the dresser trying to keep himself from falling making the sign of the cross. Marie seizes the mirror just before it hits the floor and shatters, *Abuela* she cries holding on tight to one of the leafy vines that make up the handle. *Abuela* she cries again finally turning the mirror upright are you okay, Louise looks little worse for wear, I am well angel she says, a fine introduction to your *Tia* Hilly dropping her to the floor, and after all these years Louise scolds her nephew. Marie is holding the mirror tightly as she helps the stunned Hilly into the nearest chair and sits down next to him. After a moment, the color returns to his face and Hilly's hands stop shaking, what is this he says almost in a whisper? *Tio* I do not know how to explain and I wanted to wait for the right time, the right time Hilly interrupts. Well I guess there isn't a right time to account for this, honestly how can I, Marie finally gives up and says Louise meet your nephew Hilly, Hilly meet your *Tia* Louise. *Sobrino* Louise says softly looking directly into Hilly's eyes, I have waited a long time to come home can you not welcome me. Who are you, are you of the devil Hilly questions, his voice shaken with fear making the sign of the cross. No *mi amour* my spirit has been kept safe in the mirror waiting for Marie to bring me home where I can be free once more. But, how

Hilly asks Louise not taking his eyes from her face, no this cannot be, I need to get Pilar, she will know what to do. Marie looks at Louise and nods *Tio* I will bring the two *Tia*'s and, Emilio here, you are too shaky to walk I think, yes, please the old man says. Marie decides to take the mirror with her turning the reflective side toward her chest I will be back in a minute walking out of the room but leaving the door ajar. In the hall, Marie looks at Louise, well *Abuela* that did not go, as we attended, no, angel it did not. What shall we do, I think get the *Tia*'s, and Emilio Louise answers. I know all will be well once they see me I have not been trapped in this mirror so many years to be forbidden by my family, with my freedom so close. Marie hiding the mirror goes to look for Emilio, and the two *Tia*'s, she finds them sitting on the veranda talking. Marie thinks she is the topic of their conversation as they stop speaking as soon as they see her. Maria Emilio greets her standing up do you like your room, yes very much, *Tio* Hilly asked me to find you and bring you to my room. Emilio walks over to Marie thinking she only means for him to follow, *Tia*'s Hilly wants to see you both too. Is he okay has something happened the sisters want to know, he is fine he just wants us all to talk together privately. They walk down the hall to Marie's room the sisters keep inquiring if their brother is all right, and are not satisfied as to Hilly's condition until they see him sitting in the chair Marie left him. *Hermano* both sister rush to their brothers side we were worried what is this now you must speak to us alone. Marie follows Emilio into the room, holding the mirror close to her chest still with the reflecting side not showing, her emotions are on a wild ride from fear to terror and back again, yet trying to hold herself together. Hilly bids everyone sit and in a quiet voice Maria he says, please stand there pointing to the dresser where we all can see you. Emilio has a concerned look on his face as he chooses a chair close to Hilly seemingly to protect his brother from what is to come. The room has an air of expectancy as everyone waits to hear what Hilly has to say, *Hermano* Emilio touches his brother's arm, what it is; Hilly clears his throat it would seem that our *Tia* Louise is not dead, what are you saying Pilar interrupts; holding her rosary, this is the devil's business. Hilly looks at Marie, no she exclaims please listen before you judge. Emilio stands, I think you must tell us what you have come to say, his voice is stern. I do not know how or why only that my *Abuela*'s spirit has been trapped in this hand mirror for the past ninety years. I know there are things of God we cannot explain Marie looks directly at *Tia* Pilar No, she is an evil demon Pilar says as she jumps up holding her Crucifix out in front of her invoking Mary the Mother of God to save them. We must call the priest only he can rid us of this devil. Flora has been quiet through this spectacle and looks lovingly at her brother Hilly then at Marie, how do you know this Flora asks. Please Louise whispers to Marie, turn the mirror so my family can see me. I know because Louise is here with me Marie answers *Tia* Flora, and wants to meet you. Marie looks pleadingly at her uncle Hilly who nods, yes he states let the family see, and Marie turns the mirror. Looking directly at her aunts and uncles is Louise as young and beautiful as the photos on the walls prove she was. Pilar screams and faints hitting the floor with a loud thud. Flora puts her hand to her throat and mutters Cristo; Emilio is on his feet ready to lunge at the mirror when Hilly grabs his arm-holding firm, permit her to speak he says looking at Louise. Pilar is recovering trying to sit up, still holding her rosaries when she sees Louise and faints once again. I am sorry I have upset the family, only please I am real, and I have waited so long to come home I will not hurt you please, I have much to tell you of my life, and my death, tears run down Louise's face. *Abuela* Marie cradles the mirror trying to comfort Louise I am so sorry, the room has become transfixed on both Louise and Marie the silence is as loud as a marching band. Pilar has recovered and is sitting next to her sister it is Emilio who speaks. You say you are not dead, but your ashes have been kept on the altar of our Lady for all the years I can remember. Louise tries to speak, but Emilio silences her let me finish, only evil spirits are trapped on this earth turned out of heaven by God. Yet you say God has kept you until the time you can return home, and your spirit is freed but I think not, your mama fought *La Llorona* for your son's soul and she has never walked on our land again. What is the sin your soul must do penance for tell us. Marie speaks there is no sin, if there is any sin it has been committed against Louise, I have not asked you Emilio states, please keep silent. Marie is taken aback again, by the sternness in his voice, Pilar, Emilio calls, his sister bring me the crucifix from the wall, she does as she is asked. Hilly come let us sit together, come Pilar, come Flora the four sit in a semi-circle close together, Emilio holds the crucifix up in front of them and requests Pilar to do the same with her rosary now speak he demands of Louise. The sin I am guilty is the sin of loving too much, that is not a sin Pilar says God loved us so much that He . . . Louise interrupts it is not God's love that is the sin, it is the love that blinds us to to the wishes of others. It is love that consumes us, so we want nothing but to please the one we love no matter what the cost that is my only sin. I died in a house of hate because I left the family who loved me to follow the man I cherished, so his wishes to have our child born in his family's home' in America' could be realized. I died with only hate for company, but I protected my child so evil could not destroy him until his father returned and I knew Charles Marcus was safe. Only his father was weak and could not protect our son from the demons in himself, the only noble choice he made was send the baby here to be nurtured in tenderness, love, and safety, every day I thank God for that, so if that is my sin I am guilty. Flora is in tears, but Emilio and Pilar seem unmoved, Marie looks to Hilly please we have come so far only you can end this and bring us peace. They hear the grandfather's clock striking the dinner hour it is our duty to tell our loved ones at dinner they must know Pilar declares. The family will stick together as always and pray to rid us of this evil spirit, *La Llorona* has returned to seek revenge on our family because of her defeat so many years ago by the prayers of Maria, Pilar is working herself up to near hysterics. You know this how Hilly asks his sister, do you have a direct line to God, the last time I looked I was head of this family with Emilio at my side . . . . But . . . . Pilar tries to speak, enough Hilly exclaims, I have heard enough. We will go to dinner the family is waiting, Maria you will come with us Louise will stay here, and Pilar you will act with the dignity that is required as an elder sister. Flora? I am fine *Hermano*, Emilio? Yes, the family is waiting he replies as he takes Marie's arm to escort her to dinner.

After the evening meal the family members who can retire to the veranda off the reception room for coffee and desert most of the men still have work to do in the corals and will return later in the evening. Everyone has questions for Marie about her life in America, she looks to Hilly for direction, who says remember Maria has had a long journey and must be tired. Before Hilly leaves he asks has anyone seen Ramon, he phoned and said he will return tomorrow morning business has kept him longer in Guadalajara then he has expected Deanna answers her grandfather. Humph, business, Hilly comments shaking his head in frustration at his grandson's irresponsible behavior. Turning to Flora Hilly says you and, Pilar make sure our Maria is not tired out, Emilio, and I will return soon, he smiles at Marie, and the two men walk into the house and down the hall to Marie's room. Opening the door Hilly calls to Louise, *Tia* as he and Emilio quickly enter and close the door behind them. I am here she answers as both men walk to the dresser where Marie has braced the mirror up in its stand. Looking at Louise Hilly says you are as beautiful as I remember. I was a small boy when you were married, and I thought you looked like an angel, so long ago, yes Louise replies so long ago. Tell me I am not a religious man, but I believe in good and evil, and not always, as the church sees them, how this can be. I remember *Abuela* Maria, and the sorrow in her heart when she was told you had died, my grandfather Marcus who rode his horse out into the desert like a madman his grief so great. Your Senor Burton brought your ashes home when he came to bring Marcus to us, this I remember. There is an urn at the feet of Our Lady of Guadalupe in the next room with your name engraved in gold letters this I know, yet you are here, and I see you and am speaking to you, but of this I do not know. Louise looks at both her uncles *Tio* Hilly, *Tio* Emilio I am not asking you to understand what has happened to me for there are things we experience that cannot be explained away so easily. I know my body is dead I felt myself die in the arms of my husband and yet my spirit is here confined to this mirror this small part of my home I brought with me to America. Please do not turn me away allow my spirit to be set free and find the place it belongs.

Hilly looks at Emilio, and says to Louise I have been head of this family since my father, your brother died he was a wise man, and I have tried to follow in the way he has shown me. With my brother at my side, I have always decided what was best for everyone in the family. Our blood is mingled in this earth together making us one with the land and you are part of that heritage, but I do not know what you want of us. To set me free Louise replies, you say to set you free Emilio now speaks, Pilar thinks we should call the priest, and he will banish you to hell . . . . Please, Louise cries no, I don't think the priest can do much here with all his religion. At first I thought to destroy you when I saw you, and now Louise utters quietly, as with my brother Hilly my heart has softened there are things I will never understand and you were, excuse me, are family Emilio states. Your presence must be known to only the five of us, Hilly agrees with his brother, and says we have decided the family must never know about you, and what we must do to free you this night, is that settled, so soon Louise says, yes the both men exclaim the sooner the better for all concerned. There is a knock on the door and Hilly goes to see who it is, Marie and the two *Tia*'s are in the hall, may we come in Marie asks, Hilly opens the door wider and the tree women enter the room. *Abuela*, Marie walks to Louise is everything well, yes my angel, tonight I will be free, no Marie cries, please my angel it is the only way. Marie looks over at Hilly, and the rest of the elders of the family, Louise is right no one else must know of this tonight, Louise will guide us in what must be done. Marie during all these months never thought much about what Louise's freedom really meant, it was just a word, now before her was the reality she would never see Louise again and she started to weep. What must we do Hilly asks Louise, take my ashes out into the desert and the mirror also Marie, Louise looks at her great-granddaughter you must be the one to scatter my ashes to the wind. *Abuela* how can I, you must or I will never be free to find my place, you are so much of my life I will be alone without you. You are not alone Maria, Flora puts her arm around her niece we are here and we will be with you tonight and always. Pilar also chimes in saying you are home with your family now Maria you must do this for *Tia* Louise so she can find her way. You said Louise and I are of the devil, I know what I have said Pilar replies, I cannot always know the ways of God in Heaven, but I must always show His love and Mercy and if I cannot to my own family how can I to strangers. Then it is settled Louise declares, yes, Hilly replies, what time Emilio asks, we must wait until everyone is asleep Flora says, after midnight Pilar expresses, yes, Flora agrees. Hilly looks at the clock we will meet back here at 1 a.m. the house will be quiet by then, now we must leave so Louise and Maria can say their good-byes alone.

Marie looks at Louise after everyone has left the room, I am *frightened Abuela* she cries, no, no angel I will always be with you, how? Marie asks. I am part of you and you of me I thought you understood we are one. But . . . . Marie interrupts, angel please believe me I will be here have faith.

The time seems to fly, and before Marie knows it there is a quiet knock on the door opening it she finds Hilly, Emilio, Flora and Pilar, so soon she says, yes, the house is silent we must go Hilly replies. *Abuela*, I am ready angel Marie has started crying again and Flora comforts her, please Louise tells Marie I want to be free now please. Marie holds the mirror close to her heart, and the family walk out of the *hacienda* through the gardens where Louise's wedding celebration was held amidst the laughter and joy then out into the desert where *Abuela* Maria battled *La Llorona* for Charles Marcus's soul. The air is cool and the sounds of the land play on the the breeze, Marie is holding the mirror high with one hand so Louise can see, and with the other she holds the urn with Louise's ashes. Hilly stand on one side of Marie and Emilio on the other with the *Tia*'s standing each one next to a brother forming a semi-circle. Here Louise discloses this is the place, look the full moon is passing out through the clouds I can hear it singing to me. Please, let me go, set me free, Marie fumble with the urn Hilly holds the mirror to help, and faces it to the stars, Marie now also holds the urn high as a strong cold wind sweeps over the vessel and send the ashes soaring into the air. *Tio* Marie cries out looking up at the moon as the ashes form a sword that plunges down to pierce Marie's heart as the glass in mirror shatters. The two sisters scream Hilly and Emilio hold Marie keeping her from falling to the ground. Maria, Hilly shakes her, Maria, Jesus Christo's, Maria, Pilar is saying her rosary, and Flora is summoning all the saints in heaven for help. Maria say something to us Hilly pleads as Emilio pats her hand. Maria sighs deeply and looks at her family Maria, Hilly says are you safe, Maria? She looks at her uncle who is Maria *Tio* I am Louise.

CPSIA information can be obtained at www.ICGtesting.com
Printed in the USA
BVOW01*2035111113

335546BV00005B/3/P